PERFECT

The Fray

SCARLET D'VORE

Nutmeg and Riley... luv you.

@ScarletDvore (Twitter)

www.PerfectsRule.com

Book Three

Books 1 & 2

Perfect: The Call

Perfect: The Revolt

(Reviews are king. Please consider leaving one on Amazon.com)

CHAPTER 1

ELISABETH

MY STARRY CHARIOT WHISKED me into the realm of the humans, my sad excuse for a home away from my beloved. Only one thing in the human world kept my heart from breaking fully, shattering into a million reflective shards.

Glenn—and only Glenn.

Because of him, my just punishment seemed bearable in the midst of so much displacency and dimness. His love helped me endure my guilt for allowing the Fearians to stand in my way, preventing my mission of acquiring The Seal.

Before tonight, that is.

Though it took longer than the Mother Perfects had hoped, I had achieved the Holy Grail. The Seal was in my possession at last, and I wouldn't let go of it now I'd experienced its glorious luster. Even after being exposed as a traitor among my enemies, I still managed to use my resources to sneak back into the realm of the most hated.

The mounting odds fighting against me? Astronomical, at best.

The risk involved almost cost me my life, just as it did my precious freedom. Not to mention my sanity, but it was well worth it to ensure our enemies had no advantages. I had pulled the fangs from the angry beast, and it could no longer attack and destroy my kind. But the Fearian Counsel was far from being powerless. They just weren't all powerful, not without The Seal in their hands, and that meant I could breathe a sigh of relief for a little while longer.

Of course, not every member of my species would be pleased with the decisions I had made, but that too was something I was prepared to live with for an eternity. Some will even label me an evil backstabber, once the truth of my actions fully came to light, but new love caused me to view things a little differently now.

This revelation had broken me like a wild stallion being tamed, softening my sharp edges and my resolve. I had been prepared to be a murderer when I first entered the realm of humans—now all I desired was to be with Glenn, forever, dispensing coral love in exchange for a cruel death sentence: blatant murder.

Could I walk away from the sweetness of its brutality, as its authority lay in the palm of my hand? I believed I could. I was willing to try anyway.

A foolish request for an inhuman looking to humanity for redemption, I know, but I had to risk it—it was the only choice that seemed absolute.

My ultimate decision was a selfish one, and incomprehensible to boot; neither side will understand my line of thinking, and my hell will be torturous when it came time to pay the piper. History will not be kind to my legacy. The elders will see to it, written in the holy scrolls. Plus, the bloody war my actions shall set into motion will be swift and violent to both sides: the condemned and the innocent.

The burn of my bicep ceased crying out my name, and my bruised muscles stopped aching. The black canvas of the backpack strapped to my back had the warmth of a loving hug, though its content was like a hand grenade, waiting for the metal pin to be pulled away from its oval body to create chaos and mass destruction.

Kaboom!

My swift withdraw was calculated, but not without casualties: a few guards, and two members of the Counsel had fallen by my hands, dead: murdered in cold blood.

And my breathing, as well: does it count as a casualty? Perhaps to some, but my magnificent life as a Mother Perfect among the entire species of Perfects—it too was no more. But The Seal in my possession also had the power to anoint me Almighty Perfection over both realms, if I wished it so … if I longed for the hungry lust of a world-conquering dictator.

Luckily for both sides of the battle, I understood what that would cost me in the end. The hefty price forced upon my soul in the middle of so much torment already.

No thanks.

The doorway ahead dazzled like a priceless gem as I glided toward it. My stomach fought off the fluttering nausea and head whirls, and I stepped over the threshold and into my bedroom without flaw, my balance staying in tune as my feet touched the carpet.

I took a moment to refocus to the illumination inside my human domain. My room was pretty plain, with the exception of the multitudes of teen heartthrob posters plastered on my walls. The posters were an attempt at deceiving any who ventured inside into believing I was an ordinary high school girl.

I slipped the straps off of my shoulders. It left damp stains on my shirt then I hung the backpack from the wooden bedpost, and glanced at the clock on the dresser.

Ten o'clock? That's amazing, girl.

I had rushed away unnoticed in the deadness of the night, stolen a priceless treasure from a power-lusting species in another realm—essentially starting a war of the ages—and all while making it back before mom's usual bed check. I grinned, though I failed to find it humorous. I wasn't sure if I should've been impressed by my punctuality, or condemned by my lack of remorse—still, I was damn glad to be a Mother Perfect, above all else.

I picked at the blood-soaked rag wrapped snug on my bicep. It loosened its grip on my limb, and I unraveled its itchy tail and inspected the skin. The rawness was no longer there. Like the pain, it too had vanished from sight.

Awesome!

The deep gash in my arm had healed itself in the time it took me to make it back from my savage outing. Super cells in the body were a benefit of being a Perfect, and fast healing was almost assured, so long as the injury wasn't a lethal one.

My appreciation was short-lived, as I was eager to inspect my treasure more closely. I tossed the pillows to the side of the bed and pulled back the sheets, exposing the mattress. I used the back of my hand to wipe away any dust and dirt, then grabbed my backpack and kneeled on the side of my bed. Although my eyes lost their vibrant glow of burning fuchsia, they stayed dilated with anticipation just the same.

"You can come out now," I nudged. "The fighting is over."

I tugged on the zipper securing the largest compartment, reached inside and took out the golden canister.

"Do not fear me. I won't let anything bad become of you," I promised.

My assurances failed to bring any response.

"I just cannot allow you to become what you were created to be. That would be the death of us all," I said, as if my heartfelt words nullified my deviant actions.

The gold container was the same size as urns cherished in the human world, with rubies and diamonds encrusted on the surface and intricate hieroglyphs carved upon it. It was meant for the noble eyes of the Fearian Counsel: royalty.

The shiny lid was a single gem, a large diamond shimmering in the light of the bedside lamp. I lowered my eyes with a request, and the lid responded by unscrewing itself and levitating a foot above the rim of the canister, and then onto the mattress in front of me, resting on the clean woven fabric.

Okay. Here we go.

"Let's see what all the hubbub is about," I joked, tilting the opening of the container toward the bed.

Nothing happened, though I felt slow movement from inside the golden canister. Seconds more, and a thick transparent fluid, laced with sparkly crystals, poured from the lip of the vessel and onto the mattress, like thick southern molasses.

"Wow ..." My eyes blinked pink. "Am I seeing what I think I'm seeing?" I hesitated with a shrewd hint of intrigue, tickling my curiosity.

My eyelids twitched. My heartbeat fluttered, causing my breathing to elevate.

The sparkly fluid made a puddle on the bed, then began to expand. It flowed out to the left, then squished to the right. The whole time, the center of the puddle stayed in the same place—like it was flexing its liquidy crystals. I couldn't take my eyes off the spectacle. It was beautiful, but it was also like baby scorpions, born already blessed with the power to sting, and the ultimate will to kill.

The ooze divided into three portions on the mattress. The trio glowed, though I could still see the patterns of the mattress fabric underneath them.

The three sparkly puddles bubbled, then morphed into three newborn babies, shimmering in the bedroom light: one cute male and two precious females, all three identical to the other, and filled with grace, and all three just as deadly to the touch.

"That was amazing," I said aloud. "Truly astonishing."

If only the others could've witnessed it too, maybe then their views would've been somewhat equal to mine. Maybe then things could have been ... much different.

At that moment, angst of death was the last thing on my mind. The trio possessed such innocence, and their existence was truly unique. Their skin was succulent, and their cheekbones were flushed garnet red. Their eyes were a striking hazel (unlike others on earth), and their ears were pointy.

I snapped my fingers and rubbed my hands together until heat ignited from the friction, and then caressed the tips of their ears, making them morph until they looked more humanistic and ordinary.

"That should hold you until you grow hair," I smiled. "You will like it here on earth. Hopefully, the same way I like it here."

The females seemed content as they cooed, bouncing gentle gestures back and forth as if involved in a lazy conversation on a summer day. But the limbs of the male tossed about and he cried out. His agitated voice grew louder and louder; the veins on the side of his skull bulged, and he forced the bedroom lights to flicker off like an electrical short was occurring. As his fussiness blossomed, his pleasant features wrinkled.

"Hey. Stop that. It's okay," I soothed.

But the boy kept crying. The intensity shamed my heart. I hoped his sadness wasn't related to the selfish deeds that had brought him and his sisters into the realm of humans, but a lie is a lie no matter how you sliced it—and mine were sliced paper-thin.

"Shush now," I said, reaching to pick him up, "you're going to get mom's attention, and–"

She knocked on the door. "Izzy? Are you in there?"

For a second I froze, and even held my breath, as if it would help hide me from scorn.

"I'm here," I said, still propped on my bended knees.

"Sweetie, is there a baby crying inside of your bedroom?"

"No. Yes! I mean..." I lost my words and glanced about, fidgeting.

"May I ask where you got a baby from?"

"It's not real," I said, thinking fast. "It's like a robot. It's for school. Home economics."

"Really?"

"Uh-huh. It's 'take a baby home for a passing grade' week." I hesitated. "A lot of girls in our senior class had to do it before graduation."

"Ooooh," she gestured long.

It got quiet. I knew that quietness well. Mom was nowhere near being convinced.

"Sorry for the extra noise. I'll try and keep it down."

"It's okay. It just sounds so life-like. If I didn't know any better, I'd swear you were hiding an actual live baby in there."

"I know, right?" I giggled on purpose, trying to throw her off my guilty scent, but the smell was too strong. "What will they think of next?"

The baby boy continued to cry with more intensity. The bedroom lights flickered off again. A sharp spark shot from the light bulb, and I held my breath and stared at the space underneath the bedroom door, knowing mom's acute investigative senses would be able to detect the bright fluctuation of lighting.

Oh, crap!

"Should I be making you a pot of black coffee just in case your night is long?"

"Naa. But thanks for the love. I got it covered, I think," I stammered.

The Fearian god continued to fester.

"Are you sure? It doesn't sound like it."

"Uh-huh …" I lost my words, snagged in the throes of a baby tantrum. "I …"

"Judging by the amount of activity coming from that *doll,* maybe your home economics teacher isn't a fan of the school's homecoming queen."

"You think?" I asked, sounding as passive as I could.

"Not that I'm condoning cheating or anything of that nature, but perhaps I could come in there and help out some, being I know a thing or two about the subject of baby care. Just this once."

I freaked. "Come in, you say?"

"You know, until you get the hang of things. Senior class or not, you sound a bit in over your head." She twisted the doorknob, but the lock prevented it from moving.

"Quiet little one, before you get your siblings going," I whispered to him, scanning the bedroom for a solution. "You're making things real hard for me."

"… Elisabeth?"

Uh-oh. I knew that tone as well!

Mom was seconds from turning her polite request into a stern command, and then I was up the creek without a paddle, with little to no options that would offer me a satisfying resolution, or allow me to continue living a teenage lie. I grabbed a plastic bottle of water from the floor and doused my hands quickly, washing them clean, then slipped a knuckle in the mouth of the agitated child. It soothed him into partial silence, with an occasional cooing. Enough that I could get a pass … I silently pleaded.

"All good. See? Thanks for the offer, though. Goodnight. Love you," I rushed, my heartbeat racing a mile a minute.

"…You too, sweetheart," she answered, her voice reluctant, though losing steam.

I didn't blink until I heard her bedroom door come to a close.

"I think it's safe to assume you three have worn out your welcome in this house."

I released a sigh, knowing the last thing I wanted to try and explain to Mom was how her adopted daughter ended up with three newborn babies with pointy ears and no birth certificates. I would have to tread on eggshells.

If my older sister Jamie still lived at home, I could have bribed her into running interference, but with me being the only child left in a big two-story house, what I was up to was never far off from her mind, even with me on the verge of adulthood. An involved human parent wasn't always the best thing for a Mother Perfect pretending to be a teenage girl to have. Now that I was at 'that age,' she felt a special need to ask me awkward questions, whether it involved me being alone with Glenn (handsome, manly and with a light mustache), or just me being alone by myself.

My eyes wandered to the newborns cuddling on top of my mattress.

If you only knew what your lives meant to our world.

I had way too much to lose to put my faith into the hands of the very ones I was trying to reform.

"Most of my kind wants you three destroyed … but, I can no longer see it their way anymore. So, I have a much better idea in store for your futures, instead of the usual brutality and death. You can thank me later, hopefully," I said.

I reached underneath my bed and pulled out a folded stroller I had hidden earlier. I grabbed a crocheted blanket off the back of my chair and tucked the three in, snug as a bug. I scooped up the golden canister and hid it inside an empty shoebox and wheeled the stroller to the closet door.

"Okay, you three. This is going to feel a bit strange, but I imagine you won't remember a thing." The closet door opened and the starry swallow flourished. "I have to get you somewhere safe before my host finds a new reason to enter my bedroom ... then acquire me a fake baby from school tomorrow," I muttered, with an eye roll. "Crap."

WOOSH!

I let go of the stroller handle and it stayed in place in front of me. The three Fearian babies inside didn't seem to notice, and sat calmly during the ride. I trailed the stroller out of the portal and into the darkness of evening, stepping out of a shed and onto the back lawn of a white, two-story colonial home, with its interior lights turned off. I peeked inside the stroller at my young passengers, to find them still resting peacefully.

Only babies, right?

I pushed the stroller on the grass toward the steps, then stepped onto the porch and knocked on the rear door. The porch light turned on, illuminating half of the back yard beyond the baby stroller. The door of the house opened and two odd, but familiar, figures appeared within the shadows behind the closed screen door.

"Good evening, friends. I hope all is well. Please feel safe to assume your natural forms." I egged on with my hands.

The pair nodded, though I could tell by the look in their eyes they were still trying to catch up. The man opened the screen door and the two of them stepped outside. They had big, soft blue eyes, and fish-like gills fluttered at each side of their bulky throats. Although they had on human clothing, they were both taller than the average human.

The pair looked like two gawky statues, guarding a haunted house on Halloween, but the Loafers were actually peaceful and loving. Also, they were hated by the Fearians, and many of their kind had been killed. But *the enemy of my enemy is my friend*, and so they were even more beloved in the eyes of Mother Perfects.

"I have a gift for you."

They peeked around me at the baby stroller.

"Thank you," he said.

The woman behind him smiled.

I had chosen well.

"It is I who should be thanking you. Care for them. We are not to fault them for who they are." I handed the female a large stack of money. "I will stop in and check on them from time to time until they come of age."

"That will be nice," he said.

My words comforted her expression.

"If something tragic were to become of me, you are to honor my wishes by raising them as mortals. Teach them of this realm's one true God. They will find Him blissful in dark times."

"I will," he nodded.

"They must never know where they come from, though it will be inevitable with their intelligence for them to wonder ... and one day they will even question their full existence. They will ask why their human lives feel so unfulfilling. Remember all that I have told you and it should be sufficient ... let's hope anyway."

The woman nodded, and gazed down at the children again.

"Now, about your appearance." I tilted my head.

The female shook her face vigorously, and the male followed suit. Their faces transformed into attractive human features—the forms they had assumed in this world.

"Better?" he asked.

"Awesome. Never take them off."

"We will comply with your request," he said.

"It's who you are now," I said. "This is now your home. You are human beings ... just with a beautiful secret, like me, that makes you ... unique and special."

"I like special," he grinned.

I caressed his hand. "Don't we all."

"So you find this pleasant to your eye?" she asked.

"I've always found your kind pleasant to the eye."

They smiled at my kind words, causing their cheeks to shade light crimson.

"Goodbye, Elisabeth," she said.

I returned to the stroller and its sleeping occupants. "May you find peace, little ones ... it is the only way you and I can coexist along with the human beings."

I walked back to the shed near the edge of the property, and the door swung open as I neared it. I looked back, watching the Loafers becoming more acquainted with the nobles from the very species that had murdered their own.

Life is funny that way sometimes.

CHAPTER 2

GENEVE

THE DEPICTION PLAYED OUT on Lauren's bedroom wall like a historical thriller created for the ages, full of twist, turns and coldhearted rebellion. I watched, motionless, as the revelation of what really transpired that fateful day hit my cortex. Elisabeth's narcissist traits allowed her to deviate from our original plan and left me feeling vexed and dismayed as a result. The thick darkness hovering within me churned at my aching soul and birthed nothing but great disappointment and sorrow; so much sorrow that its reeking bile could have choked the very life from me if I weren't already prepared to swallow both the unexpected taste and the vileness of backstabbing.

Why did you save The Seal from its deserving destruction, girl? That was not our plan.

Living among humans had made her soft. Her time here upon earth had created an odd conscience where the will of Mother Perfects no longer reigned supreme in her heart. How tragic and pathetic.

So much for being tormented by past actions.

Izzy was one of the strongest of Mother Perfects, like myself, and yet her unjust acts were cowardly in my eyes. And they would be seen as treasonous if the others were alive to judge the fullness of her betrayal.

Once the images of her actions vanished away from the wall, so went the written words on the end pages of the diary, turning blank once more. With my niece battling her own demons and being oblivious to the gift of kinship, I knew she was clueless as to her mother's secret, hidden from prying eyes of the undeserving: imperfects.

Lauren tossed and turned in her bed, no doubt flustered from the contagious plague of humanity, but failed to wake from her rocky slumbers. She looked so much like her mother, and so much like me. If only she possessed the true spirit of her true creation, then her love affair with mortal things wouldn't be such a salty addiction to break free from: so sad.

But her mistress required gentle hands in order for me to pry her loose. Mother Perfects were used to getting their way. Izzy had allowed her emotions to guide her into trying to be different than what she really was, and it forced me now to be the bad guy. Lucky for her, I hadn't an issue being bad, no matter how distasteful the actions required.

I just wish Elisabeth had felt the same. Both realms would have been better off for it in the end. Still, the truth would do more harm than good to Lauren at this point, so I ripped out the blank pages from the diary to keep their pathetic treasure lost forever. I folded the old pages and tucked them into my back pants pocket. Only I would know of Elisabeth's poor excuse for flogging her own kind, explained in writing—only I would know what selfish deed she had taken upon herself to set into motion without consent.

I smothered my disappointment with my pride until it was as lifeless and dead as Izzy herself, then set the diary onto the dresser and drifted toward the closet door like a jaded phantom searching for a wounded victim to finish off. The lack of a sacrificial lamb to inflict my rage upon made it quite difficult to accept the painful consequence of Izzy's naked truth. But I had no choice in the matter. And I despised not having any choices. The whirling interior of the closet seemed as pissed as I was, as it met my smoldering gaze and my clenched hands. My cute bangs rocked as I tarried forward like a villain.

I need to think.
WOOSH!

CHAPTER 3

DISON

THE GLARE OF MIDDAY hit my viridescent eyes and I stepped out of the lit doorway. The glass office door closed behind me, and I looked to the sun burning above. It felt warm, inviting, and shined against my brown skin, and I basked in the radiant glow of its succulent caress. As I walked on, I took solace in the solitude, broken only by the clunking of my black shoe heels and the swishing of my creased fitted black blue jeans.

Tall walls surrounded me. Five sides in all, caging my body like a fancy concrete fortress. The barricade was scattered with office windows, too many to number. Each connecting crook possessed a pair of glass doors, a walkway, and a path to a courtyard surrounded by luscious landscaping. Lines of pear trees and the occasional berry bush dotted the green yard, and several humans, most in uniforms, lounged about the area. I glided past a statue with an owl perched on the top and onto the quad, and shut my eyes.

WOOSH!

The unique sound was welcoming to my eardrums, and repeated several times over in the span of seconds. Madison approached me from the opposite side of the courtyard. She strutted like a long-legged supermodel, her hands planted on her twisting hips and red hair sparkling in the sun. I saw Charlotte nearest to me, then Zoe, a fair-skinned brunette, just beyond her, both converging onto the quad. Their presence made me wistful, but I kept it hidden within like a cherished secret, for fear of seeming silly.

I looked over my right shoulder. Wyatt, a close friend of my old family, and Jacob approached on two other sidewalks, one moving briskly. We came together, face-to-face, standing out like a whale out of water, with a pinkish silhouette radiating off our bodies.

"Thank you for meeting with me," I greeted.

"So, what's up?" Zoe asked.

Madison tilted her brow. "Yes. I too wish to know what was so important that I drop everything and come here."

Jacob hooked his thumbs in his pants pocket. "You and your creepy old human castles, girl. I swear, sometimes I think you were born in the wrong realm."

Madison released a grin. "I love Ireland. And what can I say? My castle is the perfect home away from home."

"Right. If you say so." Jacob chuckled. "Anyway, I do hope this little powwow is worth us putting ourselves at risk among the mortals."

Wyatt nodded in agreement, but held his tongue, and his subtle smirk as his eyes twinkled.

His words pricked at my skin. "Last time I checked, you were the honored among our species."

Jacob's sauciness changed on a dime. "Your point?"

"We weren't meant to live in the shadows in any realm, especially the likes of this one."

"I'm in agreement, Dison." Madison stepped forward. "Humans can be fickle."

"She's right," said Charlotte. "Last thing any of us want to do is award ourselves with unwanted intrusions. Read up on the violent history of this crude civilization. Fear has birthed much anger and division, and gotten many slaughtered in the process."

"Precisely," Zoe scoffed. "Their naïve culture adores confusion, death and destruction."

"Do not tell me you're now scared to die at the hands of a human being?" I asked.

Madison's face turned blank. "We didn't say that."

"You kind of did." I sized up her value. "Besides, you three insisted we meet on neutral territory. I would say this is as neutral as it gets, or have you forgotten how to be Perfects? Now, let's get to the real matter at hand. We have a problem."

Wyatt hunched his bushy eyebrows. "Problem? What now?"

I lowered my head and mourned. "Mother Harlen."

"What about him?" he asked.

"He is no more upon the Earth ... or any other realm, I am sad to announce today."

"Excuse me?" Zoe perked up and bounced glances off the others. "Did I hear you right? Did you say he is ..." her words went away.

"You heard me correct ... Mother Harlen is dead." I sighed. "Mother Isabelle as well, I'm afraid."

Everyone unleashed wide-eyed gasp.

Zoe covered her mouth. "Oh, no."

Charlotte's eyes raged coral. "Impossible!" She clenched her fists. "I would have felt it in my core!"

Zoe consoled Charlotte. "We don't believe you, Dison."

"I knew word of this would be hard to receive. It was for me, too, I assure you," I said.

"You're damn right!" Charlotte snapped. "You're trying to get me to accept Mother Isabelle, my Mother Perfect, is somehow gone long before her time!"

Jacob took a step. "She's right. And Mother Harlen was skilled at battle, not to mention he surrounded himself with the authority equal to a talented destroyer."

I curled my eyes. "And yet both are still dead just the same."

"Heresy!" Charlotte wiped streaming wetness from her crinkled face. "Prove your words!" She demanded, puffing out her chest. "If it's true then prove it to me!"

Zoe tried to soothe her, but Charlotte jerked her arm free. "I said prove it, damn it!" she shouted, her arms trembling from the unwanted attack of bad news.

Charlotte's emotional outburst had so far failed to get the attention of the human beings, but our luck couldn't hold. The raw essence of Perfects wouldn't permit it to do so.

I bowed gracefully, calming the tension in the air. "As you wish, Charlotte. We'll play it your way. Just know it was not my intention to bring harm upon your lovely spirit."

Charlotte squinted. "Whatevs."

I faced her with the presence of a king. "If I may make a humble request of you, Madison?"

"You may," she replied.

"Please honor Charlotte's request. Ease her agony. Give her the affirmation she seeks."

"Your wish is granted."

She tightened her body and lowered her head. Her long hair flowed over her sad face, and her pink eyes stayed visible within the red strands. Her body glowed pinkish with a haze of light and hummed with a vibrant noise, increasing its intensity by the second.

Suddenly, phantoms of Harlen and Isabelle appeared to the sides of us, standing on the lawn. Isabelle's face showed dark weariness in a time of her vexation, but Harlen's expression glowed confidence and retaliation as his arms slashed in heated battle.

The ghostly visions fought off their unseen attackers before the upper hand was soon lost, and one by one, each Mother Perfect fell victim and collapsed to the earth. Mother Harlen's expression displayed coldness and disbelief as his apparition deteriorated from sight.

Madison opened her glossy coral eyes and scraped her bangs off her face. "It is recorded. It is so." She looked to Charlotte with a soft gaze of sympathy. "I am sorry, sister. Dison is telling the truth."

"No ... Mother Isabelle." Charlotte broke down, kneeling to the earth in shattered strength. "But ... I don't get it. How did I not know? How? You were my love ... my Mother Perfect ... and I let you down."

Wyatt and Jacob turned away, barely containing their boiling fury, their eyeballs glossy.

Zoe fought back her salty tears. "It can't be ..."

"I too am angered by these events, but the light of truth is incapable of any kind of fabrication."

"He's right," said Wyatt. "Even if she desired it so, Madison could not lie about such things. Not to us."

"Who would dare do this?" Charlotte stared at her high heels, as she stood upright.

"I will find out the answer," Wyatt said.

"And I will help him. To defy the order with such treachery is an abomination, and must be avenged with extreme brutality!" Zoe sneered.

"I fear the answer you all seek will dampen your fire for justice, my brothers and sisters," I said.

Wyatt's eyes narrowed more. "Why would that be, Dison?"

"Yes. What are you saying?" Jacob asked.

"Vicky is the sole traitor. She is the culprit behind your torment and dismay," I said.

Madison pounded one fist against the other. "Very well, then. If we must destroy one of our own for this unspeakable act then let's not waste any time pondering mercy!"

The others nodded.

Charlotte sneered. "So long as I get to wrap my fingers around that ambitious murderer's neck, I'm good."

"Wish I could grant you that, which would deliver you solace, but the deed has been taken care of by another, I'm afraid."

Zoe's eyes widened. "What? By who?"

"Vicky suffered the same fate she selfishly dispensed, yet by her own vile making."

"No," Madison gasped.

Wyatt gritted his teeth.

"Impossible," Jacob mumbled. "It has to be."

"You know, Dison, you were quite the pair back in the day," Madison said in a condemning tone. "Thick as thieves, you two were."

"It is true. Vicky and I shared strong affections for one another at one time," I confessed.

"And yet you want us to believe you knew nothing of her infecting the order with the likes of silly human beings?" she asked. "Do we look that dumb to you?"

The others stared my way with collective animosity, and frustration, but I avoided the mounting guilt.

"Believe what you must. But I was more intrigued by her delectable body parts than what was on her overzealous mind—the view was always better from that angle."

Madison crossed her arms. "Huh. How convenient for you, Dison. How convenient indeed."

Jacob prowled closer. "Or did you decide you could finally live with yourself by turning a blind eye, while Victoria did the dirty work for you both to enjoy?"

"That would be my guess," said Zoe.

Although their anger shifted toward me, I kept my cool. "If I thought your words were more about truth and less about jealousy, I'd say, *prove it*," I bolded.

Wyatt shielded me. "Stop it! All of you!" He faced me. "How many? How many human beings did Victoria infect the order with, Dison?"

"By my count, three teenage girls."

Zoe cut her eyes. "Are you joking me? Three human beings?"

"Hybrids …" Charlotte looked on in awe. "She created real hybrids," she mumbled.

Jacob turned serious. "And what does Mother Geneve say about this filth and wickedness?"

"She is aware, and as unhappy as we are," I answered with a hint of slyness in my voice.

Wyatt glanced to Jacob. "Did you say she's unhappy?"

"Mother Geneve should be ready for war!" Jacob yelled. "I sure as hell am!"

"The circumstances have left her in a precarious situation, to say the least," I said.

"They need to be wiped off the planet!" Madison declared with a mean snarl. "Now!"

"She feels the same. But Madison, there is another Mother Perfect in play," I shared.

She snickered. "Inconceivable—explain how?"

"Elisabeth. She created a child while amongst the human beings before our asylum."

"Is that possible?" Charlotte asked.

Jacob's lips parted. "Why would she do that?"

"A daughter, who has yet to accept her lineage," I added.

"A Mother Perfect who doesn't desire to be so?" Zoe asked. "Can there be anything more tragic in all of existence?"

"She has befriended the hybrids, and has accepted them into her fold," I said.

Zoe took a deep breath. "I had to ask..."

"A Perfect who is a friend to an abomination: Quisling ..." Madison professed.

"No. Screw that!" Charlotte pouted. "Friend or not, these damn hybrids must die a cruel death!"

"Then perhaps I can assist in that regard," Penelope spoke out, as she approached us from behind, a swagger in her arrogant strides.

"Penelope. You knew of this vileness in our midst and did nothing?" Jacob asked.

"Like you, I am too catching on to what Victoria has done to the order. Yes."

Wyatt grunted. "Apparently not fast enough to persuade her to cease her efforts."

Penelope stepped in front of Wyatt. "Forgive me, Wyatt. I've been busy dealing with the Fearian Counsel, and their restless antics."

Wyatt's tone softened. "Really? I did not know."

"And the fact Nolum and the other pointy-eared monsters wish to make this realm their new kingdom," Penelope went on.

"Crap..." Zoe sulked, then perked in curiosity. "But they've failed to find the Shadow dagger and The Seal?"

"Being humans still walk the earth, and we're still breathing, one or the other has yet to be taken into possession by the Counsel," Penelope said. "Though time is running short, I'm sure."

"Why didn't she destroy it when she had the chance?" Zoe asked. "That's why she was chosen. Why?"

"I cannot answer that. One may never know, and I dread Elisabeth the wanna-be human took the answer to her grave," Penelope said.

Charlotte slapped her leg. "Damn it, Elisabeth! What have you done?"

"Nolum is resourceful. It will be only a matter of time before they're successful in their quest to restore the Counsel to its fullness and glory," Jacob predicted.

Madison puckered her lips. "And once they are successful in becoming whole, all of humanity will be lost."

"Most of it anyway," Penelope said. "I'm sure Nolum will enslave a select few."

"And we know what will befall us Perfects," Zoe said, darkly. "Total extinction."

Penelope stopped in front of Jacob. "If you have forgotten how to kill your enemy, now would be the time to do some practicing," she said, her eyes flickering pink.

Her proximity caused Jacob's senses to tingle, and his eyes flickered bright coral in response.

"You're a Mother," he muttered. The others turned to her in awe. "Penelope, is this true? How is it you have done this?"

Charlotte faced Penelope. "Jacob, are you certain of this?"

"Of course I am," he said. "Can't you sense it too? She reeks of the cycle from head to toe."

"As always, Jacob is correct," Penelope grinned. "My rebirth is nearing completion."

Madison shook her head. "No. Please no. Say you didn't, Penelope? Say you didn't become heartless?"

"I did not. But, before she perished, Isabelle showed me favor in her time of great grief," she said. "I too was as surprised as you are now, but appreciative none the less." She grinned.

Charlotte charged Penelope. "You're a damn liar! You did something evil to my crown jewel!"

"Charlotte?" Zoe tried intervening.

Tears fell down her skin. "I cherished Mother Isabelle!"

"I know," Penelope said, coldly.

"Then you also know she would have never selected the likes of you to continue her legacy! Hell, anyone else but you!"

Penelope smiled. "Perhaps."

Madison stepped beside her. "Calm down, sister. I know how you must feel, Charlotte," she said. "But-"

"No, you don't know! Every last one of you knew Mother Isabelle! And you know she would have taken her essence to the grave before handing it over to Penelope to relish!"

Penelope arched her shoulders. "Perhaps you are correct … or maybe she just liked me more than she liked you." She winked.

Charlotte gnawed. "No one likes you. You're a shape-shifter in the embodiment of a slithering snake. No matter how many times you shed your skin you will be vile."

"Careful, sweetheart. You're about to dance toe-to-toe with a Mother," Penelope advised with a serious tone. "And any contestation is an offense I will not take lightly."

Suddenly, I found myself holding my breath. Being a Perfect amongst Perfects, Penelope knew her taunts were seconds from setting Charlotte off. I wasn't sure if that was her sole intention, or an unavoidable consequence of something more beneficial to her survival. Either way, the tension was about to explode and the heavy shrapnel would cause casualties to one or the other, and also to the remaining keepers of our heritage.

We knew Mother Isabelle well, and the actions Penelope described were simply out of character for her. Isabelle had never liked Penelope's heart. Not many of us did.

"You're no mother, and you're no Isabelle … you're a sneaky opportunist … and now an essence-stealing thief," Charlotte snipped. "And we all know the truth of you."

Penelope's eyes sparkled in the light. "Prove it, darling."

"Charlotte, we weren't there," Zoe said. "So as much as I regret saying it—"

"My sentiments exactly," Penelope said. "I guess you're going to have to take my word for it along with the others." She grinned widely. "Okay, pumpkin?"

I knew Charlotte was in pain, and was trying to find peace with how things were playing out, but it was becoming a losing battle. I saw it in her eyes. It was in her DNA and seeping from her pores.

"Either that … or challenge you for its dominance," she replied, storing up bravery.

"Charlotte, no!" Zoe said.

"Mother Isabelle was her Mother, Zoe," Wyatt said.

"It is Charlotte's birthright to contest for her favor if she so desires it, according to the order," Jacob added.

Charlotte glared at Penelope.

"Well. It seems you now have the green light, for … whatever," Penelope dared.

"So it does," Charlotte said.

Their eyes flashed fuchsia, much brighter than the glow of daylight.

The pair dove headfirst into a fierce tango: Penelope back-stepped a step, evading Charlotte's lethal swipe for her neckline. Dust ascended from the tousle, as the battle raged on. Charlotte fought well. Her bravery mixed with endearing thoughts of Isabelle elevated her skills to a level even I had never witnessed from her. But it wasn't enough to overcome. Penelope fought with the mastery of a Perfect, and dominated her foe with the essence of a true Mother. Her attacks were equal to Isabelle's great talents and she wrapped Charlotte in a gust of wind, lifted her high into the air, and slammed her to the pavement.

The force sent a wave of energy in every direction, shattering office windows in the building. Charlotte's body trembled and her blue eyes rolled into the back of her head in defeat. Her stunned expression unveiled steep confusion, and her breathing seeped.

The fight had finally attracted attention, and the humans in our midst were startled by our presence, as our silhouettes flickered from sight. Some stood frozen. Others fled.

"We are exposed to the humans!" I alerted.

"Whatever you two are going to do, I suggest you do it quickly!" Jacob said.

Wyatt glanced at the human commotion. "I concur!"

Penelope pinned Charlotte to the sidewalk, with her knee to her chest. Charlotte's lungs pleaded for air, but Penelope's assault was relentless and mean spirited and offered none.

"How about that? Your disobedience was just the thing needed to resurrect me to my fullest beauty."

"I wasn't trying to help," Charlotte quipped, gasping.

"And yet you did anyway. As you can tell, Isabelle breathed fiery life inside of my tender loins—almost as if she and I were destined to be united," Penelope gloated.

"Just goes to show even a Mother Perfect can be a slave to a fool under the right circumstance."

"Your defiance is—breathtaking, at best. So. Shall I end you now?" Penelope asked.

Charlotte hesitated, fighting off a tear in her eye. Then managed to moisten her brittle throat. As the dryness faded, so went her pride and her strong will. "No."

"I guess you now belong to me. Unless you intend to further rebuke our ways."

Charlotte held her rebuttal a moment longer. "Mother Geneve will become irate once she catches wind of what you have done."

Penelope's eyes glistened. "Looking forward to it, dear."

"Me too. I hope I am a true testament to your day of reckoning when judgment befalls you."

"You hope you are a true testament—what?"

"Mother … Penelope."

"There you go," Penelope grinned.

Charlotte's rage was broken. "Now what?"

"I think … I will let you live." Penelope stood up and dusted herself off. "To all whom my voice reaches, I invoke Oracle Six of the Perfect Order. How shall ye respond to my calling?"

The others shared glances among themselves, shocked, as if hoping for a mutiny, though none came. Even I, too, failed to contest Mother Penelope's authority.

"...We shall honor the order," Madison said.

We nodded in agreement with what equated to a forced submission to an arranged marriage—with a double barrel shotgun pointed at our heads and wobbling in our knees.

Penelope blew pretty sparkling dust from her hands and it forced us to inhale its presence. "I give the gift of a destroyer. No other mother has ever done that for you … and you're welcome."

The fine dust overtook our lungs and made us cough.

"A battle looms, at which time I shall beckon and you will come," Penelope ordered. "And I expect to see your sexy face up front, Charlotte. Ready to die for me."

Charlotte hid her aggression from view. "Yes … Mother Penelope."

"Now was that so hard?"

Charlotte snatched her angry glare into a new direction and said nothing.

"We need to wrap this up quickly," I said. "The humans are stirring, and they are…"

A barrage of soldiers emptied out the doors on either side of us, twenty or so, dressed in military fatigues and carrying M-16 machine guns. They aimed at us.

We turned our backs inward, on guard, without being told to do so, preparing for what looked like a brutal war with mortals.

"Great. And this is why I stay in my secluded castle," Madison muttered with a sigh.

"Get down on the ground, now!" a soldier demanded. "You got five ticks to surrender!"

"They're not letting us walk," I mumbled.

"You wanted to be a Mother Perfect, well, here is your chance to do so," Charlotte jeered.

Penelope stepped toward the leader. "Hello. Any chance you fine Marines will believe our GPS gave us bogus coordinates?"

"Right. You have trespassed onto federal property!"

"I see."

"This is the Pentagon! And no GPS brought you here," he fumed. "On the ground now or you're dead!"

Penelope shrugged. "It was worth a shot. Perfects?"

"About time!" Jacob said.

Jacob's eyes flashed flaring pink, and he attacked the nearest three soldiers with lightning speed before any of them possessed a chance to respond to his advances.

Penelope, Zoe and Madison did the same while Charlotte and Wyatt and myself vanished from sight, reappearing behind the perplexed soldiers, desperately trying to catch up to speed.

Machine guns combusted, firing bullets at Perfects who were there, but then suddenly weren't. Madison and Wyatt released energy pulses, causing small explosions to erupt, powerful enough to toss soldiers into the air from the potent blasts.

The courtyard turned into a war zone, and the soldiers left began to comprehend the gravity of their grave situation, getting darker by the moment. No armed soldier had a clear shot at the enemy. No Perfect stood still long enough to be aimed at by a human.

The battle turned into a hand-to-hand combat of strengths and skills between trained mortals and Perfects, and one by one the soldiers were left subdued and disarmed.

Several of the humans groaned from the throbbing injuries that their limp bodies endured from battle.

Penelope jerked the slack from her designer outfit. "Boom."

"Retreat! Retreat!" the soldier shouted, as he shuffled backwards. "Retre ..." his voice lost its sting once he saw he was the last one standing. He lowered his weapon.

I motioned the scared human forward, and his body slid toward me as the momentum forced him to drop his M-16 to the pavement. The toe of his boots scraped across the concrete, and he landed in my grasp, with his feet dangling above the concrete.

"Afternoon, soldier," I greeted.

"Don't hurt me!"

"Not my call," I said.

Penelope approached us like a runway model. "That would be my call. Don't ever point your toy guns at my beautiful face ever again." Her eyes raged coral.

The soldier dared to look at her eyes. "Please don't!"

"Don't beg," she replied.

"I..."

"Don't speak at all, in fact!" Penelope snatched him from me like an unappreciated rag doll and slammed him to the earth on his back. The force left him winded and weak as she lifted him to his knees. "It's time we announce to the world there is something far greater than human beings in this realm." She wrapped her hands around his neck.

"No!" Zoe and Madison shouted, with their arms stretched out and eyes widened.

"Mother P, I'm also in agreement on this," Wyatt said.

Penelope sighed. "Which agreement?"

"Well. If you decide to kill him then-"

"I have decided to kill him."

"Okay. Your discretion."

"Thank you?" Penelope slanted her brow.

"Your actions, although warranted, will set an ugly precedents and ultimately be bad for us," he said.

"He's right," Zoe said.

Madison and the others nodded.

"Who cares?" Penelope asked. "We are Perfects, living in a world where they're not!"

I rolled my eyes, failing to speak, because evidently 'vanity' was the new decorum when facing humans on earth.

"Mother Penelope," Jacob said. "With everything else going on right now, do we need to make more enemies to have to deal with?"

"An enemy who is used to ruling by himself?" Zoe added.

"This is a battle that will come. We know this. But until then do we want this kind of hateful attention," I said. "Although the damage is done, it would be prudent I think to back away from the ledge some. Call a truce, if you will."

Penelope considered his words, while more soldiers invaded onto the courtyard, with more weapons in tow.

"They are lucky I have kindness dwelling deep within me." She looked to the soldier in her grasp and dropped his limp body. "Consider this a severance package, and a dire warning."

"Halt!" the soldiers ordered, firing off several rounds, but missing our bodies.

"Meeting adjourned!"

We chased after Penelope, and she skirted toward the rear door, the only door not pouring out armed soldiers onto the courtyard.

"Await my voice!" Penelope ordered.

The glass door swung open as she neared it.

WOOSH!

We stormed inside the starry swallow, and the others left my sight within the blink of an eye: the beautiful benefit of our lineage. None of us knew what was in store for our futures, but things were looking grim with Mother Penelope running the show.

Her spine-tingling arrogance was intoxicating to our seven senses, and although it was an alcoholic beverage we thirsted for daily, I myself included, it also meant our lives would be in great peril if it were allowed to quench our spirits. It would change everything on earth for us … and for the human beings. The same characteristics we longed for were equally lethal and deceiving, as well. It all depended upon the angle we looked from.

CHAPTER 4

KAIDEN

HOLDING MY BREATH FOR long periods of time proved much easier than I first anticipated, and I sliced through the depths down to the sandy floor. The liquid soaked my blue jeans, making the webbed fabric heavy, but failed to hinder my body's descent. I was determined to see it through. Even the blindness of truth became an eager advantage. With the Counsel having the ability to manipulate the length of days or shortness of nights, I knew the trio was secured away, guarded by their warriors as they gathered strength for the inevitable war that was sure to come. The power of their glory was unmatched when wide-awake, but when they visited the elusive dream state, its sticky allure made their sweet omnipotence temporarily inferior to their closest ally: me.

This is my one chance!

Not even the slight annoyance pricking at my open eyes would be enough to deter my sneaky intentions, nor ease my hunger for success.

Being the last of the most trusted, I knew my actions would go unseen. I loved my species, but I didn't always embrace the wisdom of every decision made by the Counsel. I had to ensure my rightful place in the universe, if for no other reason than to accurately portray our historical relevance to the true god's that ruled over all logic and discernment.

With eyes wide open, I used my hands to swipe clear the head of the entombment and layers of settled sand scattered within the unfolding depths, exposing a foggy glass-looking cover. I placed my palm to it and the coffin illuminated with an energized light, burning the pores of my skin in the process, though I endured the waning discomfort.

The thick fog obstructing my view faded into nothing, as I had hoped it would've and I pushed on the coffin lid, which encased a precious image I'd once honored for a long time. The suction of the seal was great, but my deepest desire was greatest and I was able to cause it to finally budge and give way.

In the end, the depths agreed to hold my dark actions a myth so I swore to never share the promise buried deep below. The air bubbles foaming around me assisted my weightless ascent back to the water's surface. As my eyes emerged, shielded by the tossing waves, my thin locks pressed against my skull, I stepped onto the sandy shore.

"All hail the new gods." I smirked.

Muscles were tight from the swim and my clothes clung to my thighs, yet I persevered. Even from a far I betted against detection as I blended in with the wooded terrain and green overflowing leaves of the rain forest ahead of me.

My eyes were reddish with irritation, but I didn't care. What I held snug in my hand brought me to the doorstep of invincibility and would guarantee my survival, even if my beloved Counsel failed at the same in heated discord. Green water dribbled off my face and body, and I crept deeper into the foliage. They would not know I'd come home, and I was certain my queen would remain silent in her quest of eternal slumber.

CHAPTER 5

RILEY

IT WAS THE BEGINNING of midday, and I had unfinished plans that called out to me. But mom had the day off, and I sensed her demanded conversation was going to go down now, whether I liked it or not. *Crap.*

So there we were, sitting on the side of my mattress, our feet resting on the carpet and our butts inches apart. The tension between us was so evident it was as if we were complete strangers. I fiddled with my fingers, not knowing how she was taking my perfect explanation. After a moment of silence, she released a long breath and turned to me with a bewildered expression. She hesitated to speak her next words, though her lips parted. It was then I saw disbelief in her eyes, though she was trying to be tactful.

"Canada?" she asked.

I shrugged, feeling warmly condemned by my own statement. "The country of Canada."

She opened her mouth again, but the words lost their way once more, and she tilted her head as confusion weighed her skull down. "So … on top of everything else that has happened—you say—I am now to believe you can also do this magical 'thing' just by thinking it?" Her stunned words flowed out of sync.

"Just a thought and a doorway," I said.

"A thought?"

"Even a half of one really."

Her doubt only got clearer and doubled in size. I even felt the sharp pricks of her disbelief begin to torment my honesty, forcing me to shy away from the actual truth, as I suddenly questioned the validity of my own words I knew to be true.

Strange, huh?

"… Okay." She gathered her brewing skepticism and braced her hands on her bended knees. "Riley, it's not that I don't want to believe you."

She paused. "Because I did witness something unexplainable already … it's just that—"

"Just that what?"

"Well. And hear me out here," she added, trying to spare my bruised feelings.

"I'm trying to."

"I work in a place where faith and the supernatural often share a bed pan or two." She grinned, trying to find humor where none existed.

"Right."

"Where doctors are sometimes the hands of God, or at least think so, anyhow."

"Sure."

"But, honey, what you're saying is impossible."

I puckered my lips. "You don't say?"

"You're saying you can manipulate time and space. And you're not the only one who can do it, either. There's a whole species of special beings who—"

"Perfects. We're Perfects, mother."

"If you say so: Perfects. I just can't wrap my brain around something as crazy as an unknown species and door travel. I'm sorry," she said, shooting me a look of pity.

Her slighted expression conveyed ugly words of vulgarity I knew would never slip off of her pink lips without coercion, and of course a loaded pistol. And still...

My lips slanted. "I understand."

"We're good?"

No. Far from it, mother.

Ironically, proving my words to her was going to be a sight easier than actually getting her to believe what she saw was real. I knew what I had to do, and the notion of showing her, although she wasn't a Perfect, comforted me more than I thought it would.

"Mom?"

"Riley, you're not mad at me are you?"

"No, I'm not," I said. "Just try and keep an open mind—okay? Pretty please."

She hunched her eyebrows. "You got it." Her word lingered. "About what, exactly?"

I stared at my pink tennis shoes. The Nike symbols glittered silver. "Remember the place you often talk about going for dinner if you could get dad to overcome his concern of steep heights?"

The thought of it made her grin. "How could I forget? I do love the west coast."

I stood, and her eyes followed my movement. "Come. I want to show you something rather cool," I said, offering out my hand.

She looked at my wiggling fingers and placed hers on top of mine. "… Okay."

I gave her a gentle tug and she stood to her feet, and I escorted her to my closet door. She looked perplexed, but followed my lead with a sense of reluctance in her strides.

"Still have it on your mind?"

"Uh-huh. I hear they serve the best Pacific Halibut and Hokkaido Scallops in town," she said, smiling at the image now trapped in her brain.

"Perfect."

I stared at the doorknob and it began to rattle and shake. Mom's eyes took notice and her eyebrows lifted again in suspense. She squeezed my hand and I could tell she had stopped breathing for a moment.

"Riley?"

"Yes, mother."

"How are you making the knob move like that?"

I looked to her and shrugged.

"And your eyes…"

"What about them?"

She swallowed hard. "They're … different."

"How so?"

"They're glowing a pretty pink color."

I turned humbled. "Aw. You're so sweet. Thanks for noticing." I held onto her hand tighter than before.

Mother's frame began to shudder. "Okay. Honey. I think I want to get off this ride now."

"What's the fun in that?"

I snapped my lit glare back toward the closet and the door swung open on cue, exposing the starry darkness flourishing deep inside it.

Mom's lips parted and her blue eyes stayed riveted. "Holy hell!" she squeezed my hand even tighter. "What is this, Riley?"

I felt her muscles stiffen.

"Welcome to the impossible. Mother," I smirked.

"Sweetheart."

"Oh, no. It's way too late to turn tail now."

"But …"

"Let me introduce you to my world ... to the wonderful world of being a Perfect!"

I held onto her hand with even more force than before and tugged her again. Soon she had no other choice than to allow my guidance to overtake her body's momentum and forward she came with minimum resistance. That's when I saw it. Her fear had transformed into a hint of anxious excitement mixed with overwhelming curiosity—and still a little fear.

"Sweetheart!"

"Just let go, mom. Trust me, I got you covered." I pulled her over the darkened threshold.

She shrieked. "Riley!"

WOOSH!

Mom's body went limp for a few seconds and she fainted, though it didn't last and her tilted senses slammed her back into reality. When she opened her eyes again she didn't speak, hoping it was a dream—it wasn't. The starry spectacles zooming past our faces made her eyes roll back from the wooziness, though she maintained, and yet the only emotion inside me was one of privilege. I felt more powerful than a superhero, and without the flapping red cape attached to my backside. My cheekbones turned three shades beyond being flushed, my insides tingled with the orgasmic scent of melted dark chocolate and my breathing became easier—more alluring.

"Don't let go of me, Riley."

"I won't."

"Tell me when I can open my eyes," she said, clenching tight her facial muscles.

"Didn't say you had to close them to begin with."

"And yet it still seems like the most logical thing for me to do at this exact moment."

"Suit yourself. The show is stunning."

"I'll take your word for it."

I giggled.

The intimacy caused my eyelids to flutter, the thin hairs on my neck to perk and the purity of innocence left inside me to vanish from view. I felt it leave my body as my loins craved for just five seconds more to savor its joy, as the peak slowly descended.

The lit silhouette ahead drew closer and our bodies tilted upright. I stepped out of the doorway and into the brightness of day, blinking my eyes as they refocused on our new sunlit location.

I held onto mother's hand as she took a step past me before coming to a complete stop. Her body collapsed as her knees wobbled, and I held her tightly to keep her from tumbling to the black-tarred surface face first like a falling brittle redwood. Finally, Mom's feet found there footing and her glossy eyes danced from side-to-side, shaking off the cloudy haze of dizziness circling her head.

"So..." she placed her hands on her hips, like a drunk woman trying to stand still, and tried to appeared as if she had it together. "So."

"Yep."

"Yep … yep. Yep. Yep." She bounced her lips with a gust of stiff air, and her eyes danced about.

"… Feel that magnificent sunshine. The weather sure is nice out here on the west coast."

"That it is. That it is... it appears that I owe you a tremendously huge butt kissing."

"It appears so."

She sighed. "I'm sorry for not believing you, Riley," she managed, caressing my lower back with her hand. "Even while knowing you would never intentionally lie to me."

"It's okay. I'll give you a pass."

"Really?"

"Sure. In all honesty, I probably wouldn't have believed me, either ... probably."

"Thank you." She hugged me.

I broke free and spread out my arms. "Look at that majestic Seattle skyline. Simply beautiful."

She walked to the edge of the roof and gazed out at the tall buildings in our midst. "Riley, somehow, you just brought us to the very top of the freaking Space Needle."

I crossed my arms. "I did, didn't I?"

"A Perfect …" she faced the skyline. "Truly amazing, I mean if I hadn't seen it with my own two eyes… "

"Right?"

"Wow, Riley. Just… wow."

"Now that you know what I've been up too, I trust you'll take my supernatural secret to the grave?"

"Oh, I don't think that's going to be a problem for me."

"Are you sure?"

"Absolutely."

"Cool. Because I'd hate to condemn you to a life in a straight-jacket from your friendly psychiatric ward."

"That makes two of us." She blew out air from her cheeks.

"Fantastic then."

"There is one thing I have to know, though."

An eye roll shot across my brow. "No mother, I did not kill her and bury the corpse in a shallow grave."

"Are you reading my mind again?"

I scoffed. "Like I'd actually have to."

She bumped my shoulder with hers. "So what then?"

"We ... put the fear of God into her loose legs."

"Oh. Too bad."

"Excuse me?"

Mom shrugged. "What? That bony home-wrecker was screwing my man. She gets no love from me."

"Remind me to never piss you off."

She wrapped her arm around my neck and kissed my cheek. "Ditto, times two. Now, let's go get some of that rich Halibut they're so famous for preparing here."

I sucked in my cheeks. "And?"

"And you can explain how in the hell did my only daughter become a Perfect, with supernatural powers and ... are you still considered a human being? Wait. Am I still human?"

"Mom-"

"Will my grandbabies be normal or some magical weirdo with grandma's good looks?" she rambled on.

"There she is."

"What? Too much?"

"Can I have a sip or two of your red wine before I try and answer your many questions?"

"Get your own bottle. My first one is already spoken for."

"Deal."

"On second thought: half of glass."

"Only a half?"

"Be happy with that. You're driving."

I gave it thought. "You have a point."

Her serious expression caused me to laugh and seconds more she followed suit.

We returned to the door we'd exited moments ago, only this time when it opened there was no starry darkness, no majestic swallow waiting to be ravaged.

Mom released a subtle breath of relief when her curious gaze met normality instead of the unexplainable. "Thank God," she muttered.

The sunshine rushed in on our coattails and further illuminated the stairwell. I motioned her forward, and she made sure the landing was real before she ventured inside the building stairwell.

As we descended the steps, the rich aroma of high priced cuisines bloomed in my nostrils and made my empty stomach grumble. It amazed how the smell of good food could wipe away the strongest of emotions.

I was also left comforted by the fact my life-changing confession didn't send her spiraling into a deep panic, running for the Black Hills of Kentucky.

Wahoo!

CHAPTER 6

GLENN

THE MORNING APPROACHED AT a slow pace. A flock of orioles soared overhead in a V-formation, making their way south for the beginning of their migration period. The dull yellow feathers on the breast of the females and the flare of orange feathers on the stomachs of the males caught my admiration as they flew by.

They flapped their wings without stopping—deep down they knew something insane was on the horizon. I too felt the same, though my dangers were in a different form. The breeze in the air confirmed what the new color of leaves predicted: Fall was afoot. And so was the change in realities that would surely follow.

I allowed my eyes to wander over the scenery of Cyprus Park. Even after the passing of dark years, it looked the same. The grass beneath my shoe soles felt familiar and I made my way across the vast open lawn. I walked beyond a wooden picnic table, then under a swing set with a sandy earthen rut, allowing my fingers to rake the chained rubber seating, as it swung to and forth from my gentle touch.

A few steps further and I found myself standing in the exact spot where my life changed from what it once was; the place where I once lay helpless on the ground, watching the love of my life stolen from me, murdered at the hands of that Fearian coward whose existence relied upon deception and sneakiness.

I'll never forget the day. How could I? Parts of me died along with you, Elisabeth.

My tormented thoughts were much heavier than actual words, and far sharper than carved blades created for murder.

The battle scars barged onto my frame of mind, making me flinch from the terrible memories, as I relived the tragic moment Kaiden attacked us. His revenge took me by surprise, and the aftermath left me grieving and desolate. While the deep gashes were still fresh to the sight and painful to the touch, I knew I had no other choice than to leave everything behind—*I couldn't protect either of you, and it cost me my family.*

There was no way in hell I was going to allow it to cost me my daughter's life, too. So, I drowned the truth in many bottles of whiskey, but no matter how much I drank, reality was never too far behind, reminding me of my past failures.

That's why I buried the Shadow dagger under the spot you lost your life, Izzy … I left you here, so it was fitting I did the same with the Shadow dagger.

The rain had fallen in torrents that dreadful night, but had failed to cleanse me of my defeats.

Taking a breath to clear my head from the regrets plaguing the past, I knelt down by a large oak tree and removed some rocks set in the dirt. I stabbed my fingers into the topsoil until a narrow hole appeared, but it stayed hollow the deeper I dug.

Damn it!

It's gone. The Shadow dagger is gone! Elisabeth, I'm sorry. It seems you've died for nothing. Your spirit is no more, and the dagger is lost … and once again, it's my fault.

CHAPTER 7

CHARLOTTE

I'VE OFTEN ENJOYED THE travels on passenger trains ... the way the metal wheels rattle forward as the engine pushes on to its next destination, ignoring any demands from the terrain.

The mighty force combined with the gusto of grace reminded me of a Mother Perfect. But the mirage of similarities remained a poor consolation to my broken heart.

Dealing with the tragic loss of a life before its prime, in a barbaric realm not meant for Perfects, was a battle in and of itself. Having the gift to take it out on humanity made the trial feel even worse. I've found my mind retreating several times, just to stay afloat with my fragile sanity intact: the one thing keeping me from terrorizing humans caught in the wrong place at the wrong time. The vibration of the cars rolling on the tracks distracted me from my flaring torment, if only for the moment, a fleeting moment, and I was free to reflect on my crude situation, and the very real chance of it all biting me on the ass, as it came full circle.

I gazed out with my forehead pressed against the window as I sat alone inside my private coach. The surface of the glass was cool to my skin, and a breeze whipped up from the vents below my elbow, circulating through out the entire car. No other passengers were permitted within the sanctuary of my personal space. No mortal distractions tempting me into turning it into a gladiator arena. No human etiquettes to pretend I longed to display, just my troubled thoughts ... and my burning agony.

I overheard the dim sky crying, as it took pity on my broken soul. The rain leaked from the puffy greyness, and the clear drops fell to the earth, some slapping the outside of the window. Thin jabs of sun rays intruded from behind gloomy clouds as the wind pushed them along with no remorse for the empathy they honored. The ballet of the dark billows fit my mood to an exact: angered and restless, saddened and full of disgraced. Ready to fight, but not willing to lose ... so forced to submit for the time being.

"Oh, how I long to feel the warmth of your touch … the sweet sound of your soothing voice, telling me things will be better."

The savaged greenery of Honduras was ever so calming, even with its simplistic humans. Though I never saw them as anywhere close to being equals—not many Perfects would—I tolerated them so long as they stayed clear and didn't bother me with their mortal stress. But the blackness of today put them in danger of having their heads ripped off in a violent fit of rage, so I made certain to keep my distance … for their sake.

If I could have had my way, Mother Isabelle's shadow is where I would have resided for all time. I even requested as much when Earth became our safe haven, but she had insisted Razlor was more than sufficient in keeping her safe from any harm. Now that she had been taken away from me, no matter how much I dreaded its truth, no amount of wishing would ever undo the filthy mess Penelope had made of things.

I ran my fingers along the glass pane and I mourned a great loss, trying to conjure a happier memory of her. My fingerprints smudged an imperfect wake along the clear surface.

I would have protected you, Mother Isabelle!

My pleas went unanswered, and I couldn't stop the inner me from sobbing from being ignored. And I've been sobbing a lot as of late. Losing my sweet home was hard enough, but losing my Mother was proving to be much more difficult to contend with.

The train darted inside a tunnel through Mogoton Mountain, and in seconds my coach was doused in complete thick darkness. Suddenly the unknown made it awkward, and left me disheartened, realizing the heavy shade only made the hurt feel worse, as it assisted hiding the one resolution I longed to have.

WOOSH!

I knew what that sound meant. I was no longer alone because of that sound, though the torment strangling my heart to death stopped me from offering up a response.

I held fast, defeated, facing the window, ready for whatever was to become of me.

The train exited the far side of the mountain, and the brightness chased away the shadows and exposed the passenger sitting across from me. She had her tan legs crossed, a smug look on her beautiful face and her hands were stacked on her lap, prim and proper.

"Hello, Charlotte," she greeted.

I glanced at her reflection in the glass. "Mother Geneve. It's you. You came to me."

"I received word from Bray there was a dire need for a face-to-face, and I'm not one to disappoint."

"Yes, your carrier pigeon was correct."

"Well. Here I am."

"So you are."

"Tell me what ails you, child."

"Don't you feel it?"

"I feel many things, Charlotte. To which are you referring, so that we may be on the same page of enlightenment?"

I snapped my glare her way. "You, of all Perfects, have let the memory of the colony down."

"Beg your pardon?"

"You heard me."

She uncrossed her legs and sat up straighter. "Please remember to whom you are addressing."

"You allowed her to murder my Mother Perfect!"

Her face turned cold. "Are you saying someone has knowingly violated the order?"

"Not just someone. Penelope," I sneered.

She scoffed. "Ludicrous."

"Is that so?"

She took a short breath, trying to ignore my rude attitude. "Yes. It is."

"Are you sure about that?"

"I can feel Mother Isabelle's essence among us. We spoke just days ago. About you in fact."

"That comforts me." I sobbed.

"It should."

"Especially since Mother Penelope has been favored by her touch, which is why Isabelle's gifts still exist in this realm."

She jumped to her feet. "Watch your damn tongue, Perfect or else I'll end you!"

"I no longer have to. I saw with my own eyes. She exposed the truth to us all. Mother Penelope is now my Mother, and she claims Mother Isabelle made it happen for her."

"Never! Isabelle was far too smart for that. Penelope would have been the last one chosen, if any were chosen at all ... you would have been her only choice."

I faced the window. "I am in agreement."

"Heresy." I watched her reflection sit down. "I am sorry for your loss. I know you, Isabelle and Razlor were extremely close."

"We were. And now both are no more ... my family has been taken away from me without just cause—none I know of."

"I know you are feeling vexed. Yet, I promise you, Penelope's actions will not go unpunished. I swear to you on this day, she will pay for her wickedness and deceit."

"What will you do?"

"Exactly what the Perfect Order demands of me: a cruel death for a cruel and heartless tyrant."

The exact in her words delivered a heated soothe that made my breathing shudder and my eyelids bulge with tears of empathy. Not even the saltiness of wet had the power to steal away the serenity that rushed through my body, radiating fire.

"Penelope is expecting you to come for her. She expects you to test her new perfection."

"Your expectations of sunrise doesn't make it any less magnificent to the naked eye—make no mistake, she will perish by my hands, I promise you that."

"One request."

"Anything."

"May I bear witness to her day of reckoning?"

She stiffened her posture. "I'll do you one better."

"What?"

"I shall offer you up the last beats of her cringing heart and severed head once she favors you with what is rightfully yours."

"Okay."

"I vow to correct this unjust act. I swear to both you and Isabelle's memory what has been done will not remain."

Mother Geneve caressed my knee with the heat of her touch and the comfort forced my eyes to shut, and I pretended it was my loving Isabelle's hand doing the consoling.

I nodded, wiping away a tear. "I'll be waiting for the words, which will offer me relief."

"Your wait will be short. And once I am done. We will have much work to do, along with the others."

"What do you mean?"

"I have decided. The human's are no longer deserving of earth. Once the Fearians Counsel and their cronies are disposed of we will return to earth and establish a new ruling."

"But what of Elisabeth's heir and her dirty hybrids?"

"The hybrids will die. There is no other choice in the matter."

"Something tells me you'll be forced to end her as well. She is far too humanized to accept our ways."

"Perhaps … I will put that on the back burner for the time being."

"Hum."

"Once you have been favored, every perfect among the living shall return home with us."

"For what reason?"

"To battle the Fearian Counsel in their time of refreshing during the late full moon. We will attack them outright. And we will prevail."

"They will be too weak to stop three Mother Perfects."

"…And so will the humans."

Mother Geneve approached the sliding door as a conductor passed by the hall window. The door slid open, exposing a starry mass instead of the hall interior, and Mother Geneve stepped inside it with her fists clenched at her side.

WOOSH!

The metal door slammed shut behind her, and the crewman appeared on the far side of the doorway, without so much as an inkling of the supernatural existing in his midst. I took solace in knowing her anger was kindled to a point there was nothing our foes could ever offer in exchange to ease its intent.

But even if she is unsuccessful in restoring your last dying wish, Mother Isabelle, I vow to honor your life with the rest of my days, and your memory with every breath I take.

Mother Geneve was never one for head games, and I knew she wouldn't start now that revelation had sparked flames up her spine. My grief would soon be avenged at the hands of a scorned Mother Perfect.

Finally!

CHAPTER 8

LAUREN

I SAT FIDGETING IN a chair in a cold, isolated corridor. Aunt Jamie had called the house this morning, and though she spoke with just Grangy, I sensed something in the air was off. I could see it in the slouching of her posture and grimness of her murmuring.

Grangy hung up the telephone and looked to me with those sad eyes of hers, and I knew it was bad news. I went and got dressed as requested without any further inquiry, but the lack of explanation only confirmed my worst fears were at hand.

As we left the duplex silent and awkward, I began to hope against hope Alison was still alive. Even injured, but breathing would've been comforting to my soul.

I was jittery the whole ride downtown, and didn't worry once that our perfect secret had been exposed to the entire world. I just wanted Ali back safely in my arms, explaining how she had come to grips with Jeff's murder and how things would be better now she had a moment to make peace. I could imagine her corny expression, the one she used, that made me roll my eyes and forgive her for those crazy antics of hers.

Grangy drove on without making eye contact with me once or saying a single word. Her glossy eyes stared forward, and her hands gripped the steering wheel harder than normal. The longer silence was uninterrupted, the quicker my heart pounded, trying to break free from my rib cage. My midsection began to ache with each breath I took.

Then she parked at the one building I dreaded seeing: Grand Blanc City Morgue.

"Why have you brought us here?"

She exhaled. "Lauren, the authorities have found a body ... a young girl's body."

"Whose body did they find?" I shook my head, as my heart turned dark. "It's not my Alison."

"We're not sure." She caressed my arm, though it failed to offer me any support. "Not yet, anyway."

"Then why are we here? We're wasting valuable time. Ali is waiting for me to find her."

"Aunt Jamie got the call to come down and try to identify this young girl, that may or may not be our Alison."

I fought back the tears swelling in the corner of my eyes. "What? No. No. You're way off."

"She wanted us to meet them down here so we could find out together. That way we all know at the same time."

"Oh. Thank God. I thought you were certain." I exhaled a big relief. "I'm sure it's not my Ali. She's a Perf ... I mean she knows her way around this town."

"I hope to God you're right."

Aunt Jamie and Kevin pulled into the parking space beside us. And it was the most somber thing. We got out of the cars and hugged each other, but no one said much afterward. I followed them inside the building and over to the front counter, where a secretary and a middle-aged man wearing a white doctor's coat stood side by side, conversing.

The man greeted us. "Jamie and Kevin, I presume?"

"This is my mother, Margaret," she gestured.

Grangy offered him a polite head nod.

The man hesitated, giving us a look of sympathy. "Well ... let's get to it. Follow me this way please."

He escorted us along the plain-looking corridor, ending at a simple grey door. Sticking a silver key in the lock, he twisted the knob and cracked open the door.

Aunt Jamie gave me a look. "Lauren, I know you want to go inside with us, but I want you to stay put, while we do this."

"What? But ..." I glanced at the door. "I want to go in with you guys. Please let me."

"If it turns out to be ... bad news, you will be the first to know. But if it's not Ali, then I don't want you seeing something so horrific as a young girl taken off this earth."

"Jamie is right on this," Kevin added. "That is not a memory you need to live with."

Grangy touched my arm. "When we know for certain what we're dealing with, you'll know for certain. I promise. Okay?"

I glanced at the grey door for a second. "Hurry. I need to be out looking for Alison."

A jolt of betrayal shot through me and I watched the man in the white coat take them inside the room. I sat down in the chair beyond the doorway, and waiting was one of the hardest things I ever had to endure. Seconds felt like hours and minutes turned into eternity—time crawled to a standstill and made me feel anxious—made me feel nervous.

They should know by now. They should've seen the poor girl's body, said a prayer for her family and come out to me feeling relieved it wasn't Alison ... how come they haven't come out yet? Open the door ... please.

My thoughts turned torturous with each slow tick of the clock. My knee bounced so frantically I almost lost balance. I stared at the door, trying to will them to come out it. But nothing happened. I hopped to my feet and paced the tiled floor, practically running from wall to wall, like a wild caged animal seeking its freedom.

They should know it's not Alison by now—they should know, damn it! Come out ... COME OUT!

I couldn't wait any longer. It hurt like hell not knowing the truth. I rushed to the door and wrapped my fingers around the handle and pulled on it, but something hidden within my deepest fears ordered me to halt. The answers to my questions were on the other side, yet suddenly I was too terrified to receive them. I let go of the handle and took three steps backwards to the comfort zone of ignorance I was not ready to leave from. I stared at the grey door, somehow calming myself, and deciding to be brave no matter the outcome. I even maintained civility when the door seemed to stretch out of reach before my very eyes, taunting me with the one secret it knew I wanted exposed.

The door must have taken pity on my silent cries, and I was grateful when it swung open and Kevin exited, embracing Aunt Jamie. I closed my eyes, scared of what would be revealed next. I longed for a gentle touch on the shoulder, followed by their soft words of relief that it wasn't her—but it didn't come. I heard them shuffle by, weeping, theirs shoes echoing off as they rushed out of earshot. Seconds mounted so I opened my eyes and I was standing alone.

My heart broke. Like glass shattering from a steep fall and the slivers were too sharp to touch.

Grangy stepped out next and paused in front of me, looking solemn. I stared deep into her eyes and knew the truth before I even asked. She looked much older than when she had first entered the building just moments ago and I could tell the wisdom she gained was the cruel culprit.

"Was it her?" I asked. "Is the dead girl laying in that cold room my precious Alison?"

She exhaled a long sigh and offered a crippled grin. "… It's her. It's our Ali."

I went numb. I couldn't feel my own feet propping my body up. I knew I was still breathing air, I just couldn't feel my frail lungs taking oxygen into my body.

"Lauren? … Lauren? … Lauren?"

Grangy's lips motioned my name, but there was no sound to give her words life.

"Lauren!" Her voice broke through the deaf barrier.

"Huh?" I whimpered.

"I know you two were like twin sisters. I know you hurt something awful. Wish you didn't."

"There's some mistake. There has to be. She can't be dea …" I sobbed. "I just saw her a while ago and she was alive and so … Ali! Grangy, she was …"

She pulled my body in. "I know, sweetie. I know."

Her motherly grip was so snug the warmth comforted more than it smothered. But I didn't care. I was exhausted from being in denial all morning long, and it churned my insides with an aching jab that made me want to yell from the pain, and scream from the irritation. I could do nothing but surrender to the daunting notion of Alison no longer alive. It was a hard pill to swallow. The five stages of grief hit me all at once and the world wind that followed was torturous and earth shattering.

I'll never see your sweet smile again. Never hear your soft voice, your joyous laugh, or get to watch you take up for me, as though you were put on Earth to be my sole protector.

It hadn't been twenty-four hours since I had seen her last, and I was already forgetting some of her details. The small ones were the first to go, and most painful. I had to see her again, one more time, to prove it was real, and to memorize her face before the power of death began to set in.

"I want to see her … I need to see her."

"Not before they've had a chance to properly clean her up some. She looks nothing like our Alison right now."

"I don't care about any of that. I need to see Ali with my own two eyes, before I forget what she looks like."

"… Fine. I'll take you in to see her and say goodbye one last time, before … everything changes."

"Too late."

"You know what I mean."

"I do. But, no," I sniffled. "I'm going to go in alone."

She bore a grin. "I'm proud of you for being so strong."

"I'm not strong, I just need to do this on my own."

"You're growing."

"I'm hurting."

"That too."

She held my hand before I walked off. Each step made me more anxious, and the knot lodged in my throat made it almost impossible to swallow air, and it hurt when I did.

"I'll be waiting right here."

I tugged on the cold, shiny handle. It felt odd against my palm. The doorway widened, and I stepped over the threshold. The door bumped my back once it came to a rest, further jangling my rattled nerves. The odor of decay mixed with the scent of sterilization left my senses feeling out of sorts and flustered. Confusion began to set it. The white space had a hospital feel, outfitted with metal instruments and prongs you expected to see in a surgical room. I scanned the interior until I saw what I had dreaded since I first entered the building.

It's really real. She's really...

Alison looked like she was sleeping. She was lying in the center of the room on a metal slab, covered from the neck down by a clean white sheet. A medical device with a long clear tube connected to it stood a few feet off from the slab. My fingers twitched and I moved a half step closer to her covered corpse. I stared at the grey tile squares that made up the flooring and found myself counting the numbers in between Alison's motionless body and my skittering heartbeat.

Thirteen ... there are thirteen squares.

I paused beside the slab, but I didn't look up to it. I just stood there inhaling and exhaling air. But it didn't matter, my heartbeat stayed brisk. Finally, I knew there was nothing left for me to do but lift my head and view the body—so I did. I gazed upon her closed eyelids and still frame. Grangy was right all along. It was our Alison. Her stringy hair was uncombed and her complexion was dingy, like she had been rolling around in the dirt. I inspected her skull, but saw no signs of blunt trauma, no clue if she had suffered any agony or distress.

"What happened to you?" I whimpered. "How did you die?"

I gazed at her body and focused on the portion of the sheet above her midsection. There was an odd indentation, and no presence of abdomen firmness. My heart filled with dread, and I pinched the hem of the sheet and unveiled her dirty body.

The eerie sight of her body made my bones shiver and the hairs on my neckline perk.

From the chest down, slivers of raw, torn flesh hung from her skeleton like red peeling paint, spotted with huge, sick bruises. I stared at the gaping hole where her stomach should have been. Not even the section of her spine behind the hole was left intact.

"Oh, God!"

My sadness was tempered by flaring rage, until only anger was left behind. That anger refused to let the foul taste of disgust turn into vomit. As my breathing calmed my eyes narrowed and I knew someone had to pay for this travesty I was forced to endure. It was my time to fight like hell, and I was going to be a heartless warrior, a vengeful demon with a thirst for pleads that would go unanswered. And blood ... Mother Perfect blood … Aunt Geneve's blood. The venom shooting through my veins like dark plasma turned lethal, syrupy and vile. There was nothing left for me to do but strike.

I caressed Alison's skin, and it felt stiff to my touch. Leathery. She was truly gone from me, and that pissed me off the most—I stormed out of the room with only one thing on my mind.

Grangy cut me off. "Did you say goodbye to her?"

"I did not."

"But I thought that's what you went in there for?"

"I have something vital to do first … before I can say it and mean it." I slipped by her.

"Wait! Where are you going?"

"I need to be alone right now. Go on home. I'll find my way back when I'm done."

"But—"

"Don't ask me any more. I don't want to lie to you. And I can't ask you to bear the truth." I sniffled and hurried off, ignoring her questioning voice behind me.

It took all I had not to attack the first person giving me an opportunity to murder. I ignored the faces in the lobby and rushed out the entrance, bumping into Detective Neese, startling us both at the same time. Although my expression was lost in turmoil, his was business: police business.

"Lauren. Just the person I was hoping to see."

"I'm in no mood to deal with you." I tried side stepping his large frame. "Excuse me."

He blocked my exit and our bodies touched. "Get in the mood. We need to talk now."

I clenched my fists. "About?"

"Alison came to see me before any of this."

"And?"

"She watched her father's dashboard video of the day he died on that train track."

I fought off the rage trying to flash pink. "What does that have to do with me?"

"She happened to notice something strange on the video, and it angered her for some odd reason."

"Get to the part that involves me."

"Tell me what it has to do with his death."

"I haven't the slightest."

"You're lying to me."

"Prove it."

He grabbed my arm. "A beautiful girl I cared for died a tragic death yesterday."

"No shit!" I growled like an irritated lioness about to pounce. "Move far from me!" I felt my eyes flicker fuchsia, and it was so sweet to the taste I wanted more of it to savor.

Detective Neese hesitated, letting go of my arm. "You growl at me, and then your eyes flashed pink."

"I think we're done here, unless you have an arrest warrant to serve," I snipped.

He reached his hand out again. "Wait."

"I wouldn't do that. It could be detrimental to everything that you think you know."

"Fine." He lowered his arm.

I felt the uncertainty from his eyes on my backside as I descended the first three steps.

"Lauren, I cared for Alison too. A lot of good cops did."

I looked back. "And yet she's still dead—weird, huh?"

"Help me find the monsters who did this."

"You don't think I want her to pay?"

"So, I'm looking for a female?"

"I didn't say that!"

"Actually, you did." It turned quiet. "Give me a full name: Riley, or perhaps maybe …"

I backed away. "Stop. You have no idea what the hell you're talking about, detective."

"Then help me."

"Stay out of it. It would be safer for you if you did." I stormed off along the sidewalk.

"Lauren, what on God's earth put that hole in her body?"

I didn't answer. Mostly because each word I said would lead to more inquiries, all of which needed their own explanation. I stormed off through the business district of town. The world around me kept spinning as if nothing tragic had happened, while every step I took made me more volatile. The human in me desired resolution, but only the real me was brave enough to go after it—I was ready to be that monster … and it felt—perfect.

"Geneve!" I snarled. "Where are you? I want you standing in front of me right goddamn now!"

I hurried to a one-story building and entered the front entrance.

"Welcome to Provenzano's Law Office, may I help you?" the secretary behind a desk asked me.

"Sit down!" I pointed.

Her body responded to my demand, slamming back inside the chair and shocking the woman in the process. I approached a coat closet and the door swung open as I neared it, exposing a starry darkness inside and a raging funnel of wind calling out to me.

WOOSH!

CHAPTER 9

DETECTIVE NEESE

I WATCHED LAUREN STORM off, but could do nothing to apprehend her. I had a badge and loaded pistol at my side, and yet felt helpless: helpless to my calling, to Jeff—and now to Alison. There was so much more I was missing, so much beyond my comprehension. The dead bodies of the ones I cared for were piling up, and I was angered that I hadn't done my job. I glanced at the front door of the city morgue, but knew that choice would only cause me more anguish, and I could endure no more at the present.

I got inside my police car, drenched in annoyance and feathered by grief. I slapped the steering wheel much harder than I anticipated. It vibrated, but held fast, while my bones ached and my fingers and joints numbed from the pain. I despised being lied to. Lauren's arrogant stance made me aware there was more to that murder/suicide last spring, the one that involved another pretty girl with the same lethal touch as her friend.

If dead boys could talk, I would be able to expose these teenage black widows with glowing coral eyes for what they really are ... monstrous murderers.

I was far less impressed by their gift to illuminate their eyes new colors, no matter how unexplainable or intimidating it was, than the faltering of my usual talent to unravel deadly mysteries.

Plus, being defeated by dangerous teenage girls did nothing to protect my precious community or my authoritative ego.

CHAPTER 10

GENEVE

BRAY RETURNED WITH WHAT I had sent him to retrieve, and both now sat before me appearing contrite in the VIP section of the nightclub. Club Rain continued to be my safe haven, my home away from home … away from home. The loud music pulsating in the background provided more than ample cover for my private dealings, while the strobe lighting spun in erratic circles above the damp human flesh gyrating on the dance floor. The friction sparking off their closely packed bodies made the interior of Rain sticky like a hot sauna. The tangy smell simmering in the air was quite seductive.

If that weren't enough, the chaotic noise vibrating the speakers stayed a sufficient buffer between my life long foes and me. Fearians hated the sound of loud music. The odd development of their tympanic membrane made clashing noises painful for them to endure any more than a few seconds. Unfortunately for my allies, it was the same for Loafers when it came to clamoring sounds in the form of heightened melodies. Still, I needed to be set free from the darkness of ignorance that plagued me, so their discomfort was of no concern at the moment. After all, Loafers owed Mother Perfects for their very lives, having been marked for genocide by the Fearian Counsel long ago.

Matthew and Stacy, as they called themselves, were the last of an endangered species. They hated Fearians as much as Perfects did, but they were passive and lacked fighting skills. As they sat across the table from me, with Bray standing beside them, they looked on, grimacing from the noise bouncing off the VIP walls. My slyness made them jittery, and I relished in the power of silent intimidation.

"You wanted to see us, Mother Geneve?" he asked.

"Yes. But first, take off the human charade," I demanded.

Stacy looked to Matthew. "Honey?"

They hesitated before shaking their heads, forcing the human features to vanish and the grisly features of Loafers to reappear in their place. Bray cleared his throat, battling to restrain his response to their distasteful appearance. He took a deep breath and casually stood with his back to us. I understood his plight and said nothing.

Beauty is in the eye of the beholder.

"Much better," I said. "I prefer to revel in the true faces of those in my presence."

"We beg of you, Mother Geneve. We are not to blame for Mother Elisabeth's undoing," Stacy cowed.

"My wife is correct. We had every intention of raising The Seal with nothing but affection, just as she requested of us, but when the other Perfect came to our home, we could not stop her deceitful actions. We were defenseless and left at a disadvantage, to say the least."

"She possessed the scent of one unworthy, but the traits of a Mother Perfect," Stacy said. "We were caught off guard. And—"

"Only a Mother Perfect can undo the will of another Mother Perfect. I am well familiar with the Perfect Order. But my interest lies elsewhere."

They looked to each other, their expressions twitching with grimaces of suffering, as a particularly loud song came on; one of my favorites.

"What is it, Bray?" I asked, sensing his troubled thoughts.

"It seems your presence is requested."

"By whom?"

He pointed across the dance floor. "Your niece."

"Really? I'm starting to feel cherished."

I watched Lauren scan the crowded club. Once our eyes connected, Lauren darted toward me, ducking in and out of partiers without missing a beat, or disrupting any of theirs. I was unsure why she'd come, but I sensed her emotions were running high, and not in a good way.

Damn it.

"Matthew. Stacy. I sincerely thank you for your prompt attendance here before me. We will continue this conversation at a new time and dwelling of my choosing."

"Of course," Matthew said.

"Kindly escort my consorts back to where you found them, Bray. Make sure they are safe before you leave them behind."

"This way please," he said.

"May we cloak ourselves?" Stacy asked.

I grinned, keeping my attention on my approaching family member. "Certainly. Do carry on with your pleasant window dressing."

Before I finished my words, both had turned their disfigurements back into human features. They seemed appeased by the pleasant transformation, though the glaring music was still pricking at their brains.

I knew being exposed in this realm as anything other than human beings terrified them to pieces, so I let them have their sense of asylum. I had other pressing family matters to attend, apparently.

My bodyguard unhooked the velvet rope, and they shuffled out behind Bray. As they made their way down the steps, I watched Lauren squeeze by them. Lauren hesitated and stared at Matthew, and I knew a vision of Elisabeth interacting with the Loafers flashed inside her thoughts. It caught her off guard, as she watched them being whisked away. I watched her, intrigued, and entertained, as she tried to shake off the heartwarming vision clouding up her anger. As they moved from sight, Lauren regained her stiff posture and approached the velvet rope, stopping inches before the bulky bodyguard and his grim face and puffed out chest.

"May I help you?"

"Move."

He chuckled. "You're kidding me, right?"

Lauren's pupils stormed pink with rage. "Does it look like I'm kidding? Don't make me hurt you."

Although Lauren was disgruntled, I still felt an overwhelming sense of pride. At that exact moment, she didn't care who knew she was pissed— just like me in my time of discord. Whether she refused to accept it or not, she was starting to show more and more of my characteristics, which meant less of her mother's each time we found ourselves face to face.

Birds of a feather...

"It's okay. Let her pass," I said.

Lauren didn't wait for him to clear a path after he unhooked the velvet rope, and she brushed by him. I looked on, admiring her pitbull behavior. Her antics were flagrant, sour and still breathtaking. Nothing was going to stop her from getting to me, and that determination couldn't be taught. She was born with it zipping through her noble veins.

"You!" Lauren sneered.

She flicked a finger, causing the table before me to rip from its metal stand and slam against the wall. I was left impressed, but flinched none, nor did I uncross my legs. My human whipped around, his big muscles flexing, but I motioned him to stand down, and he wisely complied. Lauren didn't take her eyes off of me as she stepped forward, clenching her fists and flaring her nostrils—the way a T-Rex would before devouring her prey.

"Welcome to Russia … again," I greeted. "I trust this trip will be crime-free?"

"What did you do to her?"

I lifted my brow. "I do not know, but whatever it was, it must've been exquisite. To whom are we referring to now, dear?"

"Don't even pretend. You know exactly 'whom' I am referring to. My Ali!" her eyes watered.

Lauren unleashed a barrage of energy pulses at me with deadly precision. Energy attracted from her fingers and into a ball. I shielded myself with the palm of my hand, defusing her attack. Her barrage made me stagger a step, but the sharpness was brief and failed to steal away my quaint smile.

"Sweetheart. Haven't you and I ventured down this rocky path once before?"

She acted undaunted by her botched attack. "I don't give a damn. I want you hurting!"

Truth be told, it was the sincerity of her words that caused me the most displeasure and heartbreak. My proclivity for violence wanted to end her, but my broken heart chastised the tempting request. She was my only family and my last connection to the sister I loved and missed dearly. Lauren turned toward me again with lethal intent, but I swiftly evaded the attack by vanishing from her sight.

A mushroom of debris caused by Lauren's own handiwork blinded her a half-second before she realized I'd reappeared at her back. I winked, and each partier froze in place, their stiff limbs still hung in the air. Before Lauren could comprehend my graceful actions, I embraced her into a reluctant surrender.

"Calm yourself, child. You are making a spectacle of yourself in a public place."

"Let go of me! Let go!" she huffed. "I'm not done with you! Not by a long shot!"

"I believe that you are."

I placed my hand over her heart, and the burning of her body released a jolt of revelation into my own, exposing the true nature of her pain. In my mind, I saw her standing over her mutilated human pet, Alison, who lay dead on a metal slab. The agony that tore through her emotions made it hard for me to bear its touch, even as an innocent third party. What Lauren felt for Alison in her time of grief was the same as what I felt for Harlen in his, and now Isabelle in her predicament.

"Get out of my head. I feel you inside me poking around! Get out!" She jerked free, but remained on guard and tensed as hell.

"My condolences for your loss. I know you and the human, Alison, were close."

"What do you care?"

"Actually I don't. But I do care for you," I said. "That will never alter no matter the circumstance."

"Then how could you be so cold to someone I love? You knew Ali meant everything to me."

"I am aware of the affection you two secured."

"And I bet it ate you up with blind jealousy. I bet that's why you did it to her. Isn't it?"

"Lauren, I have no need for such human tantrums. They are beneath me—a sick addiction to possess, in fact. As for your hurt, I am not the origin of your vexation, child."

"You are a liar!" she screamed. "You wanted them dead!"

"You are correct. I still do. However, I am not the reason she is no more upon the earth."

Her eyes shone with tears. "I don't believe you. You said you were going to kill her and you did."

"Believe what you must, but the gaping hole that was left in Alison's midsection was the work of a cruel destroyer, who only desired to dispense extreme agony."

She sniffled. "What?"

"And since the only person trying to be a destroyer in any realm belongs to you ..."

"Apple? No." Lauren stared into space. "Unless ... Jeff ... Ali did confront her."

"The same honor was thought of Victoria, and yet here we are still dealing with her corollary."

She frowned from the bitter taste of revelation and choked up. "What the hell is wrong with people? How can they be so hateful?"

Lauren backed away, trembling. She began to hyperventilate and her eyes burned bright fuchsia. The illumination grew. I could do nothing but watch, knowing what was to come next: the inevitable. Lauren overloaded, and brightness filled the club with a jabbing, blinding light and she fainted, her body collapsing to the floor at my feet.

"And this is why hybrids are unlawful," I said.

Although the consequences were brutal, I wasn't the least bit surprised by them. This little experiment would always end in the same manner. Hybrids would expose the heart of their true selves: flawed and imperfect, trapped by vanity—slaves to their flesh.

I stared down at my last loved one with pity and a hint of empathy. Just like Elisabeth, living among the humans had made me soft in ways too, no matter how much I tried to avoid it. But in the end, it wouldn't be Lauren's admission of guilt that forced my hand. She would just be the one who mattered the most, mad at me for serving justice.

I kneeled to her and caressed her tender skin. It felt so inviting, and oddly enough, humanistic.

My sweet lovely...

If Lauren wasn't careful, that elusive presence of Elisabeth she tried so hard to discern would be lost forever, leaving her with only a clear resemblance to me—and I was more than okay with that.

CHAPTER 11

CHARLOTTE

SUNSET MADE ITS PRESENCE felt, but failed to bring any solace to my broken heart. As a Perfect I often pitied the humans, tormented by their weak emotions. I used to watch them, hidden in plain sight, not once realizing I only lacked the right catalyst in order to become one of them; different in many ways, and yet so much alike in one.

The lush green grass underneath my bare feet was soft to the touch, but the cruelty of Mother Isabelle's destroyed home beyond it distracted me from its precious comfort.

The hurt you surely endured—I can only imagine.

The burnt mess had been labeled 'condemned' by the human authorities, and the foul stench of tragedy still lingered in the air, though the smoldering had ceased. Last time I was here, both Mother Isabelle and Razlor welcomed me in with open arms. Now all I could do was mourn an unquenchable memory. They didn't even receive a proper burial as an offering to the gods. I think that hurt me the most. At least then I could have fooled myself into believing their spirits ascended with some form of peace, but that last request was robbed from them. Not even mortals charge their condemned to such an end.

My thoughts traveled back to the *Cave of Relics,* when the Mother Perfects elected to do something drastic in order to preserve our species. When the choice to enter the realm of humans became anything but. How I longed to be honored with just that sad moment in time. I closed my eyelids tight, begging the past would grant me that one simple wish ...

Mother Isabelle exposed the royal portal. Mother Harlen tried his best to keep Victoria, our precocious one, in check: *A hard task for any Perfect to have to perform.*

"We should stay and fight!" Victoria protested.

Harlen looked at her with disdain. "No. Too many good Perfects have fallen today already."

I turned to Mother Isabelle and grabbed her hand. "I will follow you and Razlor into this new realm."

"Excuse me?"

"Help protect you alongside him, from the species called humans … just in case."

Mother Isabelle's eyes sparkled in the light. "You are so special to me, Charlotte. I am honored to be your Mother Perfect."

"Then it is settled."

"No, sweetie. It's not."

"But…"

"You must find your own way for now. I have taught you all that I know. I'll be fine. Trust me."

"Please. You mean the world to me. If something bad were to ever become of you I'd be lost."

She caressed my face. "That is why I want you to take some time to be truly free. Grow into the beautiful Perfect you must become."

"But I am not understanding."

"In time you will." She glanced to the commotion nearby, as Razlor approached, fiddling with his destroyer glove.

"The others are ready," he said.

Mother Isabelle nodded then looked back to me. "When my days have ended, and the sun sets at my back, I wish to give you something priceless to keep safe for me."

"Okay."

"Then Razlor will be charged with protecting you both for the remainder of his days."

"May I ask what the gift will be?"

"You may, but I'm not going to tell you," she tapped me on the tip of my nose.

"I'm going to miss being with you." My eyes watered.

"I know. But we will see each other from time to time, I promise."

"If that is your wish," I said.

"Live among the human beings, learn their ways. Find yourself, but always remember you were Perfect first."

Her words were strength to my core. She kissed my forehead and ushered me into the blinding light inside the portal.

And yet here I am, now freakishly weaken from the journey.

CHAPTER 12

PENELOPE

APPLE'S BEDROOM WAS DARK, quiet, eerie, but even in the shadows of night I could detect the foul presence of counterfeit teenage popularity in my midst.

Not exactly the style of a true Perfect. But then again, you're nowhere close to being a Perfect, now are you?

Deviancy oozed from my skin pores, lifting my spirits more. The moonlight shone through the open window, though the thin curtains were able to muffle its radiant glow. I prowled toward Apple, where she lay motionless in bed. If I expected things to go my way, it would require some finessing. Unlike Victoria, whose procrastination was a trait she couldn't shake, I believed in due diligence when it came to getting what I wanted.

I stood over Apple as she slept on her back.

She was naïve prey ready for the feasting—or brutal slaughter. Her eyes were shut, and I removed a strand of hair from her forehead. My eyes glistened. No, brighter.

I'm going to enjoy taking every little thing from you, brick by brick, like a murderous mason on a rampage, until there is no hybrid left inside your corpse ...

My pupils lit up the room, but didn't disrupt her deep slumber. Her eyelids twitched again before nestling motionless. My patsy was defenseless against a seasoned carnivore with the ultimate wisdom of a tyrant and the agility of a mother.

"That's it. Rest easy, my love," I soothed.

My words were more than a humble suggestion, or even a light proposal. They were a command, off the beautiful lips of a Mother Perfect who had audacious plans for the entire world—and who would be left standing alone in it. I caressed her pulpy skin and ran my finger along the length of her forearm, riding over the tiny hairs.

Apple's closed eyelids bloomed with a sparkling light, and she inhaled a big dose of my deepest desire into her mortal lungs, though she slumbered still.

"Mm," she mumbled, as if a secret mate touched her.

"You and I are a lot alike," I murmured.

"Yes ..."

"We both hate Lauren."

"I do hate Lauren so." Her words were steady, but her voice sounded muffled and thick, and close to being slurry.

"I know how you feel." I turned conniving. "And yet I sense there's much more percolating on your dirty mind."

Apple moved her limbs before settling in place. "If only there were something that could be done." She paused, waiting.

A flirtatious discharge rushed over my notions, elevating my deviant intentions. "Actually, there is."

"I was hoping..."

"It seems you have crossed over moral boundaries recently to dominate another's conscience in your great time of despair."

"... Maybe."

"Invigorating, isn't it?"

"Yes. It really was."

"Since proper legalities aren't quite your forte, my simple request will play right up your alley."

"Excellent."

"I hope you don't mind, but I'm going to take the wheel for a spell, and you get to ride bitch while I do it. Next time you find yourself face to face with the one you are most envious of, you shall end her, only I want it done in plain sight."

"I will go to her home."

I curled my eyes: humans. "I want you and the other Diet Pepsi to have fun with Lauren while at school ... and Apple?"

"Yes?"

"Do destroy her ... again, in public. I want other humans to witness the dawn of a new era, a Perfect era. And you will never stop your pursuit until it is completed."

"As you wish."

"Being a hybrid is nothing more than a broken wanna-be version of me, so I'm going to let you sample my own unique flavor to assist in your lofty efforts."

"Anything more, Mother Penelope?"

"That is all."

"Okay." She got cozy.

"Oh. You will know when the time is right."

"I will know."

"Until then enjoy your slumber. Sleep tight."

"Good night, Mistress."

I gave her a soft kiss on the lips. Her humanistic charms ironically failed to churn my gut. "Parting is such sweet sorrow."

My new pet monkey continued to sleep, and I skipped over to her closet door. It swung open wide with a gust of wind on its tail and a sliver of creaking from its hinges.

WOOSH!

CHAPTER 13

LAUREN

I OPENED MY EYES and found myself standing barefooted and wearing a yellow cotton sundress in the middle of a vast open field, overrun with green stemmed sunflowers as far as my eyes could see. My sense of smell confirmed all I saw to be true. The blazing sun above hung by its lonesome, with no white clouds floating on its flanks. The sunrays baked my shoulders and gave my skin color.

A rainbow of content caressed me into a state of relaxation. My bare arms fell to my side, and my fingertips swayed to and fro on the soft petals of the sunflowers. I drew in a deep breath, and it was as if I stood before a colorful smorgasbord of scented beauty.

Then I heard the tenderness of her sweet voice. Its hovering was so swift I almost overlooked the gentle greeting as it rode the warm breeze passed my eardrums.

"Lauren?"

It took a second to register within me, but when it did, a fuzzy feeling helped me to break free from the peaceful calmness and my brow shifted. "Alison?"

I surveyed the open field, but there was no sign of her, though the anxiousness poking at my heart stayed relentless and unsatisfied.

My expectations wilted.

"Lauren?" her voice came again. This time it was more direct.

A grin stretched across my face because I was now certain. "Ali. Where are ..." I whipped around, excited, but my great reward was as cruel as the first time. "You?"

Alison leaned over my shoulder, as if our game of hide and seek was won. "Hey, homeboy."

The strength of her breath caressed my shoulder blade and the mint particles that I've been longing to smell once more reminded me of her perky spirit and tangy charm.

I almost lost footing trying to lug its heavy embrace.

She strolled in front of me, almost skipping childlike, wearing a flimsy silk mini dress, with her arms tucked behind her and her pretty white teeth in view. She was beautiful to admire.

"You're alive." I studied her face. "I mean, really alive … and talking to me."

"It would appear so."

Then I looked away from her smiling face, shivering, and a jolt of fear choked my heartstrings, making it hard to inhale. Ali's grotesque wound was still there and it was still sickening to look at. A foul stench from the decay lingered in the air and a cluster of blowflies swarmed at the torn skin. I tried not to notice, but I couldn't stop myself from viewing the handful of maggots eating through her dead flesh. Goosebumps popped along the length of my arms and it took all I had to endure the vile image. "How are you … still breathing?"

Ali shrugged as though it was of know consequence. "I don't know. Maybe I'm not. Maybe you're dreaming and when you wake up this will have been a new nightmare."

Tears streamed from my eyes, and my voice turned insignificant and feeble. "It will always be a new nightmare so long as you're gone away from me."

"Sorry," she dismissed, but held her pleasantries.

I conjured the courage to face her, refusing to let my eyes droop any lower than her cherry lip-gloss. "Who did this to you, Alison?"

She giggled and the creepy undertone confused my thinking.

"Answer me, please."

"You already know the answer." She winked.

"Apple?"

She gnawed on her lip. "The slut. But are you really surprised by her sneaky actions?"

"No. I'm not."

"I didn't think so."

"It doesn't matter. I am going to hurt her for this, don't you worry." I wiped off tears.

Not even the salty taste against my buds could steal away the honeysuckle flavor dripping from my thirst for malice.

She hunched her shoulders, casually accepting my words as truth. "You can if you want. It won't bring me back." She stepped away, nodding at the distance. "I think I have to go now. He's waiting for me."

"Who's waiting for you?"

She didn't answer me, though she held her smile.

I glanced beyond her and saw a ray of light appear, shining a wide path from the heavens above. The flowers that witnessed the glorious light blossomed even more.

"But you can't go yet. You can't leave me alone. I won't let you."

"Sorry Charlie." She waved.

I ran after her, but I couldn't catch up. My frantic scamper brought me no closer as she entered the path of light. "Alison!" I shrieked.

"Love…" her voice whispered in my ear.

"No. Alison!"

Before her name had left my trembling lips, her entire body transformed into a faint figure among the brightness … until I could no longer distinguish Alison from the glowing radiance—then the light vanished from sight … and I was alone with sunflowers.

CHAPTER 14

MARGARET

"NO! NO!" LAUREN MUMBLED in her sleep, shaking her head.

I sat on the edge of the bed. Her slumber was restless and self-defeating. I wanted to wake her, but believed bad sleep was better than none at all, even if it meant having to endure nightmarish dreams that stuck along for the bumpy ride. Lauren sat up in bed.

"Don't leave me!"

"Honey, calm down. It's just a dream. I'm not going anywhere."

"Grangy?"

"Morning."

She lay perched on her elbows. "How'd I get home?"

"I haven't the slightest clue. I heard moaning coming from inside your bedroom. I looked in and here you were, fast asleep."

"I ... must've dozed off. What day is it?"

"Sunday morning. You've been asleep ever since yesterday afternoon."

"So was everything else real?"

"If you mean Alison? Yes. I'm sorry. That part is very real."

"Figures."

"Maybe a good cry will help," I said. "It helped me ... some."

"Glad to hear." Lauren placed her feet onto the floor and slipped on her shoes.

"But?"

"I'm not ready to cry yet." She stood to her feet, displaying an irritated smirk.

"Where are you going?"

"Unfinished business."

"Uh. Okay."

"It won't take me long. I promise you that."

Lauren's determined look made me uneasy. "Would you like for me to tag along to keep you company?"

"What?"

"You probably shouldn't be alone right now."

"Does it matter? What's done is done. I can't change it. Besides, I'm not the one you should worry about."

"What does that mean, Lauren?"

"It means I'll be fine." She grinned with a shroud of reluctance in her response. "Understood?" Her voice sounded mildly threatening.

Prickly hairs on my neck perked up. "If … you say so."

She kissed my cheek, but her lips felt cold, and her touch felt impersonal.

"What I have to do won't take me long."

"What won't take you long, Lauren?"

"… I'm going to go now."

She walked out of the bedroom, her shoulders stiff, like a savage warrior ordered into battle. There was something sinister going on, and I couldn't help but think it had everything to do with her mother—Elisabeth's troubled past.

CHAPTER 15

LAUREN

I SLIPPED INTO LEO'S Coney Island restaurant to find it filled with its usual breakfast crowd, oblivious to the dark skies looming. Killing Ali had gotten Apple promoted to the top of my shit list, and she had clearly reached a new level to her madness. I had to put a stop to it. I scanned about and spotted her and Riley seated in a booth.

Huh. Absolute power corrupts ...

Apple didn't need to be a Perfect, she needed a damn priest with holy water to cast out the vile demons living inside of her. It had taken a long while for me to see it, but now I knew nothing good would ever come from the gifts Victoria had given them. Still I had to be careful, or more harm than good would be the end result of our love spat.

I shackled my wrath and crept onto the minefield, eyeing my flanks for inevitable explosions and pitfalls. Riley had her back to me, but Apple made sure she saw me coming for her. The true acts of a ruthless scavenger, ready to sacrifice friendship to ensure her own existence and popularity.

Hybrids ... cowards ... imperfects.

Apple's eyes lit up and she faked a grin. "Hey, Lauren!"

"Apple."

"Lauren, why don't you have a seat?" Riley offered.

I jabbed my finger at her. "Don't talk. You don't get to talk."

"Ah. Rude," she replied, with a prideful neck twist.

"Never mind her." Apple batted her long eyelashes at me and interlocked her fingers underneath her chin. "So, girlfriend, what's on your troubled mind?"

I wanted to lay into her with the power of a Mother Perfect, but there were too many witnesses, too much at stake—too many innocent bystanders, and I knew firsthand Apple would be ruthless in her retaliation. I also sensed she was aware the only one who gave a hill of beans about any others was me, and she was not above using it as leverage. I glanced from side to side, trying to keep the strangers numb to the perils existing in their midst.

"Was it you? Did you kill Ali?" I asked under my heated breath. "Did you do it?"

"You mean the sickly tramp with the shady attitude?"

Apple's words brought me to the point of no return—a point of physical contact.

"What did you call my cousin…?"

Her destroyer glove glowed. "A sickly tramp," she boasted. "Of course, the only things she'll be screwing for now on are hungry earthworms … good thing they don't have good eyesight, huh?"

Her arrogance caught me off guard, it was so blatant and way out of bounds.

Riley leaned over the table. "Apple! You said she was still alive."

Apple shrugged. "I lied." She exhaled a big breath. "Whoo! Now that I've gotten that off of my chest, I feel so much better."

"You hateful monster," I said.

"Sticks and stones, darling," she taunted. "Too bad she's still blowing earthworms."

"Apple Paisley!" Riley condemned.

"Oh, come on, Riles."

"What?"

"Like you really wanted her to be Perfect to begin with."

Riley glanced at me, then back to Apple. "Well … doesn't mean I wanted her dead … just gone."

"You're in luck. She is … just gone." Apple looked to me. "Ms. Thing shouldn't have invited her to be hybrid in the first place. Isn't that right, Lauren?" she jeered. "The way I see it, it's your own damn fault."

I lifted my brow. "Really?"

Apple came to her feet and I felt the warmth of her breath on my face as she slithered forward a step. "Why don't we chalk this ugly misfortune up as a lesson learned and move on from it?" she suggested with a mild snarl. "How bout?"

I prided myself for not succumbing to the wilds of a 'mean girl,' even after the Perfect life stepped on the scene, yet in that exact moment my fluttering eyelashes were enough to tip the scale and send be plummeting down the rabbit hole and into the darkness. When the light finally returned, reminding me with whom I was standing, an invective attribute painted my sorrow the color of fury red and choked all compassion in me to death.

"I have a much better idea in mind." I felt the strife in me sever every bulging blood vein of loyalty to the friendship we had once had, a friendship that quickly bled out.

"Do share," Apple said.

"You and I step outside those front doors so I can kick your scrawny ass from one end of Grand Blanc to the other." I swallowed up the last inch of space between us. "So I can watch you beg me for your pathetic life to end. Spoiler alert: I grant you your wish."

"Are you sure you want to go there?"

"Yes, Apple. I am sure I want to go there—and I plan on dragging you by the ankle every bumpy step of the way … wear a helmet, bitch."

"Speaking of helmets, Riles and I would hate for dear old Grangy to skydive off the Sears Tower without a parachute," Apple whispered.

"Huh."

"Brittle old bones don't bounce." She tilted her hips. "So they say."

"They say the same about young precocious brothers."

"What?" Apple hesitated.

"You heard me. You won't touch any more of my family. I won't let you, and I'm not afraid of what it could take to stop you," I sneered, and my eyes flickered coral. "I will not cease until I destroy you, and anyone else who gets in my way." I glanced toward Riley at the end of my words, and she had the decency—or brains—to look down.

My fierceness pushed Apple back a step, and her arrogance faltered.

"Cool," she said, crossing her arms. "Senior year is about to commence, so I do believe big changes are in order."

"What kind of changes, Apple?" Riley asked.

Apple didn't take her eyes off me. "It is no longer feasible for us three to remain friendly. Conflict of interest, you do understand?"

I growled, "You think?"

"Isn't that correct, Riles?"

I turned to Riley, who placed her head down again as if she was trying to swallow something hard to get down her passageway. Once she accepted its fate, she glared up at me with a cold stare, then stood to her feet and crowded me, breathing air in and out.

Her eyes were focused, so focused I could tell she wasn't at the wheel driving. It was then I witnessed her and Apple seated on the bed and Apple running her hand along Riley's skin. Her pupil exposed the truth like a crystal ball before it vanished from sight.

"Yes," Riley snarled. "Sadly, this alliance has to come to an end." Her voice was filled with hate, rage, and I knew the battle for her soul had been lost.

"You wicked vindictive hag," I said to Apple.

"So." Apple sucked her teeth. "Now what?"

I felt stuck. Patrons in the dining room had started to notice our heated trio of commotion. I couldn't let Apple win, but more importantly, I couldn't let her expose any evidence of the order, especially now that it began to unearth its real value to my core.

"This isn't over, Apple. Not by a long shot," I mumbled.

"I know. Sucks to be you, though."

"We'll see about that," I replied.

"Just be happy anonymity is the rule of the day. Otherwise, I'd put your butt on blast and unclothed your filthy kind," Apple said. "Hell, I still might do it."

"Riles, if you're in there, try and break free from her," I pleaded. "Your very life literally depends on it."

Riley's eyes flashed pink. She punched me in the gut, snatching away my breath. The force threw me backwards, crashing onto a crowded table in the middle of the dining room. My body flopped against the wooden table and it collapsed to the floor, with me on top of it. Dishes and hot food splattered everywhere. My clothes were doused. Patrons hopped up, desperately trying to evade the chaos happening in their personal space. Other people turned to stare, and my eyes raged fuchsia, but my human audience forced them to return to normal and I froze.

Riley stood over me with her fists ready, while Apple stood a step behind her, looking on like a skilled trainer proud of the neat tricks her pet had just performed for the crowd.

"Apple?" Riley asked.

"That is all for now," Apple said.

Riley's eyes returned to human, and she relaxed her stance, though she stared at me with dissension bubbling over from within.

"See you at school. Do come prepared," Riley warned. "It'll get tragic for you if you don't."

"Leave it to you to disrupt everyone's tasty breakfast: drama queen," Apple said.

The pair strolled over to the telephone booth in the corner.

WOOSH!

Embarrassed, I clawed to my feet, apologized to the family whose breakfast I'd ruined and even paid for their meals. I tried to hold my head up, but the condemning glares and faint whispering in the background started to wear me down. I noticed a young girl recording everything with her cell phone, but I was already spent.

My revenge for Alison's murder was overshadowed by my need to be protective of humanity, even though humanity didn't give a damn about me. To take Apple down, sacrifices would have to be made. Something had to give. I would have to make a selfish choice, and I wasn't sure I could live with the one decision offering me an advantage.

A brief notion of enlisting the deadly talents of Aunt Geneve to end the drama zipped through my head, but I wasn't ready to open that enormous can of worms just yet, knowing her idea of closure was a hell of a lot different than mine. I also wasn't ready to let her hear me say she was right, but she probably knew that by now. So, I guess it didn't matter when I came back crawling on my bruised knees. She'd be expecting my arrival.

CHAPTER 16

APPLE

RILEY FOLLOWED ME OUT of my bedroom closet and began pacing the floor. I could tell she was pumped, and blind as to why Lauren's face ruffled her feathers so. My will rewrote the rules for her will, and there was no coming back from it. *Ever.*

Even though deep inside I'd hoped the drama between us could've been squashed without Lauren's exile, there existed a tiny voice, barely detectable to my consciousness.

You will die, little Miss Mother Perfect. You will perish in front of the whole world.

I might even take the continent of Australia for a bride.

I didn't know if I could handle the Fearians, but I couldn't stop myself. I wasn't sure I could handle any Perfects left, either, but I still couldn't stop myself. Thank God for my gift of destroyer—and of course Riley, who'd foolishly take a stray bullet for me at a moments notice.

But what are true besties for?

"Relax, Riles. It's over now."

"That was so much fun," she said.

"You have to let it go, girl. We have to be smart from here on out. The jungle is filled with many violent predators. All we have is each other now."

"I know. So, what should we do?"

"Lauren."

"Cool ... and then?"

"We play it by ear, one scary monster at a time. Until there are no more monsters left hiding underneath the queen's bed."

"Apple, you rock. I don't know what I would ever do without you by my side."

"Luckily you don't have to wonder about such things."

The hopeful expression on her face longed for acceptance—the way a young boy expresses his first teenage crush. Riley was so smitten it was almost pathetic—hell, it *was* pathetic, if not for being so enjoyable to my inner being I would've lost interest long ago.

"Can I ask you a question?"

"Anything, Apple."

"Did you sleep with Sean?"

"What?"

"You know back when you were a long-legged robot?"

"Oh. Didn't I tell you already?"

"No. You did not. I couldn't get it out of you. Remember?"

"Huh." She shrugged it off. "We didn't sleep much."

"Really? My Sean?"

Her witless honesty, accompanied by the smell of her perfume, the very same perfume I imagined him rubbing up against, made me hot. No, it turned me jealous.

"He was mine that night." She winked. "And I enjoyed him greatly."

I fiddled on my nightstand. "Have a favor to ask?"

"Anything for you."

I turned around with a long, silver knitting post in my hand.

"Stick this needle through your palm."

"Do you really want me to?"

"I really do."

Riley took the needle from me, pressed the tip to her palm and pierced the skin. She grimaced from the pain, but she kept pushing through, eventually impaling the thick muscles and layered tendons inside her hand.

"Ah!" she cringed, as a bone inside her hand cracked, breaking in two.

She gritted with determination and sobbed, but didn't stop pushing the needle until the tip broke the outer skin and the shiny part came into view.

Riley held up her hand before me, trembling, and in agony, and breathing hard, but proud she had pleased me. I was impressed by her new loyalty, and a bit troubled by it, but not enough to experience empathy.

"Anything else?"

My eyes sparkled. Her confession had brought out the worst in me, and I wanted her to hurt for exposing the petty insecurities I'd forgotten were still there and only skin deep. It took the sight of real blood, her blood to weaken my lethal resolve and immaturity—yet still empathy was void.

"That will be it. You can take it out now."

Riley pulled the needle free from her hand, and the puncture and broken bone healed itself as the pain eased its grip on her senses. Slowly.

I wiped off the blood from the knitting needle and placed it back on the nightstand.

It was difficult for me to maintain a sense of feeling for Riley, mostly because it clashed with the joy of being empowered by my Perfect gift. Having my own crash test dummy to play with was new for me, and quite intoxicating to process.

This gun was fully loaded, and I was eager to aim it at my next unsuspecting tool. The evil part of me wanted to torture Riley a little more, just to see what would happen. I wasn't sure if that was normal—I wasn't sure of anything anymore. It was as if...

Is this how Riley feels after yielding to my overwhelming touch? Yes. It must be...

CHAPTER 17

LAUREN

LAST TIME I RODE in the back of a limousine, I thought things were finally looking up. That the two sisters I'd acquired were going to be so for a lifetime. Never once in a million years did I imagine those same siblings to be at the root of my anguish.

Never once did I imagine them capable of murdering Ali. I should have, though. I should have known. The betrayal I felt toward them, I also felt for myself—and it stung.

I stared at my reflection in the window. No amount of self-condemnation would give me back what I lost. Even worse, my family felt the same agony as I, and yet I was unable to share the real truth of my guilt, and my deep shame for dropping the ball.

The limousine crept inside Oak Cemetery and stopped just off from Ali's closed casket and freshly dug burial plot. The limo driver opened the rear door, and my family filed out one at a time. First Aunt Jamie, who I couldn't bring myself to look at, with Uncle Kevin embracing her, then Grangy, and myself. An intimate crowd of family and friends had gathered underneath the green tarp, standing somberly behind a row of velvety cloth-draped chairs positioned in front of the casket like the front row of a movie theater. Priest Doven stood at the front like a conductor waiting for his musicians to play melodies.

The dark mood choking the air made it difficult for me to breathe as we swayed through the toe-high grass and paused before the seats underneath the green tarp. My red eyes wandered among the familiar faces, and I saw Detective Neese staring back. He glared with contempt, a cold expression meant to intimidate me into a murder confession, but I was too engulfed in self-inflicted torture to give a damn about any misguided truths he was trying to create inside his head. Part of me was pissed by his self-less confusion.

What the hell did he know about it anyway? Damn human.

I gazed out at Alison's casket, while light sniffles and crying tugged on my earlobes. Aunt Jamie had all but cried herself out. All the fears and worries had drained her spirit and she simply looked out at the casket with a blank stare of bewilderment.

"Alison was a happy soul," Priest Devon described. "Her smile lit up a room on the gloomiest of days." He paused a moment, pondering on happier times, swimming in his own memory of her. "I can recall the day of her baptism. I poured holy water onto her forehead and she didn't cry once. She just looked up with those curious bright blue eyes of hers ... it was then I knew she was going to be something special, and I believe to this day I was proven right." He nodded with a confident grin, his brown eyes watering.

And he was, proven right that is ... at least I thought so.

Alison did great things, and sacrificed even more, and most of them were for me in my selfish time of struggle.

Thank you, Alison. I sniffled.

From the corner of my eyes, I spotted Penelope approaching our gathering from the far side of the lawn. I wondered what she was up to. She merged within the crowd standing behind us and stayed silent. I thought of looking back, but her eyes weren't the only ones I didn't want to battle with. Plus, my bottled anger was still volatile.

"And when sickness robbed her body, it was Alison who managed to put a grin on *my* face when I came to console *her* at the Children's Hospital," Priest Doven continued.

It comforted me deeply the same traits I cherished of her were the same as his.

"I am going to miss that precious child's glowing spirit ... until we meet again, Ali. The angels above us rejoice your homecoming." He held his Bible close to his chest.

"Amen," everyone recited.

The conclusion of his words released the crowd into a gentle disburse as they relaxed their postures, hugging and conversing with one another as the moment turned light yet still respectful. Others made their way over to Aunt Jamie and Uncle Kevin and paid their last respects, bringing up memories of the good times with Ali. I stood next to Grangy, and noticed Detective Neese looking my way as he made a path toward us, weaving through the scattering of friends and family.

"My sincerest condolences to both you and your husband," he said. "No one should go through something so tragic."

Aunt Jamie held his hand. "Thank you for taking the time to come together with us," she said. "It is appreciated beyond words."

"It was my honor. Alison is and will remain close to my heart, surely as I live and walk."

"You're too kind. So, any good news?" she asked.

Detective Neese glanced my way. There existed no subtlety in his actions, but I was the only one who picked up on it. "I have a strong lead … I believe."

"Does that mean you also have a suspect or suspects in mind?" Uncle Kevin asked.

"Nothing I care to elaborate on at this time, but be assured you'll be the first notified when I can." He glanced my way once more.

Detective Neese's odd looks caused my stomach to clench.

"Please hurry, Detective," Grangy said. "Don't let whoever did this horrible thing get away with blatant murder without punishment. I couldn't bear the thought."

"Don't you worry, ma'am," he replied with a serious tone. "I have no intentions of letting something so tragic occur."

"Good to hear."

The conversation and weird looks were making me feel awkward, and I leaned into Grangy. "I'm going to go say hello."

"Give Izzy my love," she replied.

I walked off, but could sense Detective Neese's eyes boring a hole through my back. The lawn underneath my feet was soothing, like I was walking on puffy clouds. I veered to the right and down a new row of gravestones, stopping before the one with my mother's name engraved on the front. The sounds of voices were no longer within earshot, and the beauty of the sun-filled day helped ease my anxiety. I was at peace, though its richness failed to touch the inner depths of my shattered heart.

"Hi, Mom," I whimpered. "Ali's gone, and I pray she is in heaven with you … if Mother Perfects get to go to heaven." I shrugged, unsure. "If you are up there, please watch over her for me. She's the reason I was able to endure the loss of you."

I detected the sound of footsteps before it even registered inside my frontal lobe.

"I'm sure He will make an exception for you," she said. "Being perfect himself."

I turned around to find Penelope, appearing contrite. Knowing her, I wasn't fooled, though. Her voice was pleasant, but it still sounded like fingernails on a black chalkboard, grating my soul and bashing my eardrums into oblivion. She was winsome to look at, but the coldness behind her eyes made her distasteful and disfigured—repugnant.

"You again." I frowned. "First Cali and now Michigan—stalking is illegal, you know that right? Or do I need to get a restraining order to keep you away?"

"Can't I honor my respects for a fallen comrade?"

My hips shifted. "I doubt you have any—respect for someone else, that is."

"I could say the same for you. Comrades, that is."

"Can't you arrogant demons let me enjoy being human for at least one day?"

"I swear, girl," she scoffed. "You are your mother's child."

"So I've heard." I faced my mother's tombstone. "I wish to be left alone now."

"But of course. I'll leave you to it." She started to walk off, and then stopped. "Oh. You know I'm here for you when things turn impossible to contain, correct?"

"Thanks."

"Vicky should have warned you."

"About?"

"Not reading the fine print. It's futile to train a hybrid to act like a Perfect. It would be like trying to teach an armless monkey how to eat with a plastic fork."

"Thanks for the tip," I sneered. "Now, if you don't mind. I think you've overstayed your welcome."

"Yeah? Well. I'm a true delight, they say." She pepped.

"They lied. Goodbye, Penelope."

She hesitated. "Does this mean I'm not invited to eat fried chicken at the repast? Because I really enjoy certain human food, and fried chicken seems to bring out—"

I whipped around in attack mode. "Damn it, girl! I said…" My heated words faded.

It was … him.

"She's gone already," he said.

The sight of his familiar face doused my flaring wrath. "Dad … you did come back."

"Yes." He blew out air from his cheeks. "Guess you can only lie to yourself for so long."

"So I'm finding out."

"Hanging around Mother Perfects now, I see."

"Penelope is no Mother Perfect," I scoffed. "Far from it. I mean I'm sure she wishes so, but-"

"She's like the other one."

"What other one?"

"When you first found me, wallowing in my own filth? That one. Penelope, too, is completing the Moirai Cycle."

"Wait—the what?"

"It's the amount of time it takes for a Perfect to fully receive the essence of a deceased Mother Perfect."

"How could you possibly know that, and that she's a Perfect and not a human being?"

"Blame Elisabeth."

"Mom?"

"She couldn't stop me from being human … I couldn't prevent her from being a Mother Perfect."

"Yet you can see who is different from other mortals? By just looking at them?"

"I can: Perfect, Fearian and human or other. And let me tell you, many a time I have had to ignore a flunky sent by the Fearian Counsel to watched my every move."

"That's why you left me?"

"What I once viewed as a curse is now a trait I share with my child. Go figure."

"But even I can't do that, always detect who is Fearian and who is … like me."

"Maybe I'll stick around long enough for you to pick it up," he offered.

"… I'd like that."

He looked to Ali's funeral. "Sorry for your loss. I know you and Alison were close."

"The closest."

"So please tell me she wasn't harmed as an ugly result of that other realm?"

"Believe me, wish I could … it would be another lie that's ripping me apart from the inside."

"How tragic."

"And no matter how much I want to explain to Aunt Jamie, nothing I say will ever make sense to her. So I don't try."

"Ignorance is bliss when it comes to not knowing about Perfects and Fearians existing among human beings."

I glanced at the dwindling crowd in the distance. "Yeah. Guess you're right about that."

"Lauren, you can't blame yourself for any of this."

"Then how come I can't stop myself?" I asked, as a tear fell from my eyelid.

"Because you can't stop loving those around you. It's who you are. And it's a beautiful gift to bear, and why you are so much like Elisabeth in every way."

"Her careless decisions got others around her killed ... I'd say I'm exactly like her in every way."

"You shouldn't hate her, she cared for you dearly. I'm hoping you don't hate me either."

"Dad ... I don't have enough family left alive to hate one."

"I was wrong for denying you that day at the bar," he confessed. "It was the only thing I knew to do."

"Yes. You were wrong, but I understand now."

Dad fiddled with his fingers. "I couldn't keep you safe from that other place, and I knew it deep inside me ... so I had no other choice but to distance myself from you."

"I can see how you would think that."

"Too bad the others can never know."

"They wouldn't believe us even if they did," I assured him.

"I'm going to make this easy for you. Say the word and I'm gone from your life."

"... Stay."

His eyes overflowed with tears and he exhaled deeply. "I will. I will stay here for you."

"And hold me."

He snatched me up like I was the only thing of value left in his life, and I melted from the touch of a father's love. He held me tight until my sobbing lost its power, until the suffering inside me could no longer raise hell. The heat of his touch set my body free from the metal chains of dejection and shame that had shackled me from happiness and tranquility.

"What now?"

"You're coming home with me."

"Are you sure, Lauren?"

"Couldn't be more sure of anything else in my entire life," I said, as I took his hand and led him across the luscious lawn. "Don't let go."

Nearly everyone else had left the cemetery or was in the process of doing so. We walked behind Aunt Jamie and Uncle Kevin, hugging each other, while Grangy stood beside them, talking with Priest Doven.

"Will you come and fellowship with us?" Grangy asked Priest Doven. "It would be our honor if you did."

"Now, you know me. I've never been one to turn down a delicious hot meal from a pretty single lady such as yourself." He winked.

"I know I could eat," I interjected, getting their attention.

Their eyes widened with disbelief once they spotted dad trailing a step behind me. "Glenn," Grangy said.

"Margaret. How are you?"

"Fine … I guess. Where did you come from?"

"And why are you here at my daughter's funeral?" Aunt Jamie frowned.

I stepped forward. "I made him come. He's here because I needed him to be."

Uncle Kevin glanced to Grangy with a look of tempered shock riddled on his face.

Aunt Jamie relaxed her firm posture and uncrossed her arms. "Wait. Do what?"

"With so much going on at school and with everything else, I hadn't had a chance to tell you guys he was back in town, and back in my life. Sorry about that."

"No. It's okay. We just didn't … know," Aunt Jamie said. "But it's fine. You don't owe us any explanation."

"I was going to tell you my surprise, when the time was right." I fumbled my words, extending the lie. "Surprise." I shrugged.

The group detected my sincerity and glanced around at one another.

"Sweetie. He's your father." Aunt Jamie caressed my hand. "You don't owe us a thing, so long as you are okay with it."

"I'm more than okay with it, Aunt Jamie."

"Then so are we. Welcome home, son." Grangy hugged him. "We've missed you. I for one am glad you found your way back to Lauren."

"Me too," Kevin added, making it unanimous.

"You must be hungry?" Grangy asked. "If I remember correctly, you had a hardy appetite for fried chicken back in the day."

"Still do."

"There's plenty of room in the limo for two more. Padre?"

Grangy touched my hand, winked at me then escorted the group over to the limousine.

Priest Doven rubbed his stomach. "Right behind you."

I knew once the matriarch of the family was on board, the others would fall in line no matter their personal reservations.

The ride downtown was quiet, except for the light chatter Grangy orchestrated with Priest Doven. Aunt Jamie stared silently out the window and I imagined her engulfed in positive reflection over her loss. Not even death could steal away the importance of Alison being her child. I believed she had come to that same conclusion, being I observed her relish a brief grin as the sun basked sweet rays onto her face. Dad and I didn't say much, either. We held hands and let the lingering effects of the lengthy separation fade from sight. I watched his eyes as he admired how much Grand Blanc had flourished since he'd last seen it in person. No one made his absence a hot topic, and that was fine with me. I was glad to have the grace of love flowing in the midst of so much hurt, turmoil and so much deception.

Thanks, mom. Even though you're gone, I know somehow your presence helped bring him back home.

CHAPTER 18

PENELOPE

VALENCIA, SPAIN WAS ALWAYS radiating with dry heat this time of the year. The sun's constant rays kept the buildings' trim faded, but left the old town no less stunning. The brick, villa-style buildings had rustic flares on their rooftops, and most stood so close they looked to have been constructed as a fortification to keep humans protected on the inside of the city, while holding rebellious outcasts on the outside.

Similar to the colony in my own realm.

The Spanish mortals took great pleasure in the celebration of the nearing of fall season. They are quite humorous to observe, with their simple-minded attitudes and their carefree thinking. It's almost like they don't even realize they are alive and breathing in a modern era. Like the sands of time had stopped counting well over a decade ago. If not for the spicy food I was now accustomed to, the fruity tequila I loved to consume, and the long days on this side of the continent, there would be no reason for me to come here.

I stood silent, with a double shot of tequila in my hand, utterly undetected on a private balcony crowded with a host of attractive socialites from the coast. They chattered and bragged about their pretentious lifestyles as they looked down upon the herd of half-naked humans below us, heavily engaged in the seasonal celebration known as *La Tomatina*. The object of our partial attention frolicked about in the center of Plaza Del Pueblo, covered in sloppy wet redness.

The vibrant cheers kept the fruitful image from looking gross and sickening.

Bare flesh was the rule of the day, but you could hardly tell by the multitudes of tomatoes being thrown from one mortal to another in a frantic crimson riot, a stampede of mush red vestibules trapped in the midst of a joyous mob. Shopkeepers and village authorities alike were participating in the massive food fight. The throes of excitement left the plaza drenched in heavy laughter, an abundance of tomato slop, and gallons upon gallons of wasted tomato juice. To be honest, I could rather do without the company of loudmouth mortals, cheering about their pathetic lives as they naively gazed at existence through their cloudy lens of understanding, but the Spanish tequila was really good here.

I downed the shot of liquor, then pitched the shot glass over my head, where it shattered against the back wall. Some partiers noticed the sprinkling of jagged glass, but none gave it a second thought. Instead, they focused on the frantic fingers of the shirtless musicians strumming their classical guitars, creating a fluid and chaotic rhythm. They all swayed to the melody and remained blind to my presence, though I stood in plain sight. The pink glow radiating off of my silhouette kept me invisible from their lustful glares.

Suddenly, I felt a strange disturbance in my midst. I peeked over my shoulder to investigate, and was startled by the attendance of the very one I was hoping to avoid a short time longer: Mother Geneve. Before I could respond, she grabbed me by my expensive blouse, ruffling the collar, and pinned me against the wall. Her anger was so fierce that my high heels didn't scrape the tiled floor in our abrupt movement. My back slammed against the wall, and I felt the lace on the shoulder of my outfit rip the seam.

"Hello, Mother Geneve," I greeted. "Had I known you enjoyed La Tomatina as well I would have—"

My Spanish accent failed to impress, and she cut off my words.

"Save it!" She slammed me against the wall again, causing the light bulbs inside the three-tier chandeliers to flicker. "I'm going to rip your damn head off your neck!"

I scowled. "I take it you've heard about the favor Isabelle bestowed upon me?"

The partiers in our circle braced from the shaking of the structure. Some of the women shrieked, but all in attendance maintained their wobbling balance. They bubbled with fearful glee, like it was a one-time phenomenon, and continued on partying.

Mother Geneve winked, and the humans behind her froze in place.

"Liar!" she yelled, her eyes flashing pink with rage. "Have you any last words before I deliver a torturous judgment befitting of a scandalous dog off its leash?"

"Well ..."

Her intent was to end me, painfully, savagely—like a Jurassic carnivore. And being she was all-powerful, I knew it was in her grace to do so. I had to act fast, or perish a fool's death with only humans present, bearing witness. I unfroze mortals with nothing more than a stern glance and exposed myself, forcing Mother Geneve's expulsion at the same time. The startled socialites around her caused Mother Geneve's wrath to simmer.

The sliver of advantage was precious and all that was needed. I punched her in the gut as hard as I could muster. No, even harder. Every species under God have a weakness: Fearians can't stand the sound of loud music; it drives them batty. Perfects are excellent at wielding their supernatural gifts, but not so much at hand-to-hand combat.

Mother Geneve keeled over, but I knew it wasn't going to be enough to keep her down for very long. I slapped her fingers from off my blouse, ripping the front pocket, and hopped over the private balcony. My descent was more of a float than a steep drop.

Damn it! I love this blouse!

I soared past the bottom two floors and landed on the wet street below in the center of the chaotic food fight, just missing dancing mortals with wailing arms and excited jeers. Bracing myself, I darted into the pit of tomato hell. Mother Geneve was a half second behind. I sprinted the human gauntlet and became entangled in the crowd, getting drenched with red tomato slop. I looked back and saw Mother Geneve slowing her steps in a sad attempt at locating my whereabouts within the brutal celebrating.

It took a second for her eyes to lock on mine. I gave her a sly wave and disappeared into thin air—then reappeared, standing at the entrance of a bakery shop across the street. The front door swung open on cue, and I slipped inside the doorway.

"I will find you!" her voice echoed in my ear. "Then you're done!"

The aroma of Candeal bread drowned her snarling and overtook my sense of smell, and the starry darkness swallowed me whole.

WOOSH!

CHAPTER 19

KAIDEN

THE FEARIAN COUNSEL AND I stood in the center of the destroyed colony of Perfects, flanked by a host of our fiercest warriors. Beaded sweat dribbled from their brows, while blood from our foes dripped from their blades. The once-white structures burning to the ground were now smoky old ruins. The Perfect colony was uninhabitable and hauntingly deserted from end to end, marked by mutilated bodies sprawled along the dirt. At times, death was a true friend and showed us gallant favor.

None of the enemies left alive had the will to fight back, so they retreated within the creepy darkness of failure. Cowards. Victory was our titanium trophy, yet raw death stayed unfulfilling, because none of the dead around us were Mother Perfects.

Damn it! They have foiled our attack!

Their narrow escape further fueled my desire for battle. A mild scuffle to the rear got my attention, and I watched as a path emerged within the warriors before us. My eyes lit up when a female's limp body, bruised, battered, and bloody, was drug forward and thrust before the feet of the Counsel, near my own.

Though her fingers clenched clunks of the dirt beneath her, she failed to look up or speak, and her long, tangled hair covered her face from view.

"We found this one hiding," the warrior said.

"Is that so?" Serene asked.

"And she took the life of one of our finest before we were able to subdue her."

"How?"

"She attacked with a blade when he was unaware." He snarled, kicking her hard in the midsection.

Her thin body flopped, and she grimaced.

Oplous reached down and caressed her chin, lifting her bloody face into view. Her dirty strands of hair obstructed most of her features, but her eyes still possessed a hint of defiance. As though she waited for an opportunity to attack us, even with the odds stacked against her, even though her death would be imminent seconds after.

"Perfect. Where have the others of your kind gone?" Oplous asked. "How have the Mother Perfects escaped our wrath on this fruitful day of reckoning?"

"I am not my Mother's keeper," she snapped.

"Indeed."

"And I wouldn't tell you even if I were." She spat blood onto the dirt.

Oplous folded his arms behind him. "Then you are no use to us."

She curled her eyes. "You finally got that, huh?"

"Or maybe I shall cause a change of heart in you," Nolum smirked. "I'm sure my touch is more than adequate to do the trick."

"I doubt it. Then again, I've had worse," she replied.

The Fearian Warriors surrounding her mumbled in response to her boldness and disrespect.

Nolum grinned, then stomped on her left hand with his foot, crushing the bones. Her eyes got big, and she grit her teeth as his foot pinned her limb against the ground, twisting and driving his heel into the dirt. Still she failed to cry out in agony, though it was pretty evident in her wilting expression.

Warriors in our midst chuckled.

"It would be wise for you to reconsider," Oplous said.

"My next step shall be upon your neck, Perfect."

Tears streamed from her eyes, and she tried to hide the full effects of Nolum's actions. "I won't tell."

"Where are the Mother Perfects hiding? Where!" Nolum demanded.

"End her!" Serenity shouted. "End her now!"

"Hold her pretty head to the ground," Nolum ordered.

The chief warrior looked to two of his mighty soldiers and snapped his fingers. "Do it!"

The warriors pinned her head to the dirt. The force shot dust up her nostrils and open mouth and made her cough.

"I wish this to be as brutal as possible," Nolum said. He placed his foot on her neck. "Goodbye, Perfect! May the heavens see fit to torture you further in the afterlife!"

She gagged and her eyes bulged. "Wait …" she muttered. "Wait!"

Nolum loosened his foot. "You were saying?"

"Air … I need air."

"If you have something important you wish to add, I suggest that you speak quickly!"

She sucked in more air, but said nothing of value. Yet her resistance was not only futile, it was more than I could tolerate, even with the Counsel handling the questioning.

I kneeled down to her. "What is your name Perfect?"

"…Victoria. I am called Victoria."

"Well. Victoria, my Counsel is addressing you!"

"I am aware of this."

"Then move your tongue or I will cut it off so it can never grow back!" I drew out my blade.

"… Humans. They've taken shelter in the realm of the humans," she confessed. "Without an invitation."

"Recreants!" Oplous spouted. "Your entire species is fearful!"

"Yeah? Well. I'm still here. Hand me that blade, remove your foot and I'll show you which species is fearful."

"Kill her! Kill her! Kill her!" Warriors chanted.

"Have you enough remorse left to offer up as a sacrifice before you die?" Nolum taunted.

"Nope."

Her arrogance caught Nolum off guard. "What did you say?"

"You heard me. Stop running your mouth and do it. Saves me from having to smell you any longer."

Warriors gasped and drew out their swords, while some aimed their spears at her.

"Either kill me or let me fight. Either way, I die with honor, and without following those Mothers of Sissies!"

"I like this one. Defiant until the end," Serene said.

"Blade please?" she dared, holding out her hand.

I leaned in to Nolum with a private tone. "Sire, perhaps her defiance provides an opportunity that can be used to our advantage."

"Explain."

"There is so much we do not know about the human realm, their many strengths, or their few weaknesses."

"True."

"Now that our realm has been damaged by an unjust war, perhaps it will be prudent to see if the humans' world is a more suitable environment to reign from. After all, the Mother Perfects have used it for asylum. May I negotiate with her?"

"…You may," Nolum replied, removing his foot from her neck. "But proceed with extreme caution. Another failure on your part could prove catastrophic for your bloodline."

"Understood." I kneeled down to her again. "Tell me, Vicky. Is the life of the one you call Elisabeth worth more than your own?"

She scoffed. "... Never."

"Then you shall find her hiding among the humans. You shall find out where she has hidden what was taken from us. You shall report to me of this new realm. And you shall be prudent in your seeking."

"And if I am successful in locating Izzy's whereabouts? What becomes of me?"

"The Counsel shall spare your life ... even while the rest of your kind dies a cruel and painful death," Oplous said.

"Look around you, Perfect," Serene said. "This war has taken away your realm, as well. Perhaps there is a small climate upon the earth that would be to your liking."

"And you wouldn't mess with me there?" she asked. "Or try to kill me?"

"Sire, she murdered my kin!" a mighty warrior rebuked. "She deserves nothing short of death!"

"Silence, warrior!" Oplous snapped. "It is your brother's own fault for losing a battle to a Perfect!"

The warrior turned silent, but bitterness remained etched on his face.

"Find what has been taken away from us," I said to her.

"And in exchange, you shall live in refuge upon the Earth. This is the word of the Counsel. What say you, Perfect?" Serene asked.

"...I can live with that," she said.

As Nolum helped Victoria to her feet, he used his fingernail to brand her, burning an ancient Fearian symbol into her skin. Victoria cringed from the intense heat and savoring discomfort.

Nolum grinned. "Now you're marked as my property. Don't make me have to remind you again, Perfect."

I stepped closer to her and jerked the slack from her ruffled blouse. "When you locate Elisabeth, I do not want her confronted."

"What then?"

"You will come to me, and I will deal with her lies and deceit. Is that clear, Vicky?"

She nodded, crossing her arms. "Whatevs ..."

The careless arrogance of a Perfect, even on her judgment day ...

I released a calming breath and gazed out at the ruins, as I stood alone. Each blink of my eyelids made the past falter and the ghost colony left in its place angelic and crude. I inhaled air but the smell of war had vanished with time and only the lingering foulness of death simmered in the atmosphere.

Shattered skeletons of Perfects still lay on the ground, partially hidden by unturned dirt, new growth of Crab weeds, and the occasional Talkin bush. It was near impossible for me not to enjoy the rubble and decay, a reminder everything Mother Perfects created we had destroyed; everything but the spoiled scent of their immorality. Still, nothing would satisfy my soul until I was redeemed from allowing Elisabeth to use me as her pawn.

I would not rest until I reclaimed the dagger for my gods, and The Seal had been renewed for our kind ... and the earth bowed in submission.

CHAPTER 20

LAUREN

DAD, GRANGY AND ME stepped out of the limousine outside of the duplex. Dad carried the two paper plates piled with leftovers covered in plastic wrap, and we approached the front door. I was exhausted from the day, and I just wanted to rest with my eyelids shut.

"It's good to be home at last," Grangy sighed.

"It has been a long day," Dad added.

I offered him a grin and unlocked the front door with my key. "And it's only getting better."

"Thank you again for allowing me to stay here with you." Dad looked to Grangy. "Really, you didn't have to."

"Nonsense. You're my son-in-law. You're always welcome to stay here. Plus, it would make Lauren so happy if you did."

I shuffled to a pause beyond the doorway. Although the front door had been locked, someone had been here and the evidence was blatant. The interior was ransacked and the aftermath was like a tornado had hit. Dad and Grangy bumped into my back.

Dad squeezed in around me once he saw the mess. "Uh. Is the living room supposed to look this way?"

"No. It's not," I answered.

Grangy squeezed by me next. "Sweet God in heaven … we've been robbed … or victims of vandalism, I can't tell which one."

"They smashed our television," I said. "I liked that old television."

"My antique coffee table. What's this world coming to?"

I caressed her arm. "Apparently this."

"Awfully big risk to be taking in broad daylight, don't you think?" Dad looked my way with an eerie glare and placed the plates of food on the kitchen counter.

"Watch Grangy for me." I stepped toward the back bedrooms. "I'm going to go look around."

"Lauren, let me go."

"No. I got this. Just keep an eye on her." I gave Dad a sideways look, and he nodded slightly.

"I swear, that girl of yours believes she's ten feet tall and growing," Grangy said.

"Must get that from her mother," Dad said.

I shuffled toward the rear of the duplex without answering, creeping on eggshells each step of the way, with my hands on guard. I wasn't sure if the breaking and entering had anything to do with me being a Mother Perfect, but I had my money on the likelihood of it. That had me on alert. My eyes raged fuchsia and I advanced forward, ready to do battle with anyone, from any realm. I prayed it wouldn't come to that, yet my injured faith had been tried as of late and I had had enough.

It seemed the fight I was avoiding had been brought to my front door and was forcing me to show my hand—and my courage. It didn't make what I might have to do any easier though. I pushed the door open, and it swung back to the wall with a creaking noise. That noise had been made a million times before, but this time it put me on edge. As I stood in the doorway, inspecting the tidy bedroom, I took peace in the fact that not a single thing of Grangy's was out of place. Her gold jewelry was still on the nightstand by the lamp, and even her many pill bottles were neat on the dresser.

Okay. Not exactly what I expected to see, but anyway ...

I prowled to the door and peeped inside the bathroom. It too was empty and untouched. My heartbeat slowed some. I shuffled to my bedroom, and to my surprise I found it just as I had left it: partially organized, but passable to the non-parental visitor.

Strange ... how very strange ... maybe it was a dumb crime of opportunity. Or maybe... Hum...

I returned to the living room where Grangy and Dad were already straightening up things.

"The vandals have left, and apparently they felt no need to redecorate either bedroom any more than they already were," I said. "Wasn't that nice of them?"

"Nothing damaged?" Dad asked.

"Nope." I hunched my shoulders, feeling perplexed. "Not a single thing out of place."

"Huh." He grabbed a wooden chair lying on its side, reconnected a leg to it and sat it upright before the table.

"Thank God." Grangy exhaled big. "Who would do such a thing to a little old lady such as me? I'm simply adorable."

"Probably some stupid kids trying to look cool," I said. "We have some real knuckleheads living on this block." I began to clean too.

"Lauren?"

I looked up. My dad's tone was knowing and suggestive. "Perhaps those knuckleheads were looking for something unique, you know, not exactly of this realm?"

"Say what now?"

"Something Perfect."

His words hit me like a ton of bricks and my face soured. "No! No! No!" I backed off.

"What's wrong?" Grangy asked, worried.

I didn't take the time to respond and I darted back to the rear of the duplex and out of their sight. I ran into my bedroom and over to the bed, grabbing a teddy bear from off the pillow and ripping into it, tearing it to pieces. Chunks of fiberfill tossed in the air.

"Where are you?" I stammered. "Where the hell is it?"

I jammed my hands onto my head and scanned the bedroom. My heart pounded at a frazzled pace, and I raised my hands, causing everything in the room to levitate shoulder-high. I inspected the empty floor, but failed to locate my true prize. I dropped everything back to the carpet with a violent thud as my head spun out of control.

How could I have been so dumb? What were you thinking, girl? What were you thinking?

Dad burst into the bedroom on high alert. "Lauren!"

I cupped my face into my hands and dropped to my knees. "What have I done?"

"Are you okay? What was that noise?"

Grangy hurried inside my bedroom. "Lauren, honey! Are you safe in here!"

Dad met her at the door with his hands out. "She's fine, Grangy. She's okay. Everything is good."

"What was that god awful noise?" her eyes bulged. "Sweetheart, look at your bedroom. It's a total mess. I thought you said the bed-"

"Yeah. She did. Um, something … fell over—hard," Dad lied.

It took all I had to uncover my shameful face and look up to her. A knot burned the middle of my throat and made it difficult to speak, let alone speak the truth. My eyes filled with warm tears, and I couldn't find the strength to wipe them away as they puddle.

Her face wrinkles deepened. "Sweetheart."

"Can … you give us … a second?" Dad hesitated.

"Sure," Grangy backed away with an odd look. "I'll go finish cleaning up the giant mess left in the living room. You can take care of this mess without me … I guess."

"Cool." Dad nodded.

"Feel free to join me when you're both done in here."

"This won't take long." Dad ushered her out into the hall and shut the door. He kneeled beside me. "Lauren. What's missing?"

"I hid it in one of my stuffed animals," I managed, still stunned with fear, guilt and a sense of deep failure.

"You hid what?"

"I hadn't had a chance to find a better hiding spot, with Alison's death on my mind."

Dad snapped his fingers at my face, bringing me out of my cloudy haze. "Lauren! Tell me what was taken from you."

"… The Shadow dagger."

"You had it this whole time?"

"And I let it slip through my fingers. Only God knows who has it now. I am such a freaking idiot!" I pounded my fists against my legs. "Crap. Crap. Crap!"

"How did you get it? I buried that thing just days after your mom's funeral, before I left town."

"Victoria."

"That's the one I sensed. The one who brought you to the bar." He slapped himself on the head. "Why didn't I catch that?"

"She had it when she found me, and I took it from her after she died … and now someone else has taken it from me."

"Okay. Okay," he calmed. "Maybe a friend came and took it for safekeeping. Stranger things have happened."

"Dad, you don't understand. I don't have any friends left. Just other shady Perfects and Fearians trying to get the dagger from me."

"The Seal. It's still broken, right?"

"Wait. You know about the Fearian Seal too?"

"How can I not? Elisabeth was the one selected to steal it in order to keep the rest of her kind from extinction."

"What the… do you know what The Seal is exactly? Because I haven't a clue."

The pathetic rumbling trapped inside my core caused me to scoff, though no humor in the moment was found.

"I know *what* they are."

"They?"

"Fearian babies. Royalty."

"What?"

"At least they were. They should be close to your age now. Triplets, morphed on your mother's old bed."

"My mother is a damn baby snatcher … I can't believe- wait. Was it two girls and a boy?"

"Yes. How'd you know?"

"I think I know them," I breathed, trying to calm. "And they think they're hybrid Perfects."

"Guess that's better than knowing they're the missing pieces to the Fearian Empire." He helped me stand to my feet.

"Dad, I have to find out who took the dagger from me."

"And pretty fast. The last thing any of us want or need is for the Fearian Seal to be renewed."

"I have literally helped destroy an entire species from existence. This is all my fault."

"No. It's not. Get a hold of yourself. Clean up this mess, while I go convince your grandma not to call the cops. Lord knows we don't need them involved in this."

I pursed my lips. "Too late."

"I don't know what that means, but I'm hoping it's not as bad as it might sounds."

"Trust me … it's worse."

Dad caressed my face. "This is going to work out, Lauren. I promise you. You're a Mother Perfect with a kind heart."

I curled my eyes. "I'm a teenage girl, dad, and I haven't even figured out how to be that yet."

"I'll keep an eye on your grandma while you're at school tomorrow," he offered. "Keep things normal, cool?"

"Cool." I hugged him. "I don't know what I would do without you here with me."

"Now you don't have to wonder." He smiled. "Clean up your bedroom before I ground you."

"Right."

Dad poked my nose and walked out. His actions soothed me, though it didn't last long. I overheard them talking as they cleaned the living room. I pried loose the old photograph of mom and me from the dresser mirror and stared at it a hard minute. It didn't help ease the irritation as I had hoped. As before. For the first time she seemed foreign to me, though I was her child.

Mother, I've always found your smile to be consoling in my time of struggle, and there have been many ... So how could someone so loving be so wicked and mean spirited to an entire species? ... And to me? You not only left your only child with a lot of unanswered questions, you've left her feeling a disgrace.

The more I exposed about my mother's character, the less I was admiring her memory. It took all I had not to judge her actions, because I knew deep down inside she had felt she was doing right—I just couldn't come to the same conclusion.

CHAPTER 21

PENELOPE

I LOVE POPCORN. I swaggered about the crowded Arkansas State Fairground with a bag of it in my hand, pitching fluffy pieces into my mouth and enjoying the salty snack. The southern evening was sticky, and the flashing bright lights lighting up the skyline attracted many fluttering insects, though not enough to make it intolerable. Mortals, both young and old, ran from one simple-minded manmade contraption to the other, being pulled and thrust into the air, or twisted into circles while they screamed their heads off for fun. The appeal was less than to me.

The simplest things entertain mortals, it seems.

The robust smell of corndogs, barbecue, and sweet cotton candy mixed with the foul scent of farm animals herded in pens nearby, made the environment a confusing rainbow of colorful odors. Once I finished my salty snack, I crumpled the bag and pitched it to the ground, sucking out the kernel shells wedged in my molar.

I paused and stared at a host of games humans play for giant spotted giraffes and stuffed elephants. At the second stall I saw Dison, using his Perfection to win an oversized Tiger, and of course the affection of a group of young sluts, scantily dressed and acting as if they were much older than they actually were.

Stupid humans.

"And we have another winner!" the carnie shouted, trying to convince other potential losers his game was easily played.

Dison gloated as he impressed the human girls with his worthless prize, and of course his Perfect swagger.

I grunted, finding it humorous to observe.

While keeping my eyes locked on Dison I strolled a few steps closer to them and watched him pick the cutest girl from the bunch. She was so his type, had she'd been a Perfect it would have been a match. He handed her the stuffed animal, then made his eyes flicker pink to close the deal. The girl melted from his attention then offered Dison lustful stares to tempt him.

Perfect men are so sexy when they play head games to get what they want.

I approached his backside. "Hey, stranger."

Dison looked to me. Although surprised, he managed to play nonchalant and coy. "What up, Mother P?"

The girls vying for his hand frowned at my presence and gave me glares of jealousy.

I looked off into the distance, offering him half of my observation. "Nice night for games."

"Only if you're the big bad wolf." He grinned.

"Sucks to be piglet, I guess. Don't tell me mortal females float your boat now?"

"Stranger things have happened." He winked to one girl giving him googly eyes and me an envious sneer.

"Sure. Like learning how to eat Jell-O with a spoon."

Offended, the mortal girl flipped her hair and strutted off, her clique of mean girls following and the stuffed animal in her hands.

Dison faced me looking disappointed. "You are really trying to make my day harder, aren't you?"

"Who me? Nah. You can screw mortals any day of the week. You're a Perfect, plus you're hot."

"Appreciate the kind words."

"My pleasure."

"So what do you want then?"

"I'm sure you already know."

"Why don't you tell me anyway?"

"Okay. I want what Vicky had."

"Really?"

"In every way." I gleamed.

He narrowed his eyes at me, his voice low and seductive. "Can you handle what Vicky had?"

"In every way."

"I Iuh."

I stepped closer to him and kissed his mouth, gnawing on his lip. "Perhaps you and I can come to an arrangement."

"I don't know. Vicky was pretty special."

"Are you implying my unique lineage is not?"

"And why would I do something as dumb as that?"

"I wouldn't advise it. Anyhoo. Where was I? Oh, yeah. Our tasty arrangement?"

"... In exchange for?"

"Maybe from time to time I too can enjoy the succulent taste of sweet milk chocolate."

"You know," he said, tracing my neckline, "not even Vicky was crazy enough to contest Mother Geneve for supremacy."

"I'm not Vicky," I replied.

"Clearly. Be that as it may, Mother G may come looking for you once she catches wind of your unethical enterprise."

"You think?"

He licked my neck, savoring the nectar with the taste buds on his tongue. "I have seen her bitchy side a time or two. You don't want to piss off Mother Geneve."

"Maybe. But I believe I have an ace up my designer sleeve for such an occasion," I said. "I'm in it to win it, as they say."

"Clearly. I am intrigued to hear more."

"I'll see that she's taken care of, but when I do, you'll have my back, keeping the others in line."

"... I can do that. Then what?"

"You get to rule the entire kingdom as my hot trophy wife and royal concubine, all in one."

Greed flashed in his eyes. "How very interesting."

"What say you?"

"I can be a hot trophy and much more," he smirked. "Sure you can handle my delectability?"

"Oh, I'm sure." I strolled away feeling flirtatious and empowered, then stopped and looked back. "One last request, Dison."

"Anything for you, my future queen."

"Hands off the mortal skirts."

Dison chuckled. "You're kidding me, right?"

"I am not. This queen is possessive, and I'd hate to have to murder them in their sleep ... and you know that I will."

His gloating smirk simmered some and he nodded.

I walked off without looking back again.

I had been lucky enough to learn a thing or two from the desires that plagued Victoria, but I would succeed where she'd failed miserably. She had wanted to go it alone, holding an unhealthy grudge with the clan—not my style or way of thinking. I was more diplomatic.

Phase one is a big success.

And unlike Ms. Resentful, I would have the others on my side, so when things came to a head they would receive me as Mother Perfect, once I was the last mother standing.

Mother Geneve, however, was an unsightly thorn in my side with the talent to make me bleed out if I wasn't prudent. Luckily for me, there were three Fearian gods to keep her sole attention, like feisty rattlesnakes held in a gunnysack. Lauren, on the other hand, had her own lethal quarrels to contend with thanks to good old Vicky. But if she somehow survived those insecurities, then I would just have to kill her too.

CHAPTER 22

APPLE

MY EYES FLUTTERED OPEN to a new morning, overflowing with sunshine and robins chirping outside my window. I licked my bottom lip, trying to decipher the mysterious taste that lingered there. I'd never encountered it before, a tangy zest with a hint of bitter undertone. I touched my finger to my lips to see if what I had tasted had a visual appearance, but my finger looked the same as always.

How strange.

I got out of bed and stared down at my toes resting against the floor. My toenails were polished a pretty pink and I stood to my feet.

Something is off.

My human senses weren't on alert. My nerves weren't the least bit rattled. My heartbeat didn't pound irregularly, nor was my destroyer glove glowing. I was calm and at total peace, but my consciousness remained off balance and peculiar feeling. I stood before the mirror and inspected the familiar image staring back at me, displaying the same trepidation as I felt inside my being.

I look the same ... and yet something about me is so different ... so subtle it is almost creepy and undetectable.

"Destroy," the voice whispered in the back of my mind.

I whipped around, but no one was there.

"Hello?" I asked, not knowing if I expected someone to respond to my voice of uncertainty. Then, almost too soft to hear ...

"Apple, destroy her."

"Is someone there?" I paused. "Adam, is that you playing games with me?"

He didn't respond. No one did, just dead silence.

The voice was non-aggressive, yet still possessed a tone of authority that forced me to recognize its unyielding presence—the way a mother speaks to a child refusing to sleep in the middle of the night.

I tried shaking it off, but the strange feeling stayed with me, closer than the clothing I had on. It was as if it was a part of me now.

Staring at my reflection, I swore I detected a familiar face hiding beneath my own features. The vision was somewhat faint at first, yet the more I pondered on its likeness, the intensity of her deep blue pupils, the stronger the image began to appear. When it broke the plain of overtaking my own girly looks and my curious eyes danced upon her ghostly cheekbones, the bold image lost its dominance and dematerialized from sight.

Still … the spooky vibe churning the lining of my gut remained intact.

"Huh."

CHAPTER 23

LAUREN

I WALKED INSIDE THE front entrance of school for the first day of my senior year. The summer had flown by, so fast that I didn't have a proper chance to take it in. Maybe it was because of the drama that ended with Vicky's death, or maybe it was the torment that started with Ali's murder and continued to this day. Either way, I was returning to school a new person, and the jury was out on whether that person was a step up from the old, or just more of the same in new clothing. Not many students knew Ali the way I did, or well enough to know how close we were, so I was able to find my new locker for the school year without so much as one pity pat on my back. I checked my lock combo to ensure it worked, and made my way to the homeroom number printed on the official slip the administration office had mailed to me weeks prior.

As I journeyed through the busy hall, it wasn't until the crowd began to thin out did I notice I was headed toward the far side of the building, where the future day laborers focused more on learning an actual trade than keeping up with the wavering moralities of teenage peer pressure. Not that I had anything against this crowd, many possessed laidback attitudes and most were pretty cool when met with casual interaction. The countless stresses of high school life didn't seem to exist here, and that was always a good thing when you considered the alternative and its hefty cost to play. But I was almost sure my homeroom was not way over here, and I didn't want to spend the first half of my day trapped inside the counselor office trying to rectify someone else's mistake with a herd of other unhappy teen campers.

I watched the door numbers rise until a set matched the ones on the slip in my hand, confirming my growing dismay.

What the ...

"You got to be joking. Someone assigned my homeroom on this side of the school."

I stepped inside the garage-style classroom and noticed the crowd of students socializing. The teacher stood at his desk, wearing blue jeans, a yellow school t-shirt and a pair of safety goggles strapped to his forehead.

"This can't be right. Some idiot screwed with my schedule."

"Mother Perfect!" she yelled out.

I squinted at the sound of her voice; the voice that made my gut churn. "Apple ... I should have known."

My eyes connected with Riley and Apple, both seated side-by-side, looking as pleased as the other one. Both were dressed like cute mannequins standing in a high-end display window, and an eerie tan of blind arrogance bounced off their complexions. None of what I saw felt authentic.

This can't be a coincidence.

The bell rung and a boy behind me shut the door. He gave me a casual glance as he slipped by and took a seat along with the others. My feet still refused to budge, and confusion set in as to what my next move should be.

"We saved you a seat!" Riley said, loud and girly-like.

I bet.

Riley's fake excitement only managed to increase my wariness. Heart beating and stomach burning, I shuffled near them.

"Riley, look who decided to join our homeroom," Apple cheered.

"Super cool," she shined.

"Are you stalking us?" Apple joked. "Are you?"

Her friendly behavior was too joyous, and had a lingering dark undertone.

"... No."

Apple grinned big, but her eyes stayed flat.

"Well. It sure does seem like it." She spoke in a tightly controlled voice—the way an irritated lion growls at the tip of his trainer's slashing whip.

A tiny voice of caution whispered 'flee for the hills,' but I couldn't process an appropriate plan to do so, so I stood there. I glanced at the official slip in my hand. "So, you two didn't orchestrate this little powwow?" I asked.

Apple finally grinned. "You got me."

"Yay!" Riley cheered.

Apple clapped her hands twice, causing me to back away a half step.

Riley danced in her seat, sticking her hand in the air. "Can I tell her? Can I?"

Apple nodded with a patient look. "Okay, Riley. You can tell her if you must."

"Thanks." Riley turned to me with a secret in her eyes. "Guess what today is?"

Her words left me befuddled. "Enlighten me."

She spread out her arms, as if to include the entire world. "This is the day you go out like Alison," she jeered. "Excruciatingly."

"How tragic for me."

She pouted. "Uh. Apple, she didn't get it."

"Oh. But she will," Apple snarled.

"Do it now, Apple. Do it now."

Apple stood up and spoke loudly, her voice echoing in the cavernous room. "May I have everyone's attention, please? That includes you too, teacher man."

The teacher looked up from the document in his hand. "Yes?"

"If you are not a Perfect, then I wish for you to take forty winks."

I glanced at the teacher and the other students, as they looked on, confused. "Don't do this, Apple," I mumbled.

"So sorry. It's done already." She stomped the floor. "I said sleep! Now!"

A ripple of energy vibrated around the classroom, forcing everyone who wasn't a Perfect into a deep trance, freezing in their tracks where they sat or stood.

Crap. It's going down!

"Riley, please, this isn't you. You have to remember who you are," I pleaded to her.

"I remember exactly who I am." Riley glared like I was tasty prey and she was a hungry beast about to feed. "I remember quite well."

"I don't want to hurt you too," I pleaded.

"Funny. Because I want to hurt you." Her eyes raged coral. "How about you, Apple?"

Apple's lips slanted. "Got my mind made up!"

Two empty desks behind her shot into the air and hung there in a taunting hover.

"Ditto," Riley added.

I backed off as a host of screwdrivers zipped from their wooden holder and levitated into the air, all pointed at my face. The inanimate objects appeared to be daring with life, and pissed—at me.

"Riley, last chance," I offered.

"Shut up. You're going to get screwed!" Apple said. She flexed her neck. "Let's begin, shall we?"

The screwdrivers, fifteen or so in all, and both wooden desks shot at me with an attacking descent. I dove to the left, and the makeshift missiles flew past me. Most of the tools missed their mark, sticking into the wall behind me, but two screwdrivers slammed into me; one into my left thigh and the other in the upper right side of my shoulder. I cringed from the sharp pain. It hurt something terrible, but my tear ducks stayed dry. If not for the anxiety raging up my blood vessels with lightening speed I'm positive the punishment would have seemed far greater than it did.

I yanked the screwdrivers free, keeping my eyes glued on my wicked adversaries an their evil intent. I could feel my injuries healing themselves, and the discomfort ease, as I stood firm, still trying to prolong the inevitable.

Apple celebrated. "Bulls-eye!"

Her gleaming laughter was undeserving and it irritated my spirit more than I had expected it to.

"So, you like to throw things, do you? Cool. So do I." My eyes sparkled pink.

I raised my arms and lifted Riley and Apple up into the air without their consent. Their eyes popped with agitation, and Apple flared her arms uselessly. Their looks of uncertainty were a true delight; however, it was the way I forced their bodies to fling across the classroom and slam against the wall that gave the greatest satisfaction.

Can't stand the heat, stay out of my kitchen!

The momentum dumped Riley on her head and the force rendered her unconscious. Her limp body was mine for the taking. Apple landed on her back with her legs jackknifed. Her expression stayed focused, though, and she stared at me as she clawed to her feet, staggering like a drunkard.

"Nice job," she conceded, glancing at Riley.

"I have my moments," I smarted. "Which reminds me." I nodded, and Apple's body slid across the floor and into my hands.

"Whoa!"

I gripped her by the shirt collar. "This is for hurting my Alison, you dumb twit!"

Apple's face lost its confidence and color, but I didn't care. I showed no remorse, wanting her to suffer for what she had done to my family, and to Ali. She stared into my eyes and I could tell she knew she was outmatched.

"Lauren, please don't!" she whimpered.

The Mother Perfect in me pulsed through my veins, and made the mortal side of me cower until it was nonexistent and no longer inside my body. "Yesterday, I pitied you."

Apple trembled. "And today?"

"Today, I think I'm just going to end you and call it a day. Face it, mortal. I'm better than you are."

"I know," she trembled.

"You will never win against me. It is impossible." I sneered.

The essence in my body flamed like the sun, causing an orgasmic twitch to zip up my spine. The classroom lights overhead sparked off and back on from the overload of energy, radiating from my core. With each revelation of my potential the more powerful I became. Apple's death was inevitable—so I gladly embraced the inevitability of being her executioner. It was a title I longed for. And now it was mine: calculated and raw. The shine in my pupils hit a fevered pitch, and Apple shuddered and looked away, accepting her pathetic miniscule fate: a nothing memory.

"Goodbye human."

"Wait..."

Without warning, another teacher stormed into the classroom. "What in the hell is going on in here?" he yelled.

I jumped, startled, and released my hold on Apple's throat. She fell to the floor, coughing.

"Awake!" Apple sighed with relief as she unfroze the rest of our peers in the background.

Our teacher opened his eyes and held his head, wobbling and dazed. "What happened?"

Riley climbed to her feet, using his desk as support.

Apple massaged her reddish patch of skin. "Help me! Help me! She's trying to kill us!"

"Yes. She's on drugs or something!" Riley added, approaching me with a finger point.

I grabbed Riley by the neck.

He stormed over to us. "Take your damn hands off of that student!"

I released my grip and looked into Apple's glossy eyes. I wanted to snatch them out of their sockets. "Enjoy your stay of execution."

"I only need one," Apple smirked.

"You three follow me! Now!" He shouted with a meanness that also possessed authority.

I glanced at Apple, who did the same to Riley, and they both shuffled forward toward the door. None of us were prepared to expose the fold any further, so it seemed my self-appointed position, as Guillotine Master would have to wait a bit longer. I followed the trio outside the doorway and into the hall, with as much enthusiasm as a blindfolded pirate being forced to walk the plank off of his own ship and into shark-infested waters.

CHAPTER 24

PENELOPE

I PEEKED MY HEAD out from around the corner just in time to observe the adult male mortal escort away my two foolish hybrids and one of the last Mother Perfects standing in my way of total glory.

Damn it!

All three were alive and kicking, and it left me vexed. I had hoped my extra boost of energy would have been enough to help publicly annihilate Lauren, but it seemed I'd overestimated Apple and Riley's talent for resolve, and underestimated Lauren's will.

Never send a freaking hybrid to do a Mother Perfect's job.

If I wanted to ensure it was done right, then I would have to do it myself ... or better yet—find an unlikely ally who was better skilled at killing two birds with one stone than the rest of us. The notion of what I knew I must do made my heartbeat rise, but the reward it offered tempered the singing voice of reasoning begging for my attention. The dangerous means were justified by my lofty desires.

"Plan B is a go."

CHAPTER 25

RILEY

APPLE AND I FOLLOWED two steps behind, with Lauren trailing a few more steps behind us. The hall in front of us was empty, but the *tick* of the teacher's black dress shoes clunking against the tile echoed in my ear. The rhythmic sound made our predicament feel that much more intense. I glanced at Apple from the corner of my eye, and I could see she, too, was on the verge of exploding. Her eyes glowed fuchsia and her hands to her side clenched into fists of fury.

Here we go!

Apple huffed, and before I could intervene, she winked her eye, causing the educator ahead of us to freeze mid-stride. She whipped around and closed in on Lauren. It took Lauren an extra second to register the mean-spirited intentions coming, and she stopped. Suddenly and without reason, I too was pissed at Lauren and ready to fight.

"Where were we, heifer?" Apple blasted, invading Lauren's personal space.

Lauren's eyes flickered pink. "At your slaughtering, fat cow!"

Apple sneered. "Let's do this!"

Without thinking, I slipped in between them, with only one thing on my mind: Apple's safety and wellbeing. "Apple, no!" I said, feeling Lauren's presence on my back. "Hello? School hallway! And she might hurt you this time."

"Your point?"

"Well ..." I lost the gift of speech, as two boys walked into view.

Lauren held her breath. My heart skipped a beat.

"Unwanted company," Lauren muttered.

"Why do I care?" Apple asked with a snooty tone.

"Stunned witnesses. Frozen teacher. Front page of the National Inquirer and then government dissection?" I enlightened.

"Apple, think," I pleaded.

"No. An audience is required."

I caressed her arm. "Apple, not right now. It's suicide."

Apple glanced to my fingers touching her skin and she hesitated.

The pair held their intense stare-off and no one moved.

The two boys ceased their conversation and surveyed the frozen teacher in front of them. The first paused with a perplexed expression, and waved his left hand in front of the statue's face. The angry teacher didn't blink or move.

"No way."

The second boy looked at us. "Is he dead?"

"No. He's been frozen—"

"Hypnotized," Lauren said, cutting off my explanation.

"Oooh," he replied, chuckling. He elbowed his friend. "Dude, draw a dick on his forehead."

He pulled out his pencil. "Won't be too hard. I'll just trace the one already there."

"You two don't want the same thing to happen to you next, so I suggest you kick rocks. Beat it, scrubs." Apple jerked her head towards the hall. "Or else."

The smiles on the pair simmered to an offended smirk.

"Let's roll," one said.

"Skank," the second mumbled.

Seconds later, the pair turned out of view, and our situation returned to its previous tension and death-defying glimmer.

I looked at Apple's hollow stare, but she remained dead set on Lauren's brutal demise.

"That was close. Now, where were we? Oh, I remember. We have a frozen teacher in the middle of the damn hall!" I spouted.

Apple glared at me. "She has to die."

"Sure. But the element of surprise is now gone from us."

"And?"

"And we are no longer in the shadows. Remember?"

Apple reluctantly softened her stance.

"She's right," Lauren added.

The sound of her voice made my gut clench. "Shut up."

Apple crossed her arms. "Whatever. I'm in need of a big audience anyhow."

"We'll continue this little spat later on," I advised.

"For sure," Apple said.

Lauren stiffened her posture. "Bring it. Dead weight."

Apple squinted at Lauren before whipping around. She spoke a few words in his ear and undid her incantation.

The teacher didn't miss a beat as he faced us and pointed. "I said to the office! No more talking!" he demanded. "I won't say it again!"

His biceps ripened from the confrontation.

His chest enlarged with hot air.

The blood veins in his neck bulged as he huffed.

After displaying intimidating features, the teacher stormed off, and we followed him toward the main office on the other side of the building, trailing along the maze of dull halls.

CHAPTER 26

APPLE

CAPTAIN DICK LED US to the other side of the building, where appearances mean everything. Several stragglers filtered the hall as our walk of shame cruised by like a funeral procession. By the look on the teacher's face, it wasn't hard for others to figure out we were in big trouble, and that the repercussion was going to be epic.

We followed into the main hall, but my mind was busy elsewhere, plotting a rebuttal to whatever accusations he intended on sharing with the principal. Principal Ward was known for his soft-spoken words when in a good mood, but was also known for his large stick when it came to dispensing just punishment. We entered the main office, still trailing the looks of the other students, staring and trying to appear as if they were more concerned with their own boring lives than ours.

The teacher looked to us. "Sit. You two there and you over there."

We sat in our designated spots while he walked around the front counter and into the principal's office without knocking. I winked at Riley, and she smiled back at me. We both eyed Lauren, who kept her head lowered, looking down at the white tile. I knew she could sense we were staring at her, but she refused to respond to our death stares.

"What is she thinking?" I asked Riley.

She surveyed Lauren's forehead. "I ... I can't tell."

"You can't read her thoughts? Try harder."

"I have. She's not letting me in."

"What good are you then?"

"Whatever you want me to be good at," she said, batting her long eyelashes, while caught in a wounded gaze.

Thanks for nothing, Riley. You're taking the fun out of this.

Her heart was willing to please, but her talent was lacking. It left me disturbed and hungry for what I desired most: Lauren's most inner thoughts, fears, and insecurities. Seconds later, the teacher and The Warden exited his office with the vice principal in tow, and the three stood before us. Principal Ward placed his hands on his plump hips.

"What do you ladies have to say for yourself?" he asked.

None of us answered him.

"Like I said before, I was passing out papers when my class heard this thunderous boom." He described with his hands. "It startled the entire class, me included."

"We weren't aware of its origin, but we heard the loud sound too," Principal Ward said.

"And when I rushed into the other classroom to investigate, everyone looked frozen stiff."

"Frozen?" Vice Principal Ubly asked.

"Like mannequins, only humans … like they weren't real, only they were," he said. "Very creepy looking." He shuddered.

"Huh." Principal Ward gestured. "That is most peculiar."

"Extremely," Vice Principal Ubly added.

"Everyone except for these three." He pointed to Riley. "This one was sprawled out on the floor, while she was fighting with that one. Then everyone suddenly turned real again, and I brought them here to you."

"That will be all, James. Thank you for bringing this to our attention," he said.

The teacher hesitated and walked out, and the other men turned back towards us.

"Lauren, you were one of our best students, and now you're a class bully of some sorts?" Vice Principal Ubly asked.

Lauren didn't look to him or respond.

"I know your family has suffered another great loss, but even with that, I wouldn't expect this kind of rowdy behavior coming from someone as nice as you. I can't imagine your grandmother being too pleased about all of this," said Principal Ward.

"Things aren't always what they seem," Lauren said.

"I am inclined to believe that as well," Vice Principal Ubly said. "Alright you two. Start talking." He crossed his arms over his chest.

The moment turned awkward.

"No one has a thing to say?" Principal Ward said.

"… I can explain," I said.

"By all means: elucidate," the vice principal replied.

I released a hard sigh. "It … was Lauren."

He bounced a look off Principal Ward. "It was Lauren what?"

"It was Lauren who ... broke into the school and trashed the building before summer break."

The two administrators perked up.

"Go on."

I conjured up fake tears. "She told us she was pissed about an unjust B- in Anthropology class, and how she was going to make the school pay for hiring such an incompetent teacher. Her words exactly."

They listened to my explanation, while giving Lauren sharp looks of consideration and stern judgment.

"Really?" he asked.

"Isn't that right, Riley?" I nudged her with an elbow.

"Uh-huh. She said Mr. Molsenburg was a total douche, and since you were the ones who hired him, the punishment was yours to bear as well."

"That's right," I added. "We wanted to come forward earlier, but we were kind of afraid of her. She's gotten so vicious lately. It's quite intimidating to witness firsthand."

"Her cousin Alison being murdered seemed to push her over the edge, I think." Riley added.

My long face etched in pity. "So sad, really."

"Lauren, is any of this true?" Principal Ward asked.

Tears streamed from her eyes and onto the floor between her tennis shoes, but she didn't look up or speak.

"She was angry about that bad grade," Riley added. "Something about it affecting what college she would get accepted to or something or other. I forget."

"Yep. So when we told her she ought to tell someone about it, she lost control," I said.

Our testimony was laid on pretty thick, but their faces refused to respond in the way I had hoped. The pair walked to the side out of earshot, or so they thought.

"What's your thinking on this, Fred?" Principal Ward whispered. "I, myself, am not convinced."

"I feel the same. There may be some shred of truth in what they say, but their motives are highly malicious and sneaky at best."

They approached us again.

"I believe you three are aware of our state policies regarding fighting on school grounds," Principal Ward said.

"It was self-defense."

"Yes. She was trying to kill us!" I added.

"Be that as it may, rules are rules," Vice Principal Ubly replied.

"Your parents will be notified by phone: one-week suspension for the two of you."

Riley hopped to her feet with her hands clenched. "What, a whole week? That's way too harsh!"

"Sit down in that chair and don't get up again until advised to do so," he ordered.

"Riley? He's right. Rules are rules. We're just glad the truth is now out, even if we both had to suffer great embarrassment and assault to make sure it happened."

"But ..." her words lost their way.

"Are you sure you do not wish to respond to these serious allegations? You're an honor roll student," Vice Principal Ubly said, looking at Lauren.

Lauren shook her head.

She's making this way too easy for me.

"No? I am surprised. So, with no rebuttal being expressed, I have no other choice than to expel you from high school," Principal Ward said. "Pending a formal investigation."

"Whatever ..." Lauren mumbled.

"The board of education will determine if criminal charges are warranted against you," he added.

"Do not take this lightly, Lauren. This is serious. You may need to retain a good lawyer to defend your rights," Vice Principal Ubly said. "The police will be involved."

"He's right. Your future is at hand, and we would hate to see such a bright mind as yours go to waste. It would be tragic."

Principal Ward eyed the hall monitors standing in the doorway. "I want these two kept far apart from her, and both parties escorted to their lockers and off school property."

"This way, ladies," he motioned.

I stood, and Riley followed suit. Lauren lingered a second or two before doing the same. It felt like I had been sitting forever. Even my knees had started to ache from the lack of mobility, or perhaps it was because my muscles remained tensed the whole time we were sitting on the hot seat. Either way it caused me great grief.

The hall monitor slipped in behind Riley with another one on his tail, and we walked out the door and turned left. The last one shadowed Lauren as she walked in the other direction, while the administrators paused outside the office doorway.

Riley leaned in to me.

"Don't look back. They're watching us like a hawk," I said.

"Do you think they bought it?"

"Hell, no. He wanted to expel us, too, but Lauren refused to give him any cause."

"Ms. Goody Two-Shoes will never snitch and force our hand."

"Nope."

"We're golden. Of course, he's going to notify Detective Neese," she said.

"We better make sure when he comes to investigate, he only comes for her."

"I am in agreement."

What a difference a day makes, right?

The last time we three were interviewed, our unified front proved to be an adequate shield from his accusations. But now that our union had a gaping hole, he wasn't going to be easily deterred. Every question Detective Neese asked now gave new meaning to his pursuit. He no longer had to fish for clues. He was back on familiar footing, dangling a so-called 'plea deal' from his hook for the truth.

Riley and I had handed him the bait on a silver platter, giving his old investigation validity and new life. We may have taken shrapnel in the process, but it was vital to us staying in the war—the war of killing a Mother Perfect before she took down the ship.

CHAPTER 27

LAUREN

THE HALL MONITOR HELD the door open for me to exit the building. He had escorted me to my locker, watched me take out all of my personal belongings, then hurried me toward the main entrance before the next bell was to ring. I felt like I was being paraded through a crowded prison block, and the savages were jeering my arrival. I felt anxious and embarrassed all at the same time.

"Thanks," I said, slipping by him and out the doorway.

"Hey."

"Yes?"

"Don't return without proper authorization … in writing," he said, shutting the door and checking the lock.

The coldness of his tone added to my spiraling sorrow, loneliness and descent. I walked across the front lawn and onto the student parking lot, while the hall monitor continued to survey my retreat from the glass window in the door. Three rows in, and I paused before the driver side door of the hooptie. Familiarity never felt so inviting and peaceful. I actually felt relieved my walk of shame was over, until slight movement inside the car made me focus on the seat. My heart dipped when I saw a rattlesnake curled and waiting.

The reptile focused squarely on me, and its tail rattled with rage. As I gained my startled composure, the snake's eyes glowed green and it lunged for the glass. It struck the window with its head, its fangs leaving a smeared stream of lethal venom on the glass as it dropped back to the seat.

"Ah!"

I calmed, and my breathing started again.

God, I hate snakes!

I shivered and sucked in air, and once my brain began to function correctly, I wondered where in the hell the reptile had come from in the first place. I scanned the parking lot.

Apple and Riley stood not far off, on the side of the school building, peaking from around a corner.

"Should've guessed," I muttered.

"You really should have," Apple's voice chimed in my ear, as if she was standing behind me whispering with deviant ambitions.

I curled my eyes. "You're a real piece of work."

"I know. Have fun with my pet, Igor. And if his love nibble doesn't do the trick, then we will the next time we're standing face-to-face."

"Looking forward to it," I replied.

"Tootles," Riley added.

I watched Apple and Riley stroll out of sight, then looked inside the car. The rattlesnake was no longer in view. It must have slithered off the seat and onto the floor somewhere, and I wasn't going to open the car door and go searching for him.

I pulled out my cellular phone and Google the number for the local animal control.

"Grand Blanc Animal Control, Taffi speaking, how may I help you?" the young woman greeted me.

"My name is Lauren. I'm parked in the student parking lot over at the high school. I have a rattlesnake inside my car."

"Did you say a rattlesnake?"

"Uh-huh."

"In your car?"

"That is correct."

"Wow."

"Can you send someone over to come and remove it for me?"

"Of course. First things first, leave the door closed and do not let anyone get inside the vehicle."

"I don't think that will be an issue. I hate snakes."

"Don't feel bad. I do too."

"Estimated ETA?"

"I'm sending one of our associates over right away."

"Cool."

"His name is Robbie, and he should be there within twenty minutes or less. So sit tight. Not inside the car, mind you."

"Yeah. I got that. Thanks."

She giggled. "You're welcome."

I hung up the phone, and couldn't stop my eyes from turning glossy and red with irritation. Anger was starting to get the better of me, and I questioned my choice in letting them walk out of that classroom unscathed.

Things I held dear would've been exposed, and I would have been labeled a felon, but it would have been over, and possibly worth it. But they weren't deceased—and I was still trapped in torment. I was so isolated it boiled the marrow inside my bones and jabbed at my heart. Ali was gone from me, and I couldn't change it. My whole life was now too, and I was too emotional to assess the real value of what was left. Even if I were able to accept my fate as one hundred percent Perfect, I was lost as to how to make it official and not be desolate. I felt stuck. Worse than stuck I was dead… just couldn't convince my torn body to stay down long enough for rigor mortis to set in.

CHAPTER 28

GENEVE

I APPEARED A FOOT inside the front entrance of Grotta Palazzese restaurant, my hair fluttering to a rest as I exited the portal faster than sight. The hollowed boulder-like eatery was full of elegance and a special kind of uniqueness that came from being created inside a cave. The dark hardwood floors glowed like a boat deck in Venice in the middle of spring. The recessed lighting embedded in the rocky ceiling ten feet above complemented the modern lamps fastened to the waist-high, iron gate, which separated the far opening of the cave from the calming shores of the Mediterranean Sea. Twenty dining tables with glass tops were scattered throughout the room, and a wine counter was set against the sidewall. Each glass table was occupied with well-dressed men, all seemingly enjoying their meal, while a handful of human servers roamed from table to table with plates of food or glasses of wine in hand. The tangy smell of freshly cut lemons was in the air, and the room was busy, while at the same time romantic feeling.

I eyed the descending brightness of sun in the not so distance, as it shimmered off the vast blue sea as if an artist on a demented binge created the world's beauty with the wetness from his acrylic brush. Still, my admiration was on destruction. Though the scent of saltwater mixed with succulent warmth of the Italian air tried soothing my emotions, I denied its calming taunt, holding firm to my wrath. I was irate, and on a deadly tear; a rampage that would end with Penelope's neck broken by my freshly manicured hands, once she favored Charlotte.

Mare, Italy was a favorite hot spot of mine, especially during the cold, dreary months of Russia's numbing and ruthless winters. Penelope was no fool. She would've known that, so why she would be so careless as to show her face here was beyond me.

Was her action a misstep?

I think not. *Never.* Not Penelope. She possessed more cunning DNA than our own Victoria in her prime. Still, retribution was less than twenty-five feet away, and I was ready for everything. I narrowed my eyes and prowled beyond the empty greeter's booth, and into the heart of the lion's den. My presence failed to attract the attention of the others around me, even though Penelope and I were the only two females in the room, besides a host of busy servers doing their jobs. I continued forward, keeping my stern eyes locked on my prey.

She was seated straight ahead at a table for four, but only two others were seated with her. A pair of suited men, who had the appearance of business travelers, stared at their colorful menus before them. Penelope gazed at her half-filled crystal wine glass, running the tip of her finger in circles along the rim. Even though she was seated in the company of two attractive mortals, she purposely released a cold anti-social vibe. She looked as though she didn't want to be bothered by anyone. That was a shame, because I had every intention of being bothersome. I approached Penelope, and she glanced up from her thoughts, but didn't react to my unexpected and deadly arrival. The last time we faced each other in Spain, her response had been very different, and she seemed less spooked than before. I knew there was a good reason for that, and it was most likely to my disadvantage. I pulled out the empty chair from her table and took a seat, crossing my legs. The two men seated stayed busy conversing with one another. My eyes simmered pink.

"Love your heels," she complimented, before downing her wine.

I grinned and batted my eyelashes.

"Can I offer you a menu, madam?" a female server asked me, placing a glass of ice water on the table.

"No, thank you. I won't be staying long enough to enjoy it."

I saw her nod and walk off.

"You should try the Valle d'Aosta. It's truly delectable this time of year," Penelope gleamed. "Just saying."

"Tempting, but good cheese tends to disagree with my system when eaten in the company of pure evil."

She tilted her brow. "Don't tell me you're still miffed about our little skirmish back in Spain? I promise you I was only funning."

"And I hope you didn't think that surrounding yourself with human beings will save you from my ire."

Penelope shrugged. "Figured it couldn't hurt."

"Yeah? Well … good luck with that."

"Who needs luck when you have a beautiful mind such as mine?"

"Beauty is in the eye of the beholder. And certainly another Perfect's treasure is only fool's gold to everyone else observing."

"Mother Geneve, you've hurt my feelings." She shied.

"Get use to it. It will be the last thing you feel, period."

"... I believe you. Do you have their approval?"

"Whom are you referring?"

Her eyes flickered to the side and she smirked.

The suited man seated beside me aimed his pistol an inch or so from my temple and his eyes glared. I didn't budge.

"Them."

The shuffling of wooden chairs scoffed the floor.

I stared into Penelope's wine glass, and the reflection bouncing off the crystal showed every suited man in the background was now standing, aiming their pistols and shotguns toward me. Penelope adored as revelation registered in my steady eyes.

"Boom. Now what?" she smiled.

"Am I supposed to be fascinated?"

"A little. I picked up this accessory move from Mother Harlen himself."

"So you were there?" I asked.

"... I might have been somewhere in the arena." She shrugged. "I can neither confirm nor deny my whereabouts at the moment of his untimely and painful demise."

She held her smile as she gestured to the room. "Entertain me."

I heard the trigger housing rotate and the hammer slam against the back of the bullet. It released a loud bang, followed by lead zipping from the barrel and toward my skull. In my perfection, the situation played out in slow motion. Before the bullet grazed my skin, I had already uncrossed my legs and surfed the wooden chair backwards toward the open space in the center of the dining room. I watched the bullet zoom past the bridge of my nose and into the body of another suited man on the far side.

The impact jolted him, shuddered his chest and heart, as he lost breath then his life. His muscles flinched and he accidentally rapid fired three hollow point bullets into my attacker's forehead. From the corner of my eye I saw his head flap backwards.

The other man at Penelope's table fired his pistol, but the bullet missed me and punctured the stomach of another standing behind me on my far left.

Both suited men collapsed to the hardwood floor. Dead.

I stood up from the chair, on guard, and kicked it behind me. The wooden chair flung across the floor and shattered into sharp pieces as it slammed into two suited men at the rear. Their weapons fired bullets into the floor and their injuries sent them collapsing.

The servers standing about the cave fled for cover. Hot shell casings danced to the floor as I maneuvered about the dining room like a fuming wind on the back of a tornado, killing every suited man who dared to test my resolve or had the galls to aim at my perfect body.

I snapped my glare toward two men in the corner, and willed their bodies to shoot into the air. Both collided with the rocky ceiling then smacked the floor, motionless.

A piercing pain in my forearm caused me to whip around. "Aah!"

The last man standing fired two quick rounds from his pistol that hit my chest before I could dodge. I grimaced from the attack and dropped to one knee, while he foolishly gloated at my defeat instead of finishing me off when he had half a chance.

Seconds later my wounds were no more, and his negligence proved fatal. I stood upright and willed his body to me, so fast it snatched his breath away. I snapped his neck in two before he could respond to my vengeance, and his body dropped to the hardwood floor like a sack of coal. The dining room returned to an eerie silence as debris settled.

"Penelope!" I shouted, vibrating the fixtures.

I turned to the dinner table where I had last seen my prize, but she was gone. In the midst of battle, Penelope had again slipped away, leaving her human security team to suffer the fate meant for her. But their sacrifice fell short of satisfying my blood-thirst for revenge.

Coward! I cannot believe she is a Perfect!

Her calculated move angered me beyond words, but I elected to hold my tongue and bottled my bubbling rage for the moment. I knew it would be just a matter of time.

You're going to beg me to end you, Penelope!

"Madam! Look at my home!" the owner said, hysterical. "Look at all these dead bodies! I am ruined!"

His Italian accent was rich and fluent, even more so in the midst of his emotional distress.

"To what dead bodies are you referring?" I asked him, surveying the now empty cave with its modern glass tables, neatly prepared for dining.

Amazing what a quick, Perfect cleanup can do. I saw his face change as the mangled bodies and gore vanished and the dining room returned back to normal.

He hesitated, his memory of the event now freshly wiped clean. "What ... were we discussing again?"

"I was just complimenting you on another exquisite meal," I smiled. "Thank you."

"I am glad you were pleased." He saw my dirty plate, empty wine glass and ruffled cloth napkin on the table. "It seems you had the place all to yourself once again."

"Just as I like."

I walked off, knowing Penelope couldn't hide forever, and I was sure the revelation did not escape her as well. She feared my touch like most mortals feared their crude insecurities, and I could sense her unholy presence anywhere in the universe.

And no gang of human beings, no matter how well trained, no matter how well supplied with earthly weapons, would stop my unrelenting fury the next time my sights locked in on her. This was one punishment she would not be able to outrun.

Ever!

CHAPTER 29

ZOE

I DISLIKED HAVING TO live among the humans from within the shadows. I disliked it almost as much as I despise the very existence of Fearians.

I can still recall every minuscule detail of when the Mother Perfects elected to retreat into the realm of mortals, rather than making a stand at home. Being friends with Victoria was not something I would brag about, but I felt just as passionate as she had about defending our beloved paradise. We should have stayed and fought to the bitter end; all of us should have. But we didn't fight, and our rewards now are mountains of regrets and a burning desire for ultimate revenge.

I opened my eyes and raised my head with a pink glare. The sun nearing the horizon beamed its heat against my back. The rays were comforting, and radiated a sense of valor within me. I felt it strengthen and lift my body, as I stood in the clearing alone.

I'm ready for anything!

The ten-foot radius around me was barricaded by a seven-foot-high wall of flourishing corn stalks, mere days from being harvested. The scent of yellow kernels simmered in the air, brushing up against my skin pores.

Not far away appeared a Fearian Warrior from within the corn stocks. Both of his eyes were shut and his heart was beating like a battle drum, a sword at his side.

"I feared you were afraid," I taunted.

His eyelids moved, releasing a clicking noise from each blink. The clicking sound was irritating, but my choppy breathing drowned it out. He stretched his neck and clenched his fingers, as the sight of me seemed to make him more furious by the second. The warrior parted his lips, exposing his sharp fangs, and growled under his breath. I blew him a kiss, and his glare deepened. He twirled his sword by the handle in front of his body, and the flashes of light reflecting off the silver blade blinded me for a second.

"AAHHH!"

With a mighty battle cry, he attacked. I narrowed my eyes and readied my stance as he closed in fast, galloping like a thoroughbred seeking his very freedom. My fingers tingled and I drew out my steel sword and reared it back over my head.

The warrior swung for my neck, but the blade of my sword was there to meet his, and sparks flew from the steel-on-steel collision. I sideswiped his charge like a seasoned matador, and repositioned my weapon.

His charge was so ferocious it took him several steps to stop his momentum before he spun around at the ready. His audacity brought a smirk to my face and he barreled back toward me, thrusting his silver blade at my body. I tucked my limbs and front flipped, and his jab caught nothing but empty air. I landed at his back and slashed my blade into his beefy muscles and tendons, turning him into a spout of black ash.

The brittle wall of corn stalks trembled and a line of warriors stepped out into view, surrounding me. No one spoke as we stared at each other, ready to fight ... or die if that were our fate. The breeze tossing my bangs seemed to deliver the clicking noises from their eyelids faster and much louder than before. I detected one of them bracing his foot against the ground, so I sliced my blade in his chest. He was first to pounce and the second warrior to die. My blade cut into his body as his figure turned into black ash.

The warriors shouted as one and attacked as the same.

I tossed the sword aside and punched the earth with all my might, unleashing an angry pulse of energy. The force erupted like a nuclear bomb and sent a raging ripple across the clearing, slamming every warrior to the ground with a thud. Black ash gushed into the air as the warriors died. But before the ashes rested on the earth, another line of warriors stepped out from the corn, eager to take their fallen comrades' place.

"DIE! DIE!" I shouted, shooting pulses of energy at anything with Fearian blood.

The clearing turned dark as gushing black ash blocked the sun. Bodies charged, animalistic voices raged, and limbs swung as I unloaded energy pulse after pulse, turning my many enemies into few survivors.

Suddenly, I felt a sharp stab in my back. I grimaced from the intrusion and looked down to my stomach to see the tip of a blade poking through with blood on it.

I turned around, knocking free the warrior's grip on the sword sticking through my back. I chopped my fingers to his throat, punched him two times in the chest, twice in his gut and once to the groin in the span of three seconds. I rode the velocity and roundhouse kicked his limbs, dislocating both of his kneecaps. The warrior let out a faint whimper and tumbled to the earth on his back.

I turned and shot an energy pulse at the last two warriors charging before me, readying their swords to attack. Both turned into ash before their blades had a chance to swing. I looked to the last warrior lying on the ground and aimed at his head.

I tossed my locks free from black ash. "Not even cool."

He stared up at me blank faced, but swayed my heart none, and I shot him with a pulse, turning his body into a pile of black ash. A bead of sweat dribbled off my brow, and I took a moment to slow my breathing, as nothing but the breeze moved around me. My pupils returned to normal and I relaxed somewhat, while the weight of the sword sticking through my midsection began to pull on my body and my shaky equilibrium.

Even still, my intuition forced me to eye a patch of corn stalks. "Are you going to be a creeper, or are you going to show yourself?" I asked.

Dison stepped out of the cornfield and into the clearing. "My apologies. I did not want to disrupt your fun."

"How thoughtful of you."

He pulled the sword from my body and the wound healed itself. "You know me: a heart of pure gold."

I jammed my hands on my hips. "And modest to boot."

Dison chuckled—the way a psycho does when he's found his next unsuspecting victim.

I stayed on high alert—the way a victim does when she's had enough of being the first one to die.

"I'm a Perfect. What do you expect of me?"

"Nothing less."

"Indeed." His grin widened. "Speaking of bad ass. You looked super sexy out here kicking butt, girl."

"Am I supposed to say thank you now? Be appreciative."

"You don't have to if you don't wanna. I know that you are, though."

I tilted my hips. "Huh."

Dison prowled closer, entering my personal space. "He really should have made you his destroyer."

"I'm in agreement."

"Too bad your views weren't viewed as an asset. He may still be among the living."

"Again, I share the same sentiment."

"Oh, well. Mother Harlen's loss it shall remain."

"I've never known you for small talk."

"Just being cordial."

"Like a slithering black mamba?"

"Even a serpent benefited from good conversation before the offer of an apple was given."

My face stayed blank. "What do you want, Dison?"

He walked behind me, forcing me to turn my head as he took his time before facing me again. "Can't I drop in from time to time and visit a spell with an old friend?"

"No."

"And why is that?"

"Because I don't like you."

"Huh?"

"But you know that already."

His face soured. "I did. Still hurtful."

"It was meant to be."

"Success."

"Plus I trust you about as far as I can throw you ... if I suffered from human strength, that is."

"Zoe, why do you persist in bringing guilt upon me?"

"I'm sorry."

"Really?"

"Hell, no."

"Aw. Again. Hurtful."

"Success."

"And after I was nice enough to pull this Fearian sword from your body," he said, handling the sword playfully.

"I have trust issues."

Dison lunged at me and pinned my arms behind my back, his handsome face so close to mine I felt the heat of his breath and the cherry flavor that went with it.

"Caught you slipping."

"It would appear so. Now what?" Although his actions were rough, they failed to steal the twinkle in my eyes.

His face softened, and he leaned forward and kissed me. I responded without thinking, and my arms wrapped around his neck. After a while, we pulled apart, but he held his tender embrace, and my heart.

"I missed you," he said.

"And me you. But why have you risked coming to see me in the light of day?"

"I have news to share with my beloved. Someone interesting paid me another visit."

I squinted. "And what did that praying mantis desire of you this time around?"

"Me, what else?" he gloated.

"Over my dead body!"

"You know my heart belongs to you. But, if I help keep the others in line, I will get to reign by her side. My point is Penelope is the lesser of two evils in my book."

"Dison, Mother Geneve isn't evil."

"Mother Geneve is holding onto a world that is no more."

"And?"

"And things change."

"Dison?"

"I'm not saying I wish to rebel against our way of life, but we are here now. Things change and we need to conform quickly to stay relevant."

"So it's every Perfect for himself now? Is that what you're saying to me? That's how you want your legacy remembered?"

"I'm saying we were chosen to survive while others did not … I'm saying let's do more than survive, let's thrive. Let's succeed greatly were others failed."

"And what do you have in mind ... exactly?"

He kissed me on the forehead. "Let me sweat the small stuff."

"… Fine. But be careful. Your actions will be viewed as treasonous, depending on who's doing the judging."

"I got this." He patted his chest.

"Uh-huh."

"And when the time is right, Penelope won't know what hit her." He winked softly, so soft it actually consoled me.

"Hope you know what you are doing, Dison."

"When have I not?"

"Do you wish me to create a list for you?"

"Not enough time," he replied, silencing me with another kiss.

The heated warmth of his gentle touch stole all contestation from my intellect, leaving me vulnerable and weak—love struck.

I didn't know what he was up to, but I elected to put off my concerns and enjoy the one thing I still possessed from the homeland that made me feel whole again.

I'll be damned if I let Penelope get her hands on him—not without suffering the same fate as Victoria.

CHAPTER 30

PENELOPE

I ENTERED THE BUILDING and walked across the lobby and around the bend to the host of elevators. Standing before me were bored humans, dressed in professional attire and waiting for the doors to drift apart so they could step on board and continue on with their worthless existence of rotting away at a desk for a measly paycheck.

Their pathetic lives would make me want to kill myself.

I pushed my way between them and paused near the front of the congestion. By the slanted looks I received, I'm sure I seemed out of place in my two-piece, black leather outfit and eight-inch, coral glass heels. My unique appearance clashed with the sedated impersonal decorum they were all enslaved to.

DING!

"I think this is my ride," I said.

I tossed my long hair to one side and peeled off my shoes. I moved closer to the doors parting before me, exposing a dark shaft and no elevator. The human beings at my rear shuffled forward on my heels, with no inclination of danger, and I halted them with a cautious finger. Some snapped out of their oblivious daze of conformity.

"Y'all may want to wait for the next elevator." I faced them. "I seriously doubt you humans are capable of surviving such a roller coaster ride as this."

Their eyes widened when they noticed the steep drop before them.

"Wait!" a tall, slender man warned, reaching out for me.

It was way too late for chivalry. I stepped out into the darkness. Female voices in the crowd shrieked as my body plummeted out of sight. My impulsive idea had moved into the realm of decision, and risking everything would either birth a glorious new era, or end with my death in this one. I looked beyond my bare feet, and the bottom of the shaft began to glow with radiant colors, festive and warm as I descended closer toward it.

Beautiful ... who could've imagined anything from a monstrous species being so?

The light illuminated a familiar landscape, though I used to witness it from the other side of the great divider. I heard nothing, as my body dropped, no wind whishing past my ears, just peaceful silence—nothing left to do but close my eyes and slumber.

But I was far from sleepy, and was full aware when my descent slowed itself.

The light of day pressed against my face and I landed gently on the ground. I tried to get my bearings as I inspected the clouds, but the elevator shaft was nowhere to be found, replaced by a polluted skyline. A breeze gave me chills and ignited goose bumps along my arms. The hairs on my neckline perked with caution. This side of our world has always been notorious for its cooler climate, even with its vivid rainforest-like regions.

You needed thick skin if you expected to survive in the realm of the most hated for any longer than a short spell. I shook off the discomfort, fueled by my desires, and spotted a narrow path through the thick forest of low-hanging vines, shrubs and oversized sponge-like leaves. The bended trail was more of a mild suggestion of broken and bent shrubbery than an actual route, though I managed to hold true to its winding path.

As I climbed the hilly terrain, parts of a steeple in the distance came into view and the smell of lake water hit my nose. I found myself at a wall of trees, and pulled back the branches of thick leaves to expose a quaint opening. I emerged from the forest on a sandy beach at the edge of clear, green water, where I got a full look of the damaged temple, far from its previous splendor. I was in the heart of the Fearian world, where only Perfects on a suicide mission had ever stepped foot before—Perfects who had come close to chopping off the head of the snake, yet failed to complete the mission: Perfects like Izzy.

"Halt!" Kaiden shouted.

I reached into my pocket and pulled out a silk white scarf and waved it as I approached him. "Hello."

"How dare you violate our realm with your vulgar presence!" Kaiden snapped.

I held my tongue and looked out over the calm water. I saw the leaders of the Fearian species, standing at the edge of the damaged temple.

Kaiden charged with his weapon held high and his eyes slanted. He sprang into the air and attacked me, but I blocked his advances with little effort, and no intent to kill.

His attack was fierce, but I was not afraid of the likes of him. At the same time, I refused to exploit his weaknesses, choosing instead to let him tire him self out. From the corner of my eye, I noticed his Counsel watching his futile attempts. Only his gods possessed the strength to combat the essence of a Mother. I punched Kaiden in the chest with an open hand, and the force pushed him backwards on his heels. He shook it off, bandaged his bruised ego and renewed his assault with lethal determination.

"Stop!" Oplous ordered.

"What?" Kaiden turned, surprised.

"Your efforts will remain unfruitful, for this one possesses the authority of a true Mother Perfect," he explained.

I jerked the slack from my blouse. "I'm glad someone decided to tell him the good news."

"Why have you come here?" Oplous asked.

"As much as you may dislike my intrusion, I had no other choice than to come to you," I replied.

"Perfects. You deserve nothing less than death!" Kaiden spat blood on the sand.

"Perhaps a heated topic for a new day, flunky … or I could just end your ass right here, right now." I offered.

"Try it-"

"No. Let her speak," Nolum cut in.

"Explain why you are here in our realm, Perfect," Serene added.

Although the Counsel stood on the other side of the water, the volume of their voices was as though they were beside us, close enough to touch both Kaiden and me. Their acknowledgment of my presence seemed to bother Kaiden, and I shot him a smirk.

"I come offering a delightful proposition: an alliance between you and me," I said.

"Interesting," Nolum said. "Continue."

"You three wish to eliminate those who have done you injustice, those like Mother Elisabeth and Victoria," I said.

"The likes of Elisabeth is no more." Kaiden pumped his fist. "I saw to that already."

"And yet you didn't do the same to her offspring and to Mother Geneve. So really, what have you gained'?"

"Huh," Kaiden crossed his arms.

"And then there's the small matter of a priceless Fearian artifact stolen long ago, but never retrieved: the Shadow dagger."

"What do you know of this?" Serene asked me.

"Maybe I know its whereabouts. Maybe I don't. Do you?"

"She's a liar!" Kaiden stammered. "That's what Perfects do! They lie from their soul!"

"Servant, you will refrain from talking until told to do so," Oplous demanded.

Kaiden's rage was doused with servility and embarrassment burned his dented cheeks.

"And what makes you different from other Perfects the Counsel saw fit to trust but proved unworthy?" Serene asked, with a hint of bitterness in his tone.

"I'm still alive ... and the dagger makes me virtuous."

"And if this is true—"

"Oh, it is," I assured.

"Then you want something of value in exchange for its return to the Counsel?" Nolum asked.

I tilted my head. "I only wish to usher in a new era ... with new rules to go along with it."

"Where you would be the only Mother Perfect in existence," Serene guessed my ambition.

"You got to admit, it does have a nice ring to it," I replied.

"But you require our assistance in some other way as well," Nolum said.

"Yes. Those of my kind you despise are also similarly esteemed in my own eyes," I said. "Or to put it another way—Geneve and her kin must die by your hands."

"We're in agreement," Oplous replied.

"Not to mention Vicky's weird experiment gone awry has managed to bring unwanted attention to both species before its time," I added.

"Are you incapable of challenging their dominance for superiority?" Nolum asked. "You are favored now, a Mother Perfect. This should be no problem for you. The others then will have no choice but to follow."

"Great minds think alike. And I have installed a failsafe for the remaining hybrids to die quickly and torturous," I said.

"But?"

"Mother Geneve and Lauren are quite the handful—two against one."

"You can't handle two?" Kaiden mumbled.

"I'd much rather offer them up for your recompense ... let your fierce warriors have a crack at them."

"Intriguing."

"I'll even lay the perfect snare, no thanks required," I said. "Would this be of interest to the Counsel?"

"It would," Oplous said.

"Then I'll take the continent of Africa."

"Come again?"

"Being you Fearians prefer a more glacial climate to hang your hats, I wish to take Africa to rule for a lifetime."

"And what assurance do we have of your loyalty to the Counsel?" Serene asked.

My brain jolted a warning, but my desires were already at the helm and steering me into choppy waters.

Remember your reward, girl ... it's now or never ... your last chance to transcend beyond the fray.

I released a soothing sigh and drew out the Shadow dagger. I kneeled down on one knee and lay it on the sandy beach.

I shuddered a breath then stood to my feet, my thoughts now naked and vulnerable.

"The Shadow dagger. It is home again," Kaiden gasped.

I opened my eyes to find the Counsel standing in front of me, inches from my face. The speed at which they had traveled across the large lake startled me and still amazed. The Shadow dagger glowed jade green, a sign it felt the presence of home, then levitated into Nolum's awaiting hands where he cuddled it like a newborn Fearian baby.

"Are we in one accord?" I asked.

Serene, who stood in the middle of the three, looked thoughtful. As I watched, his normally passive eyes turned sharp, and he looked at me with a strange grin. Then he and Oplous moved so quickly I didn't have time to blink or comprehend their intentions.

Oplous grabbed both of my wrists while Serene hugged me from behind and wrapped his arm around my neck. He squeezed until the tiny bones in my neck bent and crackled. My air valve became obstructed. I tried to inhale ... then everything went black.

The darkness gave birth to a blinding light and suddenly I was standing in an open space crowded by Mother Perfects: Harlen, Isabelle, Elisabeth, and three elders: Martha, Virginia and Cole.

They wore pure white robes and their fair skinned completions had not a flaw. I looked and saw I was wearing the same and was barefooted like them as well. I caressed my neck, but the tiny bones underneath the skin were intact. I couldn't help but smile from the glowing reunion, though I couldn't tell if the warm feeling was mutual.

"Is … this the after life?"

"Where else would it be?" Harlen asked.

"You came to greet me?" I marveled.

Their blank faces turned monstrous and horrid-looking. "We came to condemn!"

"We find you guilty of treason against the order," Isabelle said.

That's when I saw. Lying on the beaten path was Victoria's mutilated body. Her face was bruised and her eyelids shut, and silver death flies picked at her leftover corpse. The image was disgusting, though the smell in the air remained pleasant, like an open field of buttercups the first day of summer. My heart darkened over the eerie thought of what was to become of me.

Elisabeth narrowed her eyes at me. "How dare you conspire against my child!"

I found myself backing off in angst, though my body glided forward with each step. "No. No. It was Vicky's idea. Please!"

One by one they stabbed at my flesh with jagged steel fingernails and the pain was excruciating, yet no shrieks released from my mouth, as I bore it in torture. I tried to scream for help, but my lips melted into one. The sapphire of my pupils faded to dim, and my vision turned white and black.

CHAPTER 31

CHARLOTTE

MY DEEPEST DESIRE HAS come to pass! The Fearian Counsel had done me a solid without them even knowing, and I got my wish—I was a witness to Penelope's day of reckoning, and it savored sweet nectar to my taste buds. I only endured a slice of guilt from relishing the beauty of watching a Perfect killed by the hands of Fearians.

Did I lie to myself this whole time? Was I stuck in the gut of selfishness? Was Penelope truly the greater of two evils?

Though I'd rather the repulsive deed have been done by my own hands, I still shed a tear of joy just the same. The brutality ravaged her essence whole and calmed my nerves and cooled the flames of revenge, without me lifting a single finger to assist.

A large, flowering bush with black and yellow petals hid me from view, and from certain death by my divine enemies, I'm sure, standing sixty feet or so off. They hovered over Penelope's twisted corpse, cherishing the return of their beloved Shadow dagger.

If I were a Mother Perfect, I might've been skilled enough to take full advantage of the element of surprise, and take down maybe one of them. But I wasn't a Mother Perfect, and I would be slaughtered the moment from exposing myself to my foes.

Even in passing, your birth has spoiled our future!

Penelope's skin looked radiant, but the light in her eyes was gone, and so with it my last connection to the one I loved, who'd died a cruel death at the hands of a fool.

The Fearians began to praise the lit white stars above, lifting their hands with honor and excitement.

"Long live the Counsel!" they shouted repeatedly.

Their arrogance and their words began to irritate me.

I inhaled the smell of death one last time as it fed my lungs and then retreated with caution, disappearing into the safety of the rainforest. The violent deed was now the past, though my smirk tried breathing life back into it repeatedly with each memory. We were still at risk of extermination if things continued on south, but at least Penelope wouldn't be around to ever offer a testimony—her ambitions prevented me from ever becoming favored by Mother Isabelle, but it cost us both of our bloodlines.

The sight of the portal offered me instant comfort, yet the slow realization of the Counsel controlling the destiny of the Shadow dagger stole it away.

CHAPTER 32

KAIDEN

PENELOPE WAS DEAD, AND the Shadow dagger was home once again. I finally felt redemption, which I had sought ever since I let Elisabeth deceive me into being careless long ago. I couldn't stop the tears that filled my eyes.

"The Perfect was correct," grinned Nolum.

"A new era is at hand, but it will be without her filthy kind destroying its true nature!" Oplous declared.

I kicked Penelope's body and her torso flipped flopped into the water, where a dark shape underneath the plain caught sight of the disruption and snatched her remains out of view. Red bubbles popped on the surface of the water—then nothing. The lake returned to its eerie calmness, and the red haze lingering fought to exist. Seconds later the greenness of the water diluted the haze until it was like Penelope herself: no more.

"Feast well, my beauties. She is worth her weight in gold bars," Nolum said.

"It is a glorious day for our kind. Shall I summon The Seal to be renewed?" I asked them.

"No. We shall take the Shadow dagger to them," Serene said.

"Yes. I think it is time we see firsthand the suitability of the human realm for a superior race such as our own," Oplous added.

CHAPTER 33

APPLE

I SWERVED ONTO THE quiet avenue, where Riles had lived all of her stupid life.

"Stop here," she directed.

I parked off the curb, and could sense something on her mind as she fiddled with the strap of her handbag.

"Spit it out, girl."

"I was just wondering ..."

"About?"

"Maybe we're taking this a little too far. I mean with trying to end Lauren and everything. Maybe-"

"We went over this already, Riley."

"I know. And I'm still on your side ... I just think maybe she's had enough, and if she disappears for good then we won't have to kill her."

"She's had enough when I say she's had enough!"

"But, what if ..."

I slapped the steering wheel. "No! She must die! She must die now!"

"Okay ..." Riley cowered.

"Look, Riley. I realize you don't understand everything right now, but once it's over and done with you'll see it was for the best. You have to trust me on this."

I lifted her face to me, and my touch delivered a jolt of lustful energy into the marrow of her bones. I sensed it spilling over and making a mess inside of her soul.

"I do. I really do."

"Then it's settled. Okay?"

"Absolutely."

"Perfect. And now since we're suspended, we have an entire week to make it happen. We make Lauren disappear, and so will all the suspicions about us."

Riley opened her car door. "Was it just me, or could you tell something was different in her when we attacked her?"

"It was just you."

"So you felt it too?"

I sighed. "Yes. But no matter, together you and I can still end her."

"Give me an hour and I'll slip out the back, then I'm all yours to do with what you wish." She gleamed.

"I'll be waiting at the stop sign. Dress to kill."

Riley skirted across her front lawn and into her home. I wasn't sure, but I believed Lauren's presence weakened my control on Riley's mind and it somehow shook my resolve as well. She needed to be handled, and quickly, in order to keep success viable.

For me to be the true Perfect I was meant to become, Lauren had to be the Mother Perfect I desired: a dead one. My thoughts were swirling, like I possessed the notions of three inside my head: mine, Riley's … and then another's.

CHAPTER 34

RILEY

I TOOK OFF MY shoes in the foyer and walked into the house. I was uncertain as to the type of greeting that was awaiting me, knowing that Principal Ward had most likely called and alerted my parents of our felonious actions, which led to suspension.

"Mom? Dad? I'm home." I stepped inside the living room.

My mouth dropped and my feet shuffled to a halt.

Oh, God! Oh, God! I must be having a nightmare ...

Mom and Dad were bound and their mouths gagged. A threaded rope gripped their necks as they hung from the second-floor railing, their toes barely able to touch the stools beneath them. The stool legs looked fragile and the inevitable seemed bleak. Cruel.

"Mom!" I shrieked. "Dad!"

"Don't take another step!" Jared ordered.

"What he said," Diane sneered, with a head nod.

Diane, Pepper and Jared looked on from the landing above and their deviant expressions made goose bumps along my neck pop.

I shivered, as coldness shot up my spine.

"Welcome home, dear. Did you have lots of homework on your first day of school?" Pepper mocked.

"Jared? What the hell?" I frowned. "Why have you done this terrible thing to my parents? They were good people."

"We hate Perfects," Diane answered with a shoulder shrug.

"Pretty much," he gloated.

I hesitated. "But ... you three are Perfects. Remember?"

"Huh. Do you hear that sis?" she said.

"That's what you wanted us to believe," Pepper said.

"Do what?"

"Knowing we were the leaders of an entire supreme species!" Jared added. "How dare you!"

Their creepy taunts were foreign to me.

"I have no idea what you're talking about," I said. "You're all hateful murderers!"

"You mean we're The Seal!" Jared jeered.

I lifted my arms. "I don't know what that is."

"God, you really are dumb, aren't you?" Diane cut her hazel eyes and planted her hands on her narrow hips.

"Blame Vicky," Jared said. "We sure do."

"Okay. I can do that. But what does that have to do with my parents being killed?"

Pepper pepped up her stance. "Oh. Absolutely nothing." She shined, displaying her pearly whites.

"What? Then …"

"We just want you to hurt for contaminating us with that filth flowing through your mortal veins," Pepper said.

Jared grunted. "Hybrid Perfect … more like hybrid joke."

My body lifted off the floor and hung in the air, where I began to swirl violently. The laughing trio became a blur as my body was flung in dizzying circles. I could hear my parents' gasps of horror, and I tried to focus, remembering what was at stake.

"Do you know what it's like to have your parents ripped away from your life and not being able to do a damn thing about it?" Diane asked me.

"Don't hurt them. Please," I sobbed.

"Too late. What's done is done," Jared said.

He stomped the floor, and I saw the rippling force jolt my parents into the air as it shattered the legs of the stools. Helpless, I watched my parents' bodies drop. The terror in their eyes hit a fever pitch, moments before the ropes tightened around their necks and caused both to snap at an awkward angle, their limp bodies jerking from the momentum.

"NOOO!"

"Take comfort in knowing that death was quick and painless," Diane giggled. "Sort of."

"Looked pretty scary, though," Pepper smiled.

I sniffled. "You three are blaming me for what was done to you many years ago?"

"Damn straight," Jared said. "Pep?"

Pepper winked, then shifted into a huge, hawk-like bird.

"What the…" I lost my train of thought.

So went my survival skills.

Pepper soared off the landing and into the air, her claws erect and her fangs sharp. She latched onto my body and we hung together, but I couldn't find the strength to fight back.

I went numb.

I heard violent sounds of flesh ripping, that I assumed was coming from my body and Pepper tore at my skin with her bladed sharp beak.

It sounded foul and grotesques to the ear, but I was beyond caring, beyond the agony, beyond any comprehension. It somehow offered me comfort not understanding the full extent of my punishment.

My mother's legs twirled partially in view as she dangled.

"I'm sorry," I muttered to her memory.

My glossy eyes became heavy … so heavy … it came like a dark phantom holding a knife …

Darkness.

CHAPTER 35

PEPPER

I DROPPED TO THE hardwood floor with Riley's corpse in my arms, landing on my feet, cat-like. Riley was just the first to fall. She would not be the last, and we were going to enjoy unleashing our Fearian fury. Jared and Diane jumped from the second floor and landed beside me. The force of their impact was like an earthquake: the house shook, glass shattered, and ceiling plaster rained down on us in a white flaky shower.

"Nice, sis," Diane said. "Couldn't have done it better myself."

"Bet I could have," Jared said.

"You will get your chance before the day's end."

Jared pointed to her parents. "What about these two?"

"Leave them hanging there. They're not our parents." I headed for the foyer.

Jared knocked over a lamp in passing. "I do enjoy being a Fearian god," he said.

Arrogance dripped off my lips like syrupy nectar from a queen bee.

"We are so bad." Diane giggled.

CHAPTER 36

LAUREN

I STORMED INTO THE living room with my father hot on my tail. My emotions were shot to hell, and I felt like I had let everyone else down. I had dropped Grangy off at Aunt Jamie's house to spend some time with her, while Dad and I did the same. Which meant we wouldn't have to be careful of our words as we tried to figure things out.

"Lauren, if she has it, then …"

"That's the thing; I can't say for sure that she does. I mean it didn't come up while they were trying to bury me six feet deep during shop class." I rolled my eyes and sighed.

"I'm coming with you, Lauren."

"No, Dad. This is my fight."

"What?"

"I lost the Shadow dagger. It's on me."

"This teenage girl has proven she is quite the lethal beast, not to mention untrustworthy."

"I agree, and I know you're trying to keep me safe."

"So let me."

"I can't." I shook my head. "I just can't."

"But I owe you this, Lauren. I want to be there for you."

"I know."

"Until the very end."

"Look. You have plenty of time to restore the past. I will gladly let you do it."

"Then…"

"Apple is a handful already …"

"Are you kidding me?" he scoffed. "I married a freaking Mother Perfect, then watched a Fearian flunky slay her." He turned sad.

"I believe you. I too was there."

"I'm not scared of either. Nor am I new to this world."

"Okay." I ringed my fingers, and my eyes got glossy, as I tried to find the words to convey my plight.

"Let them bring it. I'm ready."

"But I'm not ... I'm terrified. I'm scared."

"Of what?"

"Scared, of losing my daddy for a second time. Please don't ask me to do it twice."

"Sweetheart, I can handle myself."

He wiped away a stream of my tears.

"I believe you. Just let me do this. I'll be fine, I promise."

"...Okay."

"Okay?" I perked.

"Take this." He reached inside his front vest pocket and pulled out a bracelet with charms dangling from it.

"This belonged to mom," I said. "She used to let me wear it when I was a kid. You mean you had it this whole time?"

"Izzy made me promise to keep it safe if anything were to become of her. To keep it safe for you."

I held the bracelet carefully. "I didn't know what had happened to it. I thought someone had stolen it."

"No. I took it off her wrist that last evening, before everything changed for good and I..." his eyes watered.

"It's more beautiful than I remembered."

"It was the last thing of hers I owned, and the one good reason I had to come back to my only daughter." He hooked it around my wrist and kissed it. His lips felt perfect on my skin. "To come home to you."

I wiped the tears from his face. "Thank you for keeping your word. I'll cherish it forever ... like I cherish you."

"The least I could do."

I embraced him. "I'll be back soon."

"And I'll be waiting right here."

"You better be," I grinned.

I opened the front door to find Detective Neese and a pair of officers standing on the front porch. His stern eyes and mine met and caught us both off guard.

"Oh, God!" I slammed the front door shut.

My unexpected action, which even surprised me, surprised Dad also in the moment.

"What is it?"

"Oh. Did I happen to mention the cops now think I'm a cold-blooded murderer?"

"Uh… no, Lauren. You did not."

"Ops. They're at the door now," I called back, already running down the hall as the doorknob shimmied.

"Lauren! Don't make it worse!" Detective Neese demanded, bursting into the living room. "Don't run from me!"

"May I help you, gentlemen?" I heard Dad inquire.

I hurried into my bedroom and listened at the door.

"Move out of the way, sir!"

"I don't think so! You're chasing after my daughter!"

I heard paper ruffling. "Actually a warrant for her arrest is chasing after her!"

"No way."

"Yes way." Footsteps trampled across the carpet. "You two follow me!"

I darted to the closet and the door swung open before I got there. Detective Neese barged in seconds later.

Damn it!

I wouldn't be able to explain the portal, but I had little to no choice in the matter: expose the starry darkness or go straight to jail, surrounded by metal bars … I chose freedom.

WOOSH!

CHAPTER 37

DETECTIVE NEESE

I WATCHED THE CLOSET door slam shut with a heavy wind in its wake. It felt odd to my thinking even before I tried comprehending what my eyes swore they caught a glimpse of.

My God in Heaven!

Lauren's closet looked like the doorway down at the department when Alison had disappeared into thin air. I hurried to the closet door and yanked it open, but instead of darkness filled with stars, it was nothing more than a plain closet, cluttered with clothes and stacks of shoeboxes. I shut the door and reopened it three times, but each time I found the same cluttered space, and no sign of Lauren or the supernatural. It left me feeling part relieved and completely empty.

Goddamn it! Lauren, come back here!

"Where is she, Detective Neese?" Officer Pollen asked. "Did she escape out a window or something?"

I didn't say a word, not that any worth reciting came to mind. I pondered on my weird predicament and my next response, which would either leave me sounding foolish or plain suicidal.

"We watched her come in here. Didn't we?"

"Get out," I ordered.

"Sir?"

"Both of you." I pointed toward the door.

"But…"

I shoved them out of the doorway. "Get out! Go survey the perimeter!" I slammed the door shut in their faces.

I overheard the pair bumbling down the hall as I paced the floor with a frantic sense of urgency, trying to gather my tilted bearings and keep myself from declaring insanity.

"Okay. Okay. Think…"

I was taught long ago that once you eliminated the impossible, whatever remained, no matter how improbable, must be the truth. It's staring me in the face, and yet I'm still having trouble believing my eyes ... so I know the powers that be wouldn't.

Lauren vanished. Alison did the same thing.

Who can I tell? Who would believe me?

I needed answers, and I wasn't sure if I was ready for the questions that'd tempt them my way. But right now I didn't have time to be scared. I owed it to Jeff—and Ali—to press on. I entered the living room where Lauren's father stood waiting. Gloating.

"Did you find her?" he asked calmly, as if he already knew the answer.

"No."

"I gotta tell you, Detective Neese."

"Tell me what?"

"You're pretty damn zealous for a trespassing and vandal charge on a teenage girl that hasn't even been proven."

"You think?" I faced him.

"Besides, honestly, can you peg Lauren as a vandal? I think not."

"I think Lauren is a lot of things, and when I find her—and I will find her, I'm going to prove all of them are true."

I snatched a photograph of Lauren off the wall, ripping the corners. "You don't mind me borrowing this to assist in proving your daughter is a murderer, do you?"

"Is there anything else, Detective?" he asked.

I put on my sunglasses to hide my spite. "If you happen to see that 'gifted' daughter of yours before I catch her ass, let her know she will pay for Alison's death. I'm going to make sure of it if it's the last thing I ever do upon this earth."

Absurdness shrouded his face. "You actually think Lauren could hurt her own cousin? Her best friend in the whole world?"

My officers entered the house unfruitful and stood in the doorway with their hands on their holster belts.

"Everyone wants to be ... unique." I squinted.

"You don't say?" he replied.

"Some will even kill to try and possess its mighty power," I added.

He crossed his arms. "Huh."

"So yes, I do think your daughter could hurt Alison. In fact, I think she did hurt her."

"You're way off base."

"Maybe ... maybe not."

I felt my glare focus in on his face, and I spotted the growing concern swimming in his eyes. It rendered him speechless, to the point a hint of fear appeared within his pupils. I saw it. And it saw me before it fled.

"Huh."

His lips parted, but no rebuttal followed. He simply stared back at me. What I was unsure of was, was it because he knew I could sense the truth, or because he was scared to risk sharing any more of it with me.

Either way, a day of reckoning was coming. I just hoped I'd be able to withstand the lightening storm that loomed in the distance.

"Get out."

"Certainly."

CHAPTER 38

GLENN

DETECTIVE NEESE FOLLOWED HIS officers out of the front doorway without so much as a goodbye, leaving the door wide open. I stood silently behind the screen door and watched them drive off, like cowboys into the sunset after a fruitless gunfight.

"Good riddance."

I shut the front door and locked the deadbolt. Things were getting hectic and out of hand, and now the law was trying to pin violent crimes on Lauren I was certain other Perfects were guilty of committing, or at the very least hybrids, using a gift no meant for our kind.

"I'm sorry, sweetheart," I muttered. "I just can't sit idle and let the same tragedy occur a second time … I couldn't live with myself if it happened again and I did nothing."

I entered Lauren's bedroom, each step giving me more courage than the last, and paused before her closet door.

If I'd done this much earlier, Elisabeth might still be among the living right now.

I reached for the doorknob, and it rattled. If not for the tiny screws in place it would have flung off the door. It sensed my great determination and my sincere thoughts and accepted the royal lineage, which had giving me a 'free pass' of existing in the secrets of Perfects.

The closet door swung open and the starry swallow blossomed before me like a discovered treasure. The memory of its existence brought salty tears to my eyes, because it also brought images of Izzy to my frontal lobe.

Hello old friend.

Just seeing it again reminded me of a time when I was the only human on the Earth aware of its supernatural existence. When the love of my life was still alive, loving me back. Regret burned at my heart. I couldn't stop the tears from streaming down my face, nor could I stop my feet from stepping forward into the vast unknown …

WOOSH!

CHAPTER 39

APPLE

I PARKED ON RILEY'S avenue, and the scenery put me at ease. I cruised by her house and unleashed an extra ounce of flair from the v8 engine as I passed. I knew Riley would catch the vibrating breadcrumbs I was leaving by the distinctive sound of my twin pipes. I slowed at the stop sign a few houses down and looked in the mirror, but Riley failed to show herself. I checked the clock in the dashboard repeatedly, until the minutes started to pile up.

Where the hell are you, girl?

Something was off. Even the sound of the brawly engine turned ominous and breathtaking.

I got out of the car and pocketed my keys, then made my way onto the front porch and peeked in the window. I saw no one and heard nothing. I didn't know if she had gotten in trouble with her parents, and the last thing I wanted was to connect her bad behavior to hanging out with me—whether it was a correct assumption or not.

I knocked on the front door, then jumped a bit as it swung open. I looked inside the foyer, which was dim, neat looking and deserted.

"Hello? Is anybody here?" I said. "It's me. Apple."

The tiny hairs on my neckline stood erect from the creepy silence— the way they did when I ventured into a haunted house at night. I stepped over the threshold, and my tennis shoe touched the wooden floor of the foyer, causing the panel beneath me to creak from the pressure.

My gloved hand glowed as my anxiety increased. I looked into the living room, then felt my heart drop into the pit of my stirring gut.

Riley's parents were dangling from a pair of ropes tied to the balcony above them. Their faces were pasty and their heads hung at an odd angle, as if they were considering an interesting question asked of them. By the devastation in the living room, I knew a Perfect had had a hand in this, and his/her or their vile actions were filled with gory passion.

Nervousness jolted my bones and I aimed my gloved hand at the moving shadows around me, as the will to survive a 'callous death' took the steering wheel. The living room stretched out of reach and my inner fears boiled over, but seconds later subsided once nothing dangerous occurred. Moments more and my conclusion allowed my gloved hand to return too normal and non-lethal.

I looked away and covered my nose with my collar and I shuffled inside the room feeling out of sorts.

"Riley?"

I crept around the end table and love sofa, and saw her limp body sprawled out on the throw rug. Although disappointed, I wasn't too surprised by what I saw. I knew by the way she was lying there that she'd endured great pain beforehand. Her body was twisted in ways limbs didn't normally bend, like a drunken contortionist—or someone who'd suffered a steep fall from grace. Her glassy eyes stared off into the distance, completely void of any life.

I quivered over the loss—my loss. *Damn it!*

"Oh, Riley … you went and got yourself murdered before I had the chance to use you up. What. A. Pity."

I flipped her body onto its back with my shoe.

"I wonder. Who could've been this pissed at you? Lauren? Naa." I shook my head. "Angry enough maybe, but she certainly lacks the kahunas to pull it off in any realm … this was a labor of love." I tapped my chin with a finger, then the blooming revelation came to me. "Penelope, you vindictive train wreck. I'm really starting to like you. Still… I can make this work."

I grabbed the telephone and dialed.

"911. How may I help you?"

I screamed in horror, my voice tone identical to Riley's. "Send help! Lauren is going to kill me like she did her cousin, Alison!" I gasped. "Tell Detective Neese to come quick or we're going to die!"

I yanked the cord free from the wall and the line went dead. Then I dipped my finger into the bloody hole where Riley's simple-minded heart should've been and used her blood to write on the mirror on the wall.

COME AND GET ME, DICK!

"And the Oscar for Best Supporting Actress goes to—Me!" I cheered, wiping my hand clean from the blood on a sofa pillow.

Let's see you find a way out of this one, Ms. Thang. I am going to have your neck one way or the other.

I left Riley's house of death from the back door and returned to my Mustang unseen. I waited for the sound of sirens, then watched in my rearview mirror as several cop cars arrived.

The police officers entered the house with pistols drawn. I knew Detective Neese was too much of a hardass not to be minutes behind them, so I drove off.

"Do not bungle this, Barney Fife." I squinted.

CHAPTER 40

DIANE

WE WALKED ACROSS A green patch of grass in between the sidewalk and the street, pausing on the edge of the curb. Lauren's granny was across the street, tending to some potted flowers on her front porch railing. She didn't notice her three predators stalking her position.

"Aw. Look. She's out watering the flowers," I gloated.

Pepper giggled. "Sucks to be her."

"It does if she plans on seeing tomorrow," Jared added.

"Do you think Lauren's at home?" I asked.

"Why don't we go and find out," Pepper said, stepping out into the street.

"If she isn't, then I get to at least do the mauling of dear old Grangy as a tasty appetizer."

"Certainly, brother. Just as soon as I have my way with her first," I said. "You get the scraps."

The glaring brightness of midday made it hard to see onto the dim porch, but the shape of our prey stayed visible. And close enough to attack.

A female postal worker, carrying a bag of mail strapped to her back, walked onto the property and handed her the mail for the day. The extra witness, or victim, failed to deter our intent. Someone was going to die, and it could be both if the postal worker didn't end her 'chit-chat' before we made our way across the pavement.

As we neared the curb, the postal worker walked off while granny inspected the mail in her hand, failing to notice us still. I growled when Jared touched both my arm and Pepper's at the same time, forcing us to pause our steps. We looked to him, and at the odd expression written on his face. I bounced a glance to Pepper.

Suddenly, Jared looked up. "It's Nolum. Our presence is requested elsewhere. We have to go."

"But we're about to have some fun. Did he say why?"

"Yes. They have the Shadow dagger."

Pepper looked to me. "No way!"

"Our future awaits," Jared said, hurrying away without looking back.

Pepper and I followed, while Lauren's granny went on about her day, oblivious to how close she had been to death.

Soon we would rule the world, but I had no urge to destroy its inhabitants. It just didn't satisfy me in the same manner as it did both Jared and Pepper.

I didn't have any problem enacting restitution on those who had done us wrong, but there were a lot of innocent humans who didn't deserve what came for them. And although I was happy to be a Fearian, I found it difficult to destroy the one thing I always thought I was: human. I still had one or two good friends who were human beings.

I thought maybe I could fake it, but how do you fake hating the whole world? These types of emotions came easily to Jared and Pepper, who had taken the brunt of our bullying and harassment for years, often in my place.

Being a victim of bullying was hard enough. I wasn't sure I could handle doing the same myself to planet Earth.

CHAPTER 41

LAUREN

I RUMMAGED THROUGH APPLE'S belongings as fast as I could without alerting others that I was in her bedroom, searching for signs of the Shadow dagger's whereabouts. I wasn't sure if she was the one who really took it from me, but I had to rule her out just the same before moving up the 'wicked' ladder. I could hear muffled sounds of her parents on the main floor and bumping noises from Adam's bedroom across the hall. I shuffled through school papers on her desk, searched under the mattress and box spring, the rug, and even poked and pried in her closet, but found nothing other than designer clothing, girly accessories and a large selection of high heel shoes.

I shut the closet door and scanned the bedroom, hoping for something, anything, to give me a clue. I was starting to think she wasn't the one who stole the dagger. I could confront my Aunt Geneve, but after accusing her of murdering Alison already, I wasn't sure how she would react to more accusations from her only niece. Not to mention I would have to expose more of what I was trying to hide from her to begin with: proof she was right all along and hybrids had to be dealt with in a violent way, and that I did once have the dagger. I knew it was a matter of time before she reappeared, anyway, with the plan of setting things right. And this time around I wouldn't be able to stop her—I wouldn't be able to appeal to her compassion no matter our relationship.

Not even sure I want to try ... damn it, I'm so confused.

A part of me wished things could somehow return to the way they once were, back to the night in the restroom at the prom. Only then I would have convinced Alison not to enter that portal, not to open that door, not to journey to California, and certainly not to trespass at Alex Pettyfer's house.

The regrets were starting to jab at my heart.

We would've stayed in Grand Blanc with Riley and Apple, cruised the strip and spent the night together, and our bond would have been stronger.

So strong nothing would have been able to destroy it. But we did journey through that portal, Ali and I, and we did every exciting thing that followed, which ended up bringing us two closer than ever before. And I did get to witness her joy of being cured—if only for a little while, and sadly, it and more lead to her getting killed.

I shook off my rambling thoughts, conflicted as to whether the prize was worth the enormous cost. But the past was the past now ... and Alison was dead still ... and I was on the verge of killing Apple for sure, and with it the last of my humanity.

The only ones left I cared about weren't hybrids, but Aunt Geneve would still see them as threats; dad for sure, knowing what he knew, and Grangy for knowing me. My stomach clenched when I envisioned dueling my mother's twin sister to the death. If I chose that route ... it'd be like trying to kill the one person I longed to love: Mom.

I shuddered at the notion and shoved the tasteless image as far away as I could get it—it wasn't as far away as I had hoped.

My focus was drawn to a funnel of wind against my ear. My heartbeat froze and I whipped around to Apple's closet. The cracks along the doorway lit up fuchsia, and I backed off, aiming my hand in battle mode without the faintest of hesitation, or remorse.

Great. I've become Aunt Geneve without even trying.

I wasn't scared of Apple, by no means, but I had more pressing matters in need of my attention. Plus, her dead body at a crime scene in her bedroom would not look good for me, being that'd make me one of the last two left standing. Detective Neese would have a freaking field day, and be proven correct in his eyes as far as he was concerned. I was the real murderer all along. Even worse: a serial killer.

The closet door swung open and Dad stepped out of the starry mass. I quickly lay off the trigger, trying not to faint or lose breath. I wasn't sure if I was more relieved I didn't have to murder Apple, or surprised that my dad had traveled through a doorway portal meant only for Perfects.

"Whoa, girly! It's just me," he surrendered with his hands out.

"Dad. Do you know how close I came to killing you just then?" I bent to my knees, calming my flaming emotions and my heartbeat. "How did you use that thing, anyway?"

"What, the portal?"

"No, the window!" I flared my arms. "Of course the damn portal. How did you even make it appear for you?"

"I was married to a Mother Perfect, remember?"

"You know, for someone who wanted to stay human, you know an awful lot about being Perfect."

"Have you seen your mother's eyes?"

"…Yeah. I have."

"She was bound to get her way a time or two."

"Apparently."

"Did you find the Shadow dagger yet? Do you think she's the one who stole it from you?"

"I don't think so. I can't find it anywhere."

"Let me give it a go," he said. "Fresh pair of eyes."

"Okay. Go idea."

Dad twirled his forefingers, and every piece of furniture in Apple's bedroom vanished from sight with a whistling chirp.

My mouth dropped. "Whoa…"

"You're right, Lauren. It's not in here."

"Father?"

"Yes, Lauren?"

I gestured around the empty room. "If we somehow survive this, you and I are going to have to have a long talk."

"It's a date."

I curled my eyes. "Unbelievable."

A hint of heat sparked on my wrist. I looked at the bracelet and saw the charms glowing so brightly the bracelet was starting to burn, causing discomfort on my skin. The tiny hairs on my arm relented and fell flat.

"Daddy?"

His eyes widened at the sight and he tilted his head. "Amazing."

"Is it supposed to do that?"

"Sweetie, I don't know. I've never seen it do that before. Not even when your mother wore it."

A tingling sound, like wind chimes in the middle of spring, echoed around the bedroom. Reflective lights danced on the ceiling and walls. The charms on my wrist released a fuzzy ball of light that hovered before my face. I was speechless, but more curious than scared of what might come.

"What is that?" I mumbled as the fuzzy ball grew in size. It sparkled and released what looked like tiny fairy dust.

"Lauren?" she whispered. "Do not be afraid."

My eyes watered. "I know that voice ... but it … can't be. "
Can it?

The fuzzy ball of light transformed into a soft silhouette of her body, and then into her ghostly image, then the image turned real.

Dad sobbed. "Elisabeth ..."

I stared, feeling strangely numb—and nourished at the same time. She looked just like I remembered, only much better—way better.

"Mother?"

"My sweet Lauren. Look at you. You have grown into the perfect young woman."

"It's you. You're really here," I said.

Dad reached out and touched her. "I can feel you. Honey, I ..."

She ran her finger down the bridge of his nose. "I know, Glenn. And I'm sorry for what I made you have to live with. It wasn't fair to you."

"I would do it all over again in a heartbeat for just one moment with you," Dad sniffled back tears. "I miss you that much."

"And I miss you." She held his hand, interlocking fingers, and her touch seemed to make his eyes glitter.

I touched her white gown to confirm it was real. It was silky and soft. "Mom, how are you among the living if you're...?"

"There are certain perks to being the eldest Mother Perfect of a clan. Things are going to get hectic from here on out, Lauren," she said, looking at me solemnly.

"We lost the dagger," Dad confessed.

"He means I lost the dagger," I cut in.

"It matters none at this point," Mom said.

"What do you mean?" I asked. "Depending on who has it, it matters a whole lot."

"Penelope has given the dagger to our foes. The Fearian Seal will soon be renewed, and with it, its lethal power will come with a vengeance."

Darkness filled the lining of my gut and my eyes turned watery. "So, the Fearians have the dagger." I pondered.

"That's it," Dad mumbled.

"Mom, how do we stop them? How do we stop their tirade upon the earth?"

"Glenn is right. You will not be able to," she said.

"What? That can't be. The Fearians will destroy this realm if we don't do something to stop them."

"I am sorry for bringing this madness upon the Earth. It is not for the humans to have to suffer for my poor choices."

"The people we love are here on Earth: Grangy, Aunt Jamie ... they won't survive the Fearians' reign. They'll die along with many others as a result. What can we do against the Counsel to prevent that from happening?" I asked her.

"Absolutely nothing."

I stepped away from her. "No. Don't say that to me! There has got to be a way!"

"Think, Elisabeth. Think. Help give us a chance to survive the fray," Dad said.

"… A chance."

"Anything," I said.

Mom caressed the side of my face, and the heat of her long-missed touch overwhelmed my rattled emotions. "All that I am now belongs to you, my child," she said.

"What? What does that even mean?" I pleaded.

She smiled at me, and then a jolt of hard energy hit the core of my being, rendering me damn near unconscious. I hovered a few feet off the ground, feeling a rush of warmth and confusion. A thunderous clap erupted outside the window, making me flinch, as I battled the dizziness. Then the calming caress returned and my body nestled back onto the floor.

I felt odd as I climbed to my feet: bigger—stronger. I felt … more.

"What did you do to me, Mom?"

But she was already fading from sight.

"Wait! You can't leave me again, Elisabeth!" Dad said. He rushed towards her, but grasped nothing but empty air. Her faint image was barely still detectable.

"I never left you … and I never will."

"But ..."

She kissed him, then she looked to me. "In the end, what will be … will be."

"I love you," I said, as she disappeared. "Mom."

An angry engine growled as it pulled into the driveway and stopped outside the house.

"Lauren, someone is coming."

I scurried to the window and shielded behind the nylon curtains. Apple had parked out front and was walking onto the front porch.

"We need to go now."

"Is it her?"

"Yes. And we have far bigger demons to deal with at the moment than this one."

"I am in agreement with you there."

The closet door opened, exposing the starry swallow, and I grabbed Dad's hand and hurried inside it. The force of the portal yanked my body forward.

CHAPTER 42

APPLE

I MADE IT HOME without being seen by the wrong people, and once I shut the front door, it was as if a tremendous weight was lifted off my shoulders. Riley was gone, but I was still alive so the game continued on. Becoming more scandalous with my desires and more deviant with my actions didn't bruise my conscience, but empowered it—and redefined it. The thought of everyone killing off everyone else had a positive effect on my mood swings, as the pendulum dangled from my nerves. When the smoke cleared, it would be me alone who slipped through the cracks still unscathed, and undetected, the first of a new breed: Mother Apple, the self-proclaimed and true Perfect. The notion caused my loins to tickle.

I can barely contain my breathing the succulent thought sounds so inviting. If only...

I would be my own species, and no human would be able to match my resolve or my will. I possessed an unnatural gift to force the mind to do my bidding. I possessed a transparent weapon on my hand that made me more powerful than an entire army on a battlefield. I had the wisdom to remain unseen as I manipulated the earth for all of its riches, and most of its fame.

The revelation made me giddy to say the least.

World leaders would be forced to compete for my affection, to satisfy my lusts, to gain my honorable allegiance. The world would be my oyster, and I didn't even like oysters.

I skipped into the living room where my parents were sitting on large pillows, meditating in the center of the room and trying to block out the rest of the world and the stress it caused them.

Mom opened her eyes and saw me leaning in the doorway with my arms crossed. "Hey you," she said.

"Hey."

"Just getting home, huh?" Dad asked without moving his eyelids.

"Yep. That's why I just walked in the front door."

"Cute."

"That's me. The cutest."

"Of course, I could've sworn I heard you above us rambling around in your bedroom, though." She closed her eyes.

Her words made me perk up. "Is that so?"

"Either it was your brother or else we have awfully big rodents rambling around in the attic."

"I'm sure it was those pesky rats." I backed away with my destroyer glove lit up. "Did school call already?"

"Phone line has been down most of the afternoon. Why? Are you in some kind of trouble?"

"Nothing I can't explain."

"Really?"

"Later, mom. Finish your daily meditation."

"Or you could just tell us now," she replied.

I rolled my eyes and sighed. "Why? I wouldn't want you to get high cholesterol or something."

"And what does that mean, Apple?" her voice turned firm.

"She's kidding. Apple is a good girl," Dad cut in. "I'm sure it's nothing at all. Let her go be a hot teenager. Besides, you two are starting to disturb my Zen."

"Wouldn't want to do that." I climbed the stairs.

"We will talk!" Mom yelled.

"Counting on it."

I paused before my door and stared at the knob. I narrowed my glowing pink eyes, and the door swung open until it tapped the back wall. I crept inside, far from feeling fearful, yet on alert. It took only seconds to see it was empty, but I detected the scent of someone I hated with a passion and wanted brutally dead. Still, nothing looked out of place, broken or missing, which only left me more curious.

Huh ... interesting indeed.

I grabbed a drinking glass off the nightstand and pitched its content into the air.

"Show me."

Water rained down, exposing debris of three bodies in the center of my bedroom. I prowled around the frozen images, amazed as I watched Lauren being confronted by a vision of her mother. I remembered her likeness from a photograph in Lauren's bedroom. Lauren's dad stood on Elisabeth's backside and their facial expressions were reminiscence of a romantic reunion ... or send off. And in my bedroom no less—disgusting.

"How in the hell did you bring her back?"

The frozen mirage dropped to the carpet within the drops of water and splattered on the floor.

"I will be so happy when you are killed off, Lauren." I gritted my teeth. "Both you and your deadbeat daddy."

I sat on the side of my bed, feeling flustered and a smidge vexed by the arrogance of her deceitful actions.

Kill or be killed...

If only I had Riley alive to try and read Lauren's thoughts, then maybe I'd be a step closer to enjoying the advantage I clearly had, but didn't know of. But being I had no real way of finding out the truth—outside of tracking Lauren down and beating her senseless until she spilled the beans—I'd remain oblivious to her shady thinking, for now.

Damn it!

CHAPTER 43

KAIDEN

I HAD SUMMONED THE last of our kind, and we stood waiting on the edge of the shore. It was time to renew The Seal and take over the Earth. Twenty Fearian Warriors in all had survived the Days of Sorrow, and they were hungry for war to continue and retribution to follow. Warriors knew no fear, only the will to vanquish new territories. That was the reason they existed, their one purpose for being. Our twenty warriors could only be compared to a million human soldiers, if not more.

Our females were able to overthrow the mortals, if we saw fit to send them into battle. Five winged Fury Beasts stood with a Fearian Warrior in every saddle, waiting for an opportunity to rewrite history, our history, and to make it more favorable for our kind.

The Counsel appeared from within the mystic waterfall, wearing battle armor and a confident snarl. Victory was ours on the backs of humans, and the Perfects would pay the ultimate price in the end: a brutal offering to the heavens. A new era was at hand.

All hail the Fearian Counsel!

Nolum, followed by Serene and Oplous, stepped out onto the water and crossed over to the shore, their bodies transporting across in seconds. As they neared, the warriors chanted and cheered their presence. The winged Fury Beasts reared back on their hind legs, responding to the excitement. As Nolum led Serene and Oplous onto the sandy beach, every head bowed out of respect for our leaders, and every mouth ceased talking.

"It has been a long time since we have had a reason to celebrate," Nolum said.

"This marks the beginning of a new day. The day when our enemies will be slaughtered, both Perfects and human beings," Oplous said.

The Warriors cheered.

"The day when the Fearian Seal will be reborn," Serene added.

"We shall be worshiped by the humans allowed to live, only to serve us all."

The Warriors cheered even louder, and some raised their fists over their heads.

"Kaiden, come to the front, my son," Nolum said.

I faced him, my face both solemn and contrite. "Yes, sire?"

"You have redeemed yourself." He placed his hand on my shoulder.

"Thank you."

"Think no more on the past tragedies. Put them to rest. You have made amends in the eyes of the Counsel," he said.

Serene looked to his warriors. "Now. Come together, my sons. The Earth is ours for the taking. We shall claim it, and rule for an eternity."

The Counsel escorted us into the bosom of our foes. Because of the Perfects, our world had been destroyed. But because of humans, it would be given back to us—a hundred fold, a sacrifice in fool's blood, in exchange for a ransom of awesome power.

We ventured into the rainforest, and the trees in our path parted, clearing a passage as the mighty stomps of the Fury Beast made the ground shake.

"I desire to walk upon the Earth among the humans," Nolum declared.

A gateway portal appeared before us, transparent and shimmering in the light.

WOOSH!

CHAPTER 44

DETECTIVE NEESE

I GOT OUT OF my car and walked onto the front lawn of the murder scene. The property was scattered with other police officers, casing the area for clues. Curious neighbors had gathered across the street, looking on. I retrieved a pair of latex gloves from my jacket pocket, pried my hands in them and then entered Riley's home.

I inspected the doorknob and lock, but saw no signs of forced entry. I walked into the crowded living room. Our crime technicians combed the room for evidence, and it felt like any other day. Except for the dead parents strung up by their necks and the teenage girl lying on the floor, mutilated as if a wild animal had gotten to her. But we weren't in the wild, and there were no loose carnivores terrorizing the city, none I was aware of. So I was left both disgusted and disturbed by what I'd witnessed.

I stopped at the head technician, who was kneeling over Riley's remains. "Please tell me you have some idea as to what killed her."

"Someone stole her heart ... literally."

"What?" I felt my stomach flip, and I turned cold.

"Someone took out her beating heart. Look at the abrasions here across the flesh."

"Looks an awful lot like young human fingers."

"Female fingers, by the size of the grooves."

"But that would mean ..."

"A girl or petite woman burrowed inside her chest and ripped the whole damn thing out."

"Yep."

"School has gotten a lot more dangerous since my days at Grand Blanc High."

I inspected her parents' bodies. "I was told there was a message left for me."

He pointed to the wall. "Check the mirror."

I approached the glass and read the message written in blood and meant for me. The words only managed to anger me more. First Alison was killed, and now Riley had suffered the same fate. I was fed up with being taunted by an adolescent.

I turned away from the message and walked outside. My brain was flustered and running a mile a minute and I was no closer to achieving the peace I so strongly desired. Too much had happened for it to be some big coincidence. If Lauren wasn't the guilty party, and that was a big 'if,' she was definitely involved with the murderers. She was the last one left, so I knew she had the answers I sought—I just had to find her … and fast, before she or some 'thing' killed again.

CHAPTER 45

KAIDEN

THE COUNSEL WAS THE first to emerge from the coin fountain. I appeared soon after them, followed by five Fearian Warriors on Fury Beasts, stepping out from the water and into a large shopping mall.

The portal had chosen the location, but the Counsel accepted the calling. Mortals carrying plastic bags began to take notice of our unexpected arrival. Once they started believing the gravity of what their eyes saw most screamed in terror and fled for the exits, while a few elected to hide inside stores. The Fury Beasts gawked and flapped their feathered wings as their bodies adjusted to the taste of Earth's atmosphere.

"So this is the realm of the humans?" Nolum asked me.

"Yes, sire. It is where the humans come to trade for goods," I explained.

"Interesting." He looked up at the ceiling. "The heavens are an odd appearance, and much smaller than I imagined."

"That is because we are inside, sire. The skyline is fabricated. The real sky is as blue as the waters of Kayif and just as vast.

"Hum."

"It is indeed fresh smelling and unpolluted compared to ours," I added.

"Interesting indeed."

CHAPTER 46

JARED

WATCHING THE REST OF the Counsel emerge with the last of our kind brought tears to my perkily eyes, and watching the pathetic humans around us scatter in fear was priceless and heartwarming. I could only imagine what thoughts zipped through their inferior brains as they ran for dear life. But running wouldn't help them this time. We were about to be reborn, and then all hell would break loose at the power of our hands. I glanced over at Diane, who stood on the other side of Pepper. Her look of enthusiasm seemed forced, and not on the level of Pepper's and mine. As the last of our kind cleared the coin fountain, we swaggered towards them with confidence in our strides. A reward owed to us. Nolum and the others were standing at the front of the band of warriors.

"Welcome to Earth!" I greeted. "Our home is now your new home. Please enjoy … hell, everything."

"Is that the Shadow dagger? How'd you find it?" Pepper asked.

"We didn't. It found us," Nolum said. "It will always find home, no matter what," he added. "Now, before we rule the Earth, there is a small matter of being renewed."

His hazel eyes shined with delight.

CHAPTER 47

GENEVE

I POSED IN THE VIP section at Rain, contemplating my next move to quietly expulse any hybrids created by Victoria. As far as Lauren went, I had tiptoed around her feelings long enough, but no more. It was time to do what needed to be done. Chasing Penelope across Europe had brought an end to my days of having tolerance and compassion. My 'hit list' was getting long, and it began to make me look weak and nothing like a leader.

"Geneve? Geneve?"

Her voice slipped into my subconscious, awakening me from my inner thoughts and raw frustrations.

I perked up in my seat still. "Yes? I hear."

Even with the loud bass shaking the walls, her voice was familiar, and it filled my heart with love.

"Get up, sister. The moment has arrived," she said.

"Elisabeth?" I stood to my feet. "Is that you?"

Bray looked at me, but stayed mum. He hunched his brow and scanned my personal space on guard.

"We have failed, Geneve. The Seal is about to be renewed, and the Fearian Counsel shall take the Earth from the human beings, and from you."

"No," I mumbled. "It can't be. They don't have the dagger."

"Is everything okay, Mother Geneve?" Bray asked.

I held up a finger, bringing him to silence.

A bright vision of Elisabeth's image appeared ghostly, beautiful and breathtaking on my flank. "I am here, Geneve."

"Izzy." I grinned and my eyes turned glossy. My heart burned with affection. "You're here with me?"

"There is no time to squander. You must make a choice now, and both are going to require a steep sacrifice," she said.

"You know my choice. It's the same as always. Nothing will ever change it."

She touched my hand and gave me a gift of knowledge. "Please hurry ... Lauren, you're niece, needs you."

I stood taller and flexed my fists. My eyes flashed coral, causing the nearby crowd to cheer wildly, while Izzy vanished into thin air.

"Then she shall have me," I said.

"Mother Geneve, something troubles you. I can feel its presence coming," Bray said.

"An evil entity has entered this realm uninvited."

"Why have they come?"

"To take your world away from you. And they might, if we do not stop them."

"The Fearians. What must I do?"

"Pray to God this thunderstorm passes you by."

"I will fight beside you."

"You will die."

"I don't care."

"I do."

"But..."

"Stay here. If I do not return, you are free from your life devotion to a Mother Perfect."

I removed the key and lanyard from my neck. "Take the Euros and the American currencies I have secured and seek refuge in a warmer climate."

"No-"

"Leave Russia. It will no longer be safe here."

I touched his shoulder and a gift from my essence shot into his core, causing his eyes to glow coral before returning to normal.

His knees wobbled. "Whoa."

"Some of my gifts are now your gifts. Stay humble, and they will serve you well.

"But Mother Geneve, I do not wish to be free from you. You are my world. That is my vow to you."

"And you are my ... friend. Goodbye, Bray."

I stormed past him, toward the door at the rear of the lounge as it swung open for me. The starry swallow inside was bold and daring.

WOOSH!

CHAPTER 48

LAUREN

I STEPPED OUT A doorway with Dad on my tail, but my destination left me confused. I hesitated and looked at the building in the middle of a large parking lot. It took a moment to gather my bearings, as Dad paused beside me.

"Where did you bring us, Lauren?"

"We're at Somerset Mall," I sighed. "But I don't know how we got here. This is the first time it's ever happened to me before."

Geneve stepped out of the same door Dad and I had just exited. "We have a problem," she said.

"Aunt Geneve?"

"In the flesh."

I followed her around the building, and the front of the mall came into view. "You brought us here? How did you do that?"

"I can do much, including bring you to me," she said.

Dad caught up with us. "Excuse me. Anyone want to share with me how she looks exactly like your mother?"

"Dad. Meet my aunt," I introduced.

"You look like my Elisabeth," he said.

"That's because she was my Elisabeth first."

"Your mother has an identical twin?"

"Among other things." I grabbed her by the arm. "Hello? Will you slow down a minute, please?"

"We do not have time, Lauren. What?"

"What? Why are you going toward the mall? Do Mother Perfects even shop in this realm?"

"The Fearian Counsel has entered your world, with the dagger and The Seal. Things are about to change."

My lips tingled. "The Fearian Counsel is here? Here? In Grand Blanc, Michigan?"

"Perfects are about to be exposed, as not of this realm."

"How can you be sure of this?" I asked.

"Because the Fearians are about to expose themselves … and renew The Seal, here, in your Grand Blanc, Michigan."

"Which means humans are about to be wiped out," Dad predicted. "This is not good."

"The Counsel will only enslave a select few. The rest of your kind will be eradicated at best."

My eyes watered. "Grangy …"

"She will not survive their reign," she said, inspecting my face. "You have seen your mother, as well."

"How could you know that?"

"We're going to need every bit of what she gave you," she replied, ignoring my question.

"And what was that?" I asked.

"Only you can answer. Let's go."

We advanced toward the front entrance of Somerset Mall, preparing for the worse of the unknown. It was then that I noticed the stirring dimness in the thick clouds, hovering over the building. Flashes of lightning zipped across the skyline and the wind began to turn heavy.

CHAPTER 49

KAIDEN

Nolum addressed The Seal with Serene and Oplous on his flanks. The few humans left looked on timidly and unsure how to respond to what they were witnessing.

"Are you three ready to take your rightful place among the gods? To rule over all species?"

Diane spoke first, her soft voice possessed sympathy. "What about all these innocent people?"

"The rest will suffer a deserving fate," Oplous said.

"But do we want them to see this?" Jared asked.

"Yes. We do. Let them bear witness to the dawn of a new era!" he shouted.

"ALL HAIL THE FEARIAN COUNSEL!" Warriors shouted out, while stabbing their weapons into the air.

"Guys." Diane looked to her siblings. "I don't want anyone to get hurt. These people did nothing to us. They're not like the others. They don't deserve our punishment."

"Pepper?" Jared asked.

"I couldn't care less," Pepper scoffed.

Jared looked back to Diane. "Looks like you've been outvoted, sis. Time to get with the program."

"Pity is an honorable trait. One day the humans shall love you for it, princess," Oplous said, tilting his head. "One day."

"He's right, Diane" Jared said. "We're going to rule the entire Earth, and every single person on it."

"What good is it to be royalty if you have no loyal subjects to worship you?" Pepper asked.

"I don't know if I want that. I thought we were just going to…" Diane's reluctance stole her words.

"Don't turn weak on us now, sis!" Jared snapped. "After all those years of abuse, bullying and being lied to."

"Your brother is correct, child. This is what you were born for," Nolum said.

"You were meant to help rule a proud species. Or would you prefer the Perfects had their way among the humans?" Serene asked. "I'm sure they'll show more pity than they showed to your parents."

"Only after they've learned to fear our wrath can they embrace loving the beauty of our compassion," Oplous said.

"Suits me just fine," Jared snickered.

"Me too," Pepper said.

They gazed at Diane, and their condemnation rained down upon her like a force of nature.

"Fine. Let's reign then," Diane said, slowly giving in. "I'm with you guys if this is truly what you want."

"It is," she said.

"It really is," he added.

"Excellent. Warriors, do what you do best," Nolum ordered. "Kill humans at will."

The Fury Beasts reared back on hind legs and barked, while warriors attacked all the humans in sight. Men, women and children, it didn't matter. Extermination had been ordered, and our attack wasn't going to cease until that order had been carried out.

The mall was filled with chaos, and the fiery destruction that followed in the wake of our warriors was nothing short of magnificent. Fury Beasts soared in the air, spewing twisted flames from their snouts like angry dragons, while their wings created massive tornados. In seconds, the mall was destroyed and barely recognizable as such.

Decorative glass walls shattered from the repeated bombings, and parts of the structure began to crumble. Pleas of mercy faded into whimpers and sighs of defeat. I stood with the Counsel, basking in the unfolding carnage, like an ominous dark cloud about to cover the entire Earth.

"Let us finish this," Nolum said.

Jared looked to his sisters and stepped closer. "I'm first."

"It is foretold. You shall be a great leader like your father," said Nolum. Then he stabbed Jared with the Shadow dagger, jamming it inside his chest. "But first, you must learn to follow."

Jared's knees buckled. "Ooh!"

Diane and Pepper covered their mouths.

"The blood of the Counsel shall never die. It shall flow through your veins as you reign in this realm, and many others before it is done with," he boldly declared.

Nolum grimaced while Oplous and Serene looked on enviously. I stared at Nolum's hand and watched as black essence oozed from his palm and ran along the edge of the sharp blade, while another ebony essence began filling the glass handle.

The handle was one-third full when Nolum pulled the dagger from Jared's chest. Jared groped his wound, then collapsed to the floor. He stared at the ceiling, speechless. Diane backed away a step, fearing what was to come. Jared's eyes eventually closed for good.

"Pepper?" Nolum said.

She twitched. "Uh-huh?"

"You are brave like your sibling. You shall be next in line," he said. "Your time has come."

"Sure." She stepped forward, over Jared's body. "You say so."

Nolum caressed her face and placed his hand on the back of her neck. "Worry not, my child. It will all be over shortly."

"I believe you," Pepper replied.

"No, you don't," he squinted, thrusting the dagger inside Pepper's body. "But you soon will."

"Oh, God!" Her eyes popped from the pain.

Diane screamed, but kept it muffled behind her hand.

Nolum leaned into Pepper's ear. "You are the queen of your kind. You have the power to create with just a simple thought! Through you, our species shall flourish. Like you, our kind shall be great upon the Earth!"

The sharp blade withdrew her essence into the glass casing and filled it two-thirds of the way full.

"Is that true?" she asked, tumbling to the tile.

"It is," Nolum replied. "And so much more."

Pepper went limp and her eyes shut.

Diane's pupils grew big, and she shook her head and backed off more. "I can't do this. I'm too scared of what will happen," she confessed.

"Do not dread the unknown, child. It is futile to do so," Serene said. "Especially if you truly knew what was waiting for you on the other side."

Diane looked down to her siblings. "They should be awake by now. Last time it took only seconds."

"Last time was a crude deception."

"I remember," she replied.

"Not to mention at the hands of a filthy hybrid."

"I know. But, what if they ..."

Pepper's and Jared's bodies began to glow, then both hovered a half foot from off the floor.

"You see child, the magic surrounds them. But they are held in stasis, and they will continue to be so until the third has been established," Oplous said. "They need you as much as you need them."

"Won't you join them, Diane? Won't you join us? Do not be afraid of what you are," Nolum said. "It is truly a colorful sight to behold."

"You must accept your rightful place. We cannot force it upon you," said Serene.

She hesitated before moving forward. "Okay," she whispered.

Nolum's eyes sparkled in the light in response to Diane's acceptance, and then he shoved the dagger into her chest.

"The humans have infected your identity for long enough, child," Oplous sneered.

"Those sad days of being weak and indecisive are no more," Nolum added.

"You are a god now!" Serene said.

Diane tried to withstand the violent assault, she tried hard but she couldn't stop her limbs from trembling out of control. She pondered screaming, but no sound would release off her lips. She had no other choice but to endure the agony in a vacuum of muted silence, and without the empathy of her two siblings to egg her on through the darkness.

"It hurts," she whimpered. "So bad."

"That's it. Embrace the agony," Nolum said to her. "You are the charitable one. Your servants shall follow your kindness to the ends of the Earth and back again. You are the last missing piece to a great dynasty. No longer shall you answer to Diane."

Her eyes turned heavy. "What ... then?"

"All hail Queen Aresti! Mother of the Fearian tribe!" Nolum yelled with gusto.

She made eye contact with me. "Don't forget me."

"Never," I said.

Her black essence withdrew into the dagger and filled the empty space left in the glass casing. Nolum kneeled and pulled out the Shadow dagger from her body.

"Rest easy, my love. For when you awake, we shall rule for an entire millennium!"

"Here! Here!" Oplous and Serene shouted.

Diane's body glowed and levitated like her siblings. A spark of firelight floated above them and created a shallow dome over their bodies. The protective bubble then sealed against the floor, and through it they could be seen levitating underneath the force field. The recessed lighting overhead caused a glittering effect on the surface of the dome, making it resemble a transparent gemstone and just as priceless.

Nolum ejected the ebony filled casing, and the aroma of Opium oil caressed my senses, delivering sugary images of splendor to my brain.

Home sweet home.

Nolum, Serene and Oplous shared the murky fluid until the casing was empty. They lay their hands onto the protective dome and began chanting words of wisdom beyond my understanding, and their hazel eyes glowed brightly. A bolt of energy shot from their hands and into the dome, and the bubble shaded dark grey.

"Amazing," I whispered.

CHAPTER 50

LAUREN

DAD AND I TRAILED Aunt Geneve and we stormed the front entrance of Somerset Mall. The open doors spewed out terrified patrons, running for their lives in sheer panic. Their screams said it all. Their faces worth a thousand descriptions and each began with horrid nightmares.

"So it has begun, I see," she said. "We are too late. Prepare yourselves for an inevitable war."

"We are prepared," he said.

We squeezed through the fleeing crowd behind her and hurried along the corridor toward the center of the building. In the distance, we saw angry bolts of lightning bouncing off the walls, charring, and defying the law of nature with each jagged strike.

I glanced at him. "You do see a lightning storm, correct?"

"That's exactly what I see," Dad said.

Aunt Geneve picked up her pace. "Hurry up, you two. The Seal is no longer broken. Izzy's gallant deeds have been undone!"

"It can't be."

"What does that mean?" I asked him.

Thunder erupted and startled me, causing my body to turn cold and shaky and a bit jittery.

"It means we must fight for our own existence," Dad said. "Genocide is now likely for both Perfects and human beings, at the hands of the Fearian Counsel and their evil cronies."

I held up a finger. "But there are two Mother Perfects ready to defend against them."

"And there are six Counsel members, all with superhuman strength and crazy god-like complexes, and that's not including their fierce warriors running amuck killing innocent people."

"But what of the other Perfects on Earth?" I asked.

Her face stayed grim. "I do not know. They share no allegiance to anyone but to themselves, thanks to Penelope. I'm not even sure we could stop a Fearian invasion with them at our side."

"Couldn't hurt," he said.

"Screw the selfish cowards, then," I sneered. "We can still do this alone if need be."

"I'm ready," Dad said.

"And are you prepared to die for her?" she nodded to me.

"Lauren will always be my child," he said.

She gave him an extended look. "I understand why Izzy loved you so … I too possessed a human of such nature."

I looked to her. "Bray?"

"…Focus." She stayed brisk.

A ferocious roar pierced our hearing, and the image of a lion came to mind without thinking. The elevator music chiming out the ceiling speakers made the death and chaos within our midst seem freakishly jolly. We hurried deeper inside the mall, past terrified stragglers scampering for the exit. We were the only ones advancing toward the eye of the storm. I didn't know what to expect, but I hoped Mom was wrong. I hoped we would find a way—I hoped we would find a path that led to victory.

I really hoped …

CHAPTER 51

DETECTIVE NEESE

I DROVE ALONG DOWNTOWN, looking for the most wanted fugitive in my history: a teenage high school girl with supernatural gifts to transport herself through portals and only God knows what else. I wasn't quite sure if my gas tank was running on unleaded courage or deceptive stupidity, but the only way to enlightenment was to hit the storm straight on.

I stared out my window at the passing scenery and observed the world go on around me, as if nothing out of the ordinary was knocking on the door of reality—or kicking the damn thing in with no regard for human life. Oblivious townspeople were out and about enjoying their day. If I didn't know any better ... but I did know better. A violent squall was brewing, and I wasn't sure I had the means to endure it long enough to put a stop to it. I was proving to be inconsequential compared to what I was dealing with, and that was with a shiny badge on my chest and a loaded pistol strapped to my side. But even still, I had no other choice but to fake my way to the doorstep of uncertainty, yank the knob and charge in unannounced. Hopefully, she wouldn't see the fear I was trying to cover.

I'm at a total loss.

"Where are you hiding, girl?"

"Detective Neese?" Dispatch crackled from my CB radio.

I grabbed for the receiver. "Go dispatch."

"You may want to head over to Somerset Mall."

"What for?"

"There are multiple reports of ... well ... some really strange things happening."

"How strange?"

"Flying animals, crazy looking gangs. And your teenage witch has also been spotted on the scene."

"I'm on my way! Send backup! Send everyone!"

"Roger that, Detective. Backup is en route."

I flipped on my emergency lights and revved the engine hard, zipping through a stoplight along the way.

Flying animals?

It appeared there were lots more players in this game than I realized, and if I was having trouble handling one teenage girl, how in the hell was I going to subdue a gang of whatever they were? My day just went from bad to worse, and I still didn't know what terrible monsters awaited my arrival at the mall.

Damn it! Why didn't I wear my bulletproof vest this morning?

CHAPTER 52

KAIDEN

I STOOD ALONGSIDE THE rest of the Counsel, waiting for The Seal to awake reborn. Our warriors were busy wreaking havoc and making their introduction into the realm of the mortals. It was humorous their response to our arrival. But even within all the bloody tumult we caused, a sense of peace radiated off the shaded dome on the floor.

My heartbeat thumped at an eerie pace that stayed unmanageable to my lungs.

The sound of water trickling off the statue in the fountain reminded me of the succulent pleasures of Bzar. It delivered a tear to my eye, and a thirst for blood to my spirit. With an angry growl, I gnashed my teeth and leaped into the air, landing on the shoulders of a fleeing human man. Snarling, I ripped his throat to shreds, his blood pooling on the floor. The feeling was overwhelming—and exuberating. I wiped the metallic zest with the back of my hand, smearing the blood across my mouth like the red paint on a warrior's face during battle. Death tasted empowering and supreme, and highly addictive to the senses.

"This is greater than I ever imagined," I said.

I was finally free of the lies. Free of the weak constraints of acting mortal and childish. But most of all I was free of dirty humans, and their sense of undeserved entitlement. Humanity had blinded them, but we were on the verge of restoring true sight. And things would never be the same.

Nolum gazed at the cocoon with the Shadow dagger in his grip, while Serene and Oplous bounced anxious glares back and forth between them. We all felt it ... retribution.

"This is a glorious time for our kind," I declared. "Every Fearian who sacrificed his soul shall be rewarded a king's ransom for it in the afterlife."

CHAPTER 53

GENEVE

I RUSHED TO THE far end of the corridor and rounded the next corner, where it opened into the main interior of the mall. The area was spacious, with five levels of floors. I could see humans, frantic and staring down at the Fearian fury below them.

Lauren and Elisabeth's human soul mate (or pet, I'm still unsure of which) were behind me as I shuffled to a halt, watching the Counsel congregated by a water fountain. Warriors were all around, attacking terrified humans that scrambled in circles like dizzy mice in a deadly maze: a maze that had no exits, only countless snares of deception.

Fury Beasts soared overhead and into nearby corridors, destroying the building with their wide wings, sharp claws and fiery lashes. Clunks of red bricks and slices of plaster rained down like meteor showers. The monsters bounced off the walls like drunken flies trapped in an upside down fish bowl, shattering display windows in their inebriated wake. Slivers of sharp glass sprinkled upon the many corpses lying on the floor, as if an honorable burial. My mouth grew dry, and it was hard to swallow the anger that rose up in my throat.

Those bastards did it ... they came to Earth to annihilate!

I spotted The Seal, motionless, hovering inches above the floor and protected inside their royal dome. The oval-shaped shelter was frosty and slightly opaque, but I knew what was lying inside it, awaiting a new birth to terrorize another species, just like so many other species before in times past: from Loafers, to Perfects ... to now humans.

Damn it! We're too late!

They would siphon the Earth for its precious resources, discarding all whom they found unfit to live.

"My God! Look what they've done!" Lauren gasped.

"And they're only getting started," I said. "This is why your mother did what she did, to try and prevent their tirade from reaching new worlds."

Lauren sobbed. "I see now."

"Him!" Glenn gritted his teeth. "That's the Fearian who took my Elisabeth!" He pointed across the way.

His confirmation made me bitter. "Kaiden."

"He murdered her before my eyes! I'll never forget it, or him!"

"There's too many of them," Lauren said.

"Too bad. We have no other choice but to fight." I squinted. "Even if we perish in battle."

"Let's go down fighting, then." Glenn unbuttoned his biker vest and exposed the cluster of throwing blades hanging inside like shiny ornaments on a Christmas tree. "This is for you, Elisabeth!" He snarled. "Let's take these bastards down a peg!"

The entranceways at both Saks Fifth Avenue and Nordstrom transformed into a humming starry darkness, just before three pink silhouettes appeared, running forward.

WOOSH!

Three Perfects: Dison, Wyatt and Jacob, sprang from the double doorway at Saks Fifth Avenue. Their eyes raged a brilliant coral. But before I could savor the unexpected backup, Zoe, Charlotte and Madison poured out of Nordstrom, with both eerie defiance and eagerness in their sharp faces. Bladed weapons were in their hands.

As our eyes met, a sense of relief eased the tension swimming inside my gut. Although short-lived, it was welcomed and offered me a boost of confidence. My battle stance grew stronger. It was time to kill or be killed on the battlefield, but this death would be viewed as acceptable. This death would be admired to the end of time.

"Mother Geneve? It was you who summoned us?" asked Dison.

"Yes, it was." I looked to the others. "Pick any warrior and defeat him!" I demanded.

Dison pumped a fist. "Gladly!"

Zoe tapped Madison on the arm. "Let's kick some Fearian butt!"

The two scampered into a corridor, shooting Fearian Warriors and sporadic humans who got caught up in the skirmish.

Charlotte unleashed a battle cry and stormed into a corridor by herself, firing at every warrior in her line of site. Our enemies went from pillaging the mall to having to duel both an unexpected and formidable foe: Perfects, and one brave human being.

"May death be a friend today!" Wyatt growled.

Wyatt sprinted toward a long table in the center of the room, jumped onto it and leaped into the air. He soared high and latched onto the paws of a

Fury Beast as it flew above him. The animal's rider failed to notice Wyatt until it was too late. He dove the animal into a corridor, trying to shake Wyatt off, but Wyatt held his own and climbed onto the rear of the Beast injured, though alive. The animal swayed side-to-side then out of view, as Wyatt and the warrior fought for control, and a future.

Kaiden backed away from his preoccupied leaders without saying a word, and darted into a corridor.

I eyed Jacob and pointed toward him. "Do not let that coward survive this day!"

Jacob nodded. "He's all mine!" he chased after Kaiden, shifting his body into a huge spider and scuttling along the walls. I warmed, feeling victory grow closer.

"Oh, no!"

"What is it, Lauren?"

She pointed. "Aunt Jamie and Uncle Kevin, there in the display window!"

Glenn spotted the two hiding, their heads barely in sight as they peeked out. "Don't worry, I see them."

"Get them out of here, please!" she begged. "Don't let the Fearians harm them!"

"I'm on it."

He bolted across the room, flinging sharp blades at the warriors in his path. The warriors howled, shocked by the audacity of a simple human in their midst.

Glenn made it halfway across the floor before the warriors redirected their attack towards him. But Glenn stayed fierce, even as the lethalness of battle elevated.

"Be careful, daddy!" Lauren cried.

"Die!" he shouted, and he slid underneath a diving Fury Beast and whipped a handful of blades into its feathery underbelly.

The beast cramped from the agony. It smashed into a thick glass wall, shattering the window and subduing the animal, as its legs kicked about. Sharp glass stuck out of its body.

At the end of his slide, Glenn hopped to his feet and kept running for the shop as the mayhem around him enclosed. Another Fury Beast and its rider spotted Glenn's path and circled around for a deadly strike, but Glenn dove inside the doorway of the shop with a trail of flames slapping the heel of his boots and singing the cuffs on his jeans.

Lauren sighed, then flinched at the sound of a voice just behind us.

Oplous chuckled. "Look who stuck around long enough to fight this time?"

His voice angered me. "Oplous."

"Even a weak Mother Perfect has her day of reckoning," he replied. "Today is that day."

Serene held out his hand before Oplous, halting him, and swaggered toward us. "Face the inevitable. You cannot win, Mother Geneve. You never could, oh foolish one."

"Is that so?"

"Accept your fate and I might spare your torture. After all, we want the humans to see firsthand there are such things worse than servitude," Serene smirked.

"We'll see who spares whom," I replied.

"Very well, Mother Perfect." His eyes narrowed. "Let's begin the end of your existence."

"No. Wait for The Seal, Serene," Oplous muttered, with a hint of hidden caution within his low tone of voice.

Serene's gloating smirk and weighted pride seemed to deafen him with pure ignorance. He puffed out his chest and charged forward, curving his hazel eyes and exposing his white fangs. Oplous reached out to calm, but it was a second too late. Serene broke free from the harmonious sanctuary of the Counsel and The Seal and ventured blindly into my personal space, where I was strongest.

Each step Serene stole empowered the monstrous glare in his eyes.

I blinked, and felt a potent force shooting from my core and his body flew backwards from the reverb, crashing into the ruined entrance of an empty perfume store.

The collision started a raging fire (his corpse was combustible) and quickly filled the area with dark smoke and flickering flames. The building rattled and our limbs shook from the massive blast, but Lauren and I held firm … as did the rest of the Fearian Counsel.

"Any more of those in your back pocket?" Lauren asked, a hopeful tone in her voice.

"Sorry. Just the one," I said.

"Crap. Oh well."

"NOOO!" Oplous tightened his fists.

"Look what you've done!" Nolum spouted.

"Serene has always been the weakest link, like his ignorant brother," I said. "Both of their deaths are on your head."

"YOU WILL DIE FOR THIS!" Oplous replied.

He stormed toward me in the same manner as Serene, though I already knew his strengths wouldn't allow the same outcome.

"Bring it!"

Oplous snarled, flicking fireballs with his fingers (his fingernails burned like fire), and it took all I had to withstand the massive barrage as it slammed against the protective shield I summoned to appear just in time. The strongest of the Counsel proved to be a test of wills, as we were equally matched and just as determined. I knew if I were to be victorious I would have to earn it, and I prayed favor would fall on my side when the thick dust had settled.

CHAPTER 54

LAUREN

I BACKED UP A step without thinking as Aunt Geneve and the one called Oplous squared-up for supremacy. They attack each other like kings of the jungle. I wanted to help, but didn't know how to without being more of a shameful hindrance than a welcomed advantage. My uncertainty overshadowed my right to make a choice.

They fought hand-to-hand, Oplous's growls uniquely matched Aunt Geneve's fierce roars, and their momentum pushed the pair twelve feet into the air. Neither seemed to care, and their relentless struggle continued, as they spun over our heads.

The last of the Counsel faced me and glared my way, his head slanted in offense. His back arched in combat mode, and I knew what was coming next. I felt its hot glow.

Nolum towered into the air in my direction, his fangs and claws erect like an angry hawk about to snatch its unsuspecting prey below, though I was fully aware of his deadly intentions. I observed his every move and still was caught off guard by it.

I gasped, suddenly frightened and anxious and unsure how to defend. Nolum saw the lack of conviction exposed within my high brow, and his hazel eyes illuminated.

"You haven't the heart to fight!" He opened his mouth wide and showed his sharp jagged teeth. "You're just a pathetic human trapped in a Perfect body! Fear not, I will set you free!"

"No!"

My knees weaken then I tumbled to the tile, unprepared to guard his flying assault, but he bounced off the invisible shield protecting my body. His momentum pushed me backwards and I slid across the floor before coming to rest against the wall. Nolum recovered his graceless flop with a quick flip, landing on his feet. The tile beneath his shoes cracked from the pressured impact, and my eyes widened at the sight.

"Interesting," he said, looking more irritated than impressed.

Nolum flicked his fingers and unleashed orange balls of fire in my direction. The first hits slammed against the shield before I was able to get to my feet. Thick smoke crept off the floor, a ghostly fog longing for a chance to kill my undeserved perfection.

"Fight back!" Aunt Geneve's voice urged against my eardrum.

I glanced up at her, still embroiled in a wild clash with Oplous.

Nolum prowled toward me, stomping his feet and crumbling the tile beneath him as he moved. The space between our two bodies shrunk, and so did the length of time in between the pounding of my heartbeats. But my nervousness slung me in a different direction than I had anticipated, and my eyes squinted and flashed fuchsia. I pointed to the water fountain, and a gush of water and coins rose out of the shallow pool.

His missiles crashed against my damaged barrier again, but I held my ground. Somehow.

"Make a wish!" I mocked.

A tidal wave of water and metal punched into Nolum, stunning, while soaking him into submission on the floor. Water rained down onto the tile and coins bounced at my feet before settling on heads or tail.

His coerced belly flop pleased me, and I couldn't stop my lips from slanting—I desired another taste of its delectable juicy flavor.

CHAPTER 55

GLENN

I FELT MYSELF BEING pulled away from the doorway and behind the cover of the wall. It took a moment of time for me to pry open my eyelids and gather my dizzy composure, and for the heat of my scorched boots to die down. My eyes focused on Kevin's moving lips, but I didn't hear the sound of his voice. A ringing noise sang in my eardrum, and I felt twisted and off balance. I noticed Jamie kneel beside Kevin, and slowly my hearing returned, but with a slight reverb to it.

Then everything slammed back to normal.

"Glenn? Glenn! Are you okay?" Kevin asked.

"Yes. I ... I think so."

"What the hell is going on in here, Glenn?" Jamie gasped. "What are those things? Who are those crazy looking people? And why is Lauren fighting that one?"

I caressed her arm. "Jamie, I can't begin to explain this to you. Let's just get you guys out of here before it's too late."

"But what about Lauren?"

"Lauren can handle herself," I said.

"And what on Earth gave you that idea?"

"Because Lauren's a Mother Perfect. This is hers and Izzy's world."

"Mother Perfect? What the hell does that mean, Glenn?"

"Trust me, Jamie. She's ... prepared. Can we go now?" I asked.

She looked to Kevin, hesitant and confused, and then we stood to our feet. A Fury Beast spewed hot flames towards us, and we hid in the Juicer Hut while it flew by. Then we slipped back into the corridor, hugging the wall. The mayhem around us continued and made each step feel dangerous.

"Stay close to me. Both of you."

"Don't think you have to worry about that," Kevin said, eying the strange events feet away.

I grabbed Jamie's hand and shuffled off, with Kevin close behind. We dodged fireballs and pink-eyed Perfects battling fierce warriors, with Fury Beasts flying not so high overhead. Kevin's anxiety turned into trembling fear, and he stopped moving.

Damn it, Kevin! Goddamn it!

"I'm… not going to make it, sweetie!" Kevin stammered.

"Yes. You will." I assured him. "Keep your eyes on me, and keep your feet moving forward!"

"Honey, keep up! You can do this!"

"I can't! They're … they're too many of them! And they're everywhere! We won't make it out alive!"

"Stay calm, Kevin! You're freaking out!"

"No! We have to go back and wait for the police!" he grabbed for Jamie's arm.

"Honey! Let go!" Jamie said.

He halted our progress but I overpowered his intent. I lay my eyes to his, but it was too late. He had stopped behind us, and was staring at the crazy devastation unfolding before him. The more Kevin witnessed, the weaker his resolve became. His hesitation left a gaping space in between him and us, and a Fury Beast barreled toward him, like an out of control bomber on a suicide run.

"Kevin!" I shouted.

Jamie reached out to him, but fear had caused his brain to shutdown and his body to freeze.

Kevin screamed as the Fury Beast and its Fearian rider trampled him under its mighty feet.

"Kevin!" Jamie shrieked.

I spun her into my chest as the Fury Beast spilled toward us. It roared and hovered inches over our heads, its claws digging into my back. I cringed in pure agony, then grabbed three blades and flung them at the Fury Beast's head. One blade clipped the tip of his left ear and severed a slice off. The other stuck in his right eye. Green goo spilled from the socket, and the beast screeched in torment. It bucked its Fearian rider and he almost lost balance.

I shielded Jamie against the wall as the animal slashed by us, so close the hair from its underbelly tickled my nostrils. With a final moan, it crashed onto the floor, rolling over onto its rider and smothering him whole.

"Glenn, please don't let me go!" she screamed and trembled, as her eyes bulged in fright.

"I've got you, Jamie."

"I don't want to die!"

"I won't let you, just focus on me."

The beast flopped around on the tile in front of us, its wings beating a death march on the floor. The tile cracked and jagged chips flew in the air, like bomb shrapnel. Some stabbed the walls and ceiling and some beat tender bruises on my back. I cringed, and inhaled a breath to create an inch of space, and we skimmed by the kicking animal. The broken warrior appeared from underneath its breast. His swollen red eye connected with mine and he reached for a weapon to kill us, but I kicked his forehead with my boot tip and broke his neck.

Jamie squeezed my hand so tightly I lost feeling, but I paid it no mind, hurrying her out of the danger zone and toward the front doors. The brightness of day flashed our faces and brought a surge of relief, though our hearts pounded like battle drums.

CHAPTER 56

JACOB

THE CORRIDOR WAS A bloody battlefield, with mangled bodies sprawled all about the pitted interior. It had been a time since I tasted the sweet nectar of savagery against a Fearian soldier. The last time I'd faced one I had been successful at defeating him. Today would be no different. If not for the sheer number of warriors back then, perhaps the Days of Sorrow would have possessed a different outcome.

But it did not.

However, this time there were far less than before, and no one to command us to flee instead of standing firm and fighting to the death, their death. The Fearian blood on the palm of my hands was a symbol of bravery and strength, like a great eagle's tail feather added to a decorated war bonnet of the ages.

I peered up to the skylights and took death deep into my lungs, accepted the call to transform into the beating heart of a martyr then scanned the corridor for my elusive reward; my eagle's feather: the flapping wings of a Fury Beast. I picked up on his battle cry and descent and it caused me to whip around without hesitation or fright.

Finally! I snarled.

Its body was massive as it soared my way; it's eyeballs stone black and haunting in appearance.

It took a brief moment for my brain to comprehend what I was witnessing. The beast had Charlotte's limp body clenched in its mouth, her head and legs dangling from the sides. My insides turned cold and anxiety stabbed at my spirit and jolted my nerves until they felt numb.

"Charlotte!" I yelled.

The callous animal dropped her beautiful corpse before it veered around to attack me, and Charlotte's body plummeted to the floor below. The sight was devastating to me, and yet I couldn't look away. It was the one thing left I could offer to her memory, my last chance at honor and respect. I shuddered, forced to watch her remains crash onto a wooden cart in the center of the floor. The structure caved in from the collision, and although I didn't see the impact of her body, the irking thud made tears run down my rosy cheeks. I winced from the vile image inside my head. My cruel imagination filled in the blanks. It saddened me … then it tortured me … then vexed me.

I faced my foe, who crouched low on the backside of the soaring beast as both nosedived in assault mode. Its steep angle caused the sliced wind to scream out. I unleashed a barrage of energy pulses at the filthy animal and its evil handler. The beast stayed defiant and gained speed as it neared me, but I refused to retreat. My distraught wouldn't allow it, and my tainted heart was hell-bent on payback.

My first few shots were evaded easily, but I meant it to be so, cause I would not be denied on this day. I had studied its evasive maneuvers, bottled my pressured rage, gritted my teeth to the point they almost crumbled and then my incendiary slugs turned heat seeking, locking in on the creature's chest feathers.

The Fury Beast let out a building-shaking squawk.

It took a slow moment for my earlobes to stop humming.

"Come to me!" I demanded, motioning with my fingers. "Come and get what you deserve."

My piercing pulses punctured its left wing, its underbelly and then its neck, partly severing the head of its warrior. His body lost all control to sit steady on the animal.

The beast roared, and flames spewed from its mouth, though the pain in his eyes was quite obvious. The heat burned my eyebrows, but otherwise left me unscathed.

Both the Fury Beast and its dead rider missed me as it slammed onto the floor and slid to a bumpy halt. I ran to it and filled the beast's body with pulses of rage, much more than was needed to ensure its demise, but I didn't care one lick. Even in death I wanted it to suffer for what the pair had done to our beloved Charlotte, and for what it had forced me to witness and record in the tablet of truth.

As I stood over the dead beast, no closer to basking in pleasure, I caught Kaiden sneaking out of a clothing shop in the distance. He headed toward an exit, tiptoeing over shallow mounds of debris.

"You're not getting away that easy, coward!" I muttered. "Not by a long shot."

I gave chase, in attack mode, knowing my day would be just a little bit sweeter with the Counsel's number one flunky listed as one of my confirmed bloody kills. The thought made my heartbeat elevate with anticipation.

"Do not run from death!" I shouted at him. "It won't be ignored!"

Kaiden didn't respond, though he picked up speed in his retreat. He swerved in and out of the rubble, trying to evade my fierce aim and my unrelenting determination. I fired on a line of fancy chandeliers hanging from the ceiling, and they dropped to the floor like air bombs, shattering into a starburst of heated glass on both sides of his body.

The exploding glass splashed into his face, stopping him abruptly. I came at him from the side and aimed at his forehead, blind with rage and an unquenchable thirst for immediate redemption. Kaiden had no other choice than to raise his weapon, shuffling backwards, timidly, until his back pressed against the partition.

Got you now!

"There's no way out for you, flunky!"

"Oh, yeah?"

"Damn right."

"Well, who said I was looking for a way out?"

"Your feet. Idiot."

He chuckled. "You damn destroyers are all the same; you think every world is yours to command."

"There is one difference between us."

"And what's that?"

"I am going to be the one who gets to kill you, and no one can steal that from me."

"You're a fool. The Seal is moments from being renewed. After that, it will be a whole new ballgame for Fearians, and for you Perfects. Even if you manage to kill me, they will bring me back… and then send you straight to hell."

"Better hope they have you an extra body."

I blasted the concrete wall behind him as Kaiden shot me in the side, sending me to the floor bleeding. The pain seemed far away as I focused on Kaiden in front of me.

"NO!" he cried.

A dark cloud of dust and debris crumbled on top of Kaiden in a massive landslide of cement. When the smut cleared, Kaiden was no more; all but three limp, dirty fingers was buried from sight. My face stayed bleak, far from sympathy—and far from pleasure.

Hope this gives you some peace, Charlotte.

I staggered to my feet and spit blood on the pile of concrete. "Until we continue this in the afterlife, my foe."

The image brought a subtle smirk to my face and a sliver of content to my spirit. For a half second, I was at peace … then it vanished from in me. A frenzied howl of a Fury Beast in the distance caught my eardrum. It reminded me of the present state of things: still distasteful and malignant.

I stalked toward the sound of my next battle.

CHAPTER 57

LAUREN

I JUMPED OUT FROM around the clutter of debris, but Nolum's body was not where it should have been. I hadn't planned on looking for a fight, and yet I had no other choice in the matter. This had to end before The Seal was renewed. Aunt Geneve and Oplous had elevated their fruitless battle to the rafters above, while the interior of the mall looked like the aftermath at Chernobyl—doom and gloom.

"Scared to fight a girl?" I taunted, looking about, but seeing no one.

A fireball hit me in the spine of my back, knocking me to the ground. The force field guarding my body shuddered from the heavy blow before disabling itself and leaving me unprotected on the floor. I winced from the agony and looked toward my adversary, but again saw no one. Like a magician, Nolum reappeared, standing in the edge of my vision.

"I have respect for females."

"Could have fooled me."

"It's Perfects that I despise."

"And that's why you shot me in the back?"

"You will see this one coming."

"Thanks. How manly of you. Is that eyeliner on your brow?"

He chuckled then aimed at my face. "Vanity. Goodbye, Perfect. Human. Or whichever you claim to be."

Against my will, my body lifted a few feet off the ground while Nolum grinned evilly. A flash of fear zipped through me as I heard a loud roar, and both Nolum and I turned to look at the sound. The Fury Beast roared once more, but the rider in the saddle wasn't whom either of us expected to see sitting there.

Nolum's expression was stunned as he watched Wyatt leaning forward, riding the Fearians' treasured gem: a Fury Beast. Dison hung from the claws of its third leg, and his eyes raged coral.

"It can't be," Nolum muttered, backing off.

His connection to my levitation broke along with his focus, and I dropped to the tile and bounced up on my knees.

"Oh, but it can," I said, aiming at his chest.

Dison fired at Nolum not even a second after I did. Nolum hesitated as his aim switched from me to Dison, then he fired on Dison just as I fired on him a second time. His shot veered left, but the Fury Beast dropped and pushed Dison into its new path. Nolum's blasts struck Dison in the gut, and I saw the torture on his face. Nolum turned into black ash before he could relish in his success.

"Oh, God!" I cried out.

I scurried to my feet and prepared to catch Dison, or at least slow his crash to the floor, but Wyatt curved the beast into a corridor still in battle and out of sight, flinging Dison's body out of reach. He hit the floor and I swore I heard every bone in his being shatter.

"No!"

I ran to his twisted body and kneeled over him. Shattered bones tore through his brown skin. His eyes were closed and I was afraid to touch him. Then he looked up at me.

"Hey ..."

"Hey."

"I am sorry ... for everything I've done, young Perfect."

"You saved my life."

"Finally, I did something courageous. Do you ... believe in second ... chances?" He spit out blood.

"I do. And whatever you've done, know you will die with honor in my eyes."

"Thank you ... Mother Lauren." He slipped into darkness.

"Goodbye, new friend."

I closed Dison's eyes and stood to my feet. The just battle seemed anything but as casualties piled up. I hunted toward The Seal, lying on the floor in its hazy bubble. Their bodies glowed red and still hovered inches above the tile, but signs of life had begun to show. Diane's arm flinched, and both of Pepper's legs did, too. Jared's entire body quivered, like a newborn baby dragon, clawing his way from the cracked shell of an egg. I knew what I had to do, and there was no time for any more failures. Alas, the power to end this tragic ordeal was in the palm of my hand, and I finally possessed no qualms in doing the deed.

"This is the way it must be. You three will never live in peace, and I can't let you take this world." I steeled my tenacity. "Time for you three to cease to exist."

I narrowed my eyes, aimed by fists and fired on them—and nothing happened. Smoke rose off the bubble, but the inside remained untouched. I blasted at the bubble once more, more focused than the last time, and yet the same thing occurred: absolutely nothing.

What the...?

A light flashed off the bubble, blinding me for a second. A spark of nervousness jolted my insides, and my fingertips tingled. I shook it off and fired upon my enemy a third time—still nothing. I felt brittle and my confidence dropped suddenly.

It seemed I wasn't as powerful as I once thought, and if I couldn't stop them from being renewed, then how in the hell was I going to do anything to stop them when they were fully awake, and reborn?

CHAPTER 58

DETECTIVE NEESE

I SWERVED INTO THE parking lot at Somerset Mall, followed by a host of police cars just off my rear bumper. I was leading the swarm toward the front entrance, when the glass doors of the building exploded into a ball of fire. The commotion forced us to skid our cars to a stop. I hopped out with my eyes on the fiery entranceway, and watched a large beast appear within the flames and stomp out onto the pavement.

"God almighty! What on Earth is that?"

The crazy-acting weather made the images appear larger, scarier.

The thing had a smaller thing riding on its back with a glowing spearhead in its hand. The beast reared on its back leg, stretched out its long neck and roared in the air. The vibrating sound rocked the ground and shattered windows throughout the parking lot, causing most of us to take cover behind our cars.

A news chopper closed in for a closer look, barely able to keep steady in the gusting wind, and the rider of the beast jabbed his spear toward the helicopter as his animal shot a blast of flame from its mouth. We watched as the red fire skirted like a military missile and blew the news helicopter from the sky. The copter plummeted to the pavement in a jagged ball of heat.

I dove for cover again as the helicopter crashed on top of my police car, causing both to explode in a blast of seared heat and thick dark smoke. The chaotic scene was unimaginable and yet delivered horror to my senses.

I scampered to my feet and hid behind the nearest police car not on fire.

"Detective Neese! What the hell is that thing?"

"I have no idea. But let's see if it's bulletproof. Fire!" I ordered in a loud voice.

The others lay down a line of gunfire at the feathered creature guarding the entranceway. Bullets impacted the animal's body, but didn't give us the response we had hoped.

"Nothing is happening!" said Officer Smith. "Our bullets aren't even hurting the damn thing!"

I reloaded and aimed. "Just keep shooting!"

After a few moments of our attack, the beast puffed out its chest as though it was annoyed with our foolish attempts and unleashed a flaming trail across the parking lot. A patrol car was set ablaze as the one next to it exploded, sending officers running. The beast then flapped its mighty wings and took flight, pinning us down as it roared and circled over the flaming parking lot.

I felt useless … cornered … victimized, even worse with a pistol in my hand and an authority that gave not one of us an advantage.

CHAPTER 59

MARGARET

I SAT AT THE edge of my recliner, amazed at what I was witnessing unfolding on the television screen. The news had cut into our regular programming and was showing live feed from the parking lot of the Somerset Mall. Some kind of weird animal had sprayed a news chopper with fire and disabled it, knocking it to the earth.

Jamie and Kevin had returned to their eatery after I left their home, so I hoped they made it out safely. I called her telephone number to check, but the line remained busy.

A dark cloud of tremors overtook me, causing my beliefs to be tested in ways I'd never expected. There was only one other time in my life something even remotely as strange as this had occurred, but that was a long time ago.

Still, they had to be connected ... they just had to be.

I wiped away tears and watched Detective Neese and the others scatter like red ants being tortured with a magnifying glass by a mean bully: a bully not of this world.

"My God in heaven!" I covered my mouth. "Help us ..."

CHAPTER 60

GENEVE

OPLOUS HAD MY BODY pinned against the wall near the top of the cathedral ceiling, high above the warring factions below us. We were evenly matched, as the authority of the Counsel balanced perfectly with the power of a Mother Perfect in almost every way: the gods attempt at equality and peace. But the injuries sustained between us were starting to mount. It was a test of will to see who could outlast the other.

Oplous grabbed my blouse and slammed my back against the concrete wall. The force caused the concrete to chip away and dust to hover. It made me cough.

"In moments The Seal shall be renewed and we will reign forever!" he declared.

"Then … I guess I better kill you right now," I answered, my ears still ringing from the impact with the wall.

I looked down at The Seal and saw Lauren standing over them, but even from a distance I could tell she was having unsuccessful issues of her own—crude issues that could prove to be detrimental to our survival if not rectified quickly.

There just isn't enough time!

With a sudden growl, Oplous bit into my neck and ripped out a portion of flesh. The sound of tearing tissue and skin made me shudder and the intense tweak left me vulnerable. Desperate, I concentrated and willed the music chiming from the ceiling speakers to increase to an eardrum trembling level—it became almost deafening, even for me.

Oplous's eyes popped from the loud melody and he cringed. His assault faltered, and I jabbed my thumbs into his eye sockets, stealing his view of the world. The posh orbs squished, then gave way with a sickening softness, while some dark goo ran onto my fingers and hands. My stomach flipped, sour bile bubbled up my throat and burned my taste buds, but I dug into his sockets even harder, until his shrieks reached a fever pitch and vomit spewed off my bloody lips.

Seeing my chance, I clawed inside his chest, gripped his beating heart and yanked it out of his body with one forceful tug. The rest of his vital organs soon surrendered their functions and his body dropped toward the floor below, snatching me along with it.

Time seemed to slow as I fell, exhausted, numb, and I didn't feel my limp limbs smack against the floor when it occurred. I lay there, unable to lift my head or speak. I felt the edges of my vision going black without my consent, but I could do nothing but accept my heartless fate—leaving Lauren to suffer the calling of the Fearian Seal alone.

CHAPTER 61

LAUREN

OH MY GOD! SHE fell from the ceiling!

I ran to Aunt Geneve's mangled body and hovered over her. I wanted to help her, but I didn't want to move her and make things worse, either. I pleaded to God that her life source didn't go out like Disons did.

Her eye cracked open, but I knew that look. I knew it too well. It was the same one my mother had given moments before her body gave up its spirit that tragic day at the park, the day my life changed forever. A change I was still dealing with. I couldn't stop crying, and I felt helpless as I grazed her face with my fingers, as soft as I could.

"Aunt Geneva, please don't leave me here!"

Her eyelids didn't flicker pink. They stayed glossy—and human looking—and her lips didn't move. I wasn't even sure she could hear my words of love.

"I can't destroy them, Aunt Geneve. I'm not strong enough. I am nothing like you! Maybe I never was."

I wanted to surrender my will and die along side my mother's sister. There was nothing more in me I could give. I put my head on her chest, wanting to curl up beside her, when I heard her whisper my name in a shaky low voice.

"Aunt Geneve?"

"You will, one day... be strong ... enough."

I gazed at her face. "It's too late. I failed us. The Seal is almost renewed."

"...So are ... you."

I wiped my nose with my hand and sniffed back tears. "I don't understand."

Vibrant humming echoed from the bubble as it began to glow more intensely by the second.

"Something is happening. I have to get you out of here."

I grabbed her broken body and drug her into the entranceway of Neiman Marcus, behind a wall of glass. Portions of the display were still in place, though it'd been broken at the top corners of the window. I peeked out in the hall and observed the bubble burning ever brighter. Then, without warning, it exploded with a loud boom.

The force sent shattered slivers of bubble shell everywhere, and the blasts blew a gust of wind so powerful it shattered the remaining glass displays still standing in the main room. Damaged demo cars parked in the center of the corridor flew past us like toy cars being thrown at the hands of a spoiled toddler commanding a feisty tantrum.

My ears rang and left me dazed, and I struggled to focus. As the thick dust settled, the first of The Seal emerged from the rubble. She looked much different: stronger, bolder—renewed. Her hazel eyes beamed with an intensity that I'd never witnessed before, even as a Perfect. Her siblings then followed suit, each looking equally stronger and reborn.

It's over now...

Jared looked to the sky, past the shattered skyline. "Lauren! Come to us now!"

"Face your fate, Perfect!" Pepper demanded.

Diane giggled and balled her fists. "Or are you terrified you're now left without any help from dear old auntie?"

"I'm sorry I let everyone down." I caressed Aunt Geneve's face. "I let you down."

"All ... that I ever was ... now belongs ... to you." Aunt Geneve kissed my earlobe. It was so soft I barely even felt it, though it had the power to console.

At her touch, a surge of energy rushed through my body so swiftly I felt dizzy. I gathered my composure and looked down to her, but she was no more. She was dead ... and I was alone. I bit back tears, while the heat in me left me confused.

"What's ... happening to me?"

Then a sudden seizure hit me. My limbs jerked and shook uncontrollably and my eyelids fluttered. New impressions from both Aunt Geneve's and my mother's essences overflowed my brain. Their darkest regrets and most treasured secrets were floating inside my head, bringing me closer to their Perfect essence—and closer to mine.

In the twinkle of an eye, I knew where I'd come from, who'd paved the path before me, and where I needed to take it to fulfill the prophecy. Every question I'd pondered before had a new understanding, including what it meant to be a Mother Perfect. I was an endangered species, and yet far from being alone inside my own head.

The control of my essence belonged to another. And that 'other' wasn't done breaking me free from the rusty chains of humanity that had enslaved my thinking since birth. I sat hostage, frozen, unable to break loose from the massive flood of knowledge and wisdom being dumped inside my mind at an alarming rate. It made me an old soul.

CHAPTER 62

GLENN

I STOOD BEHIND THE Seal with blades in my hands as they called out to my only child. The trio wanted her life to end, and there was no-way I was ever letting that go down without giving my input. They were renewed, just as Elisabeth had feared and described, and everything she had sacrificed was now for nothing.

Every pain I'd endured was a loss.

The blades glimmered in the light. I zipped a handful at The Seal, striking each one multiple times in the chest before they had time to react. Although they were caught off guard, I failed to injure them at all. I watched as my blades were absorbed into their flesh. They looked to be more impressed than intimidated by my ambitious courage.

"I like this human," Pepper smiled. "I think I shall have him for a pet. To remind me of Lauren's pathetic existence."

"Come and get me," I mocked.

"I think he's referring to you, sister." Diane giggled.

"I wonder if you're half the man you pretend to be?" Jared asked, eyeing me with a snotty glare.

An unseen force hit my left leg and snapped it in two before I had a chance to brace for impact. The jabs were excruciating, torturous, and I cried and tumbled to one knee. My consciousness faltered a bit, and it took a time to gather my composure.

The trio stared at me placidly, and I felt offended by their pride. I flung the second row of ninja blades their way, my accuracy dead-on even while injured. I struck Jared in the right thigh, the left side of his stomach and square in the forehead. Jared didn't show signs of discomfort, but stumbled backwards a step. It made me grin. Then he lifted his shirt, and his skin stretched over my blades and sucked them in and out of sight.

Crap.

"My turn, human pet," he quipped.

This time I was prepared for his counterblow, but it mattered none. The ease in which his will broke my other leg was as swift as last time. It was more than I could take, and I collapsed to the floor on my back in agony.

"You may want to rethink that pet offer," he suggested to Pepper. "He's going to be awfully defective when I'm done with him."

Pepper pouted. "Oooh. But I like his spirit."

In desperation, I sat up, grabbed the last blade I had left and flung the blade at her neck. The sharp edge sliced into her skin with ease and stuck out at an awkward angle. Before I could bask in my actions, the sharp blade was swallowed whole within her skin.

"We both know it's still there." I grinned.

"Okay. I'm bored with him." She curved her eyes.

I couldn't hold my upper body any longer, and I plopped down against the floor. "That's all I have to give you," I said, staring at the sky. "I love you so much, Elisabeth … even if my efforts didn't make a difference."

The thick clouds above parted and welcomed me into their bosom. I felt the killing force caress my body again, so warmly it was deceiving at first. It became difficult for me to breathe as my rib cage was squeezed until it snapped, puncturing both lungs. Then the force gripped my neck and the bones cracked from the pressure.

I grunted with each torturous twist and turn, it was so horrific and unspeakable. I couldn't find the strength to fight it off, and I didn't try. I thought on happier times. When I first saw Elisabeth sticking out of that tree trunk, when I first saw her eyes flicker pink … when I first saw Lauren the day she was born, when I first saw...

Everything went black.

CHAPTER 63

DIANE

I SNEERED AS JARED snapped the puny human's neck in two, killing him. I'd never felt so strong in my entire life. None of us had.

Jared turned to Pepper and I. "Where were we?"

"Believe we were about to finish off his daughter," Pepper replied. "Before we claim the world as our own."

We turned back toward Lauren and stalked toward her, relishing every single step. It was finally her time of reckoning. And it would be vindictively sweet to the taste.

"No more games!" I growled. "I want some Perfect blood! I want your blood!"

"You heard my siblings. Come to us, Lauren. Bow down before your new gods," Pepper said.

"Or suffer our mighty wrath … either or. Maybe even both still," Jared ridiculed.

Every second that ticked and she didn't show her face increased our taste for more potent revenge. Then, Lauren stepped out into the main room with her hair covering her face as she stared at the floor.

"There's my soon-to-be pet," I jeered.

Lauren scoffed, so lightly I almost didn't pick up on it. Her response was so out of place it felt off. Then I noticed she was hovering a few inches off the tile. I glanced at my siblings, but it seemed I was the only one who saw it. Arrogance is blinding.

"The last Mother Perfect alive," Jared said.

"We should display her before the humans," Pepper suggested. "Show them how lucky they are they aren't her."

"You know, sis, you might have something there," he said.

"But first I want her to pay for what she put us through," she added. "And I aim to collect."

"I'm good with that," said Jared. "How about you, Diane?"

I hid my concerns. "Yeah. Sure. Make it happen. Pepper?"

"I was hoping you'd say my name, girl."

Lauren didn't say a thing as her strands of hair covered her face. It was almost eerie, though she was the prey and we were the predators. Then she reached out her hand, and Pepper's body slid forward across the glossy floor and into her awaiting grasp.

Pepper was so startled she didn't have time to call out. The move left me shook, and caused Jared to back up a step. Lauren lifted Pepper by the collar, and her feet dangled a foot off the floor. I could sense the uncertainty and panic hit Pepper's bones.

"Uh-oh," I mumbled.

"How did you do that?" Pepper asked her.

Lauren raised her face to Pepper's. Her pupils flared poppy red and her coy expression made my anxieties rush. "Really? That's the part you wish to question?"

Lauren's entire body glowed a brilliant red, so intense that Pepper's body glowed the same, until it reached a boiling point and exploded with a violent boom. Jagged pieces of tissue and bones splattered to the floor, but Lauren only lowered her head again, allowing her luscious strands to hide her face.

"Pepper!" Jared shouted.

"We should think about this," I said. "Something's not right."

"Screw that! I am The Seal!" he exhaled.

Jared's wrath had pushed him over the edge, to a place of no return. He charged for Lauren, tears of rage running down his face. I prayed for his victory, but I was none too sure of it coming true.

Lauren didn't look up as she ran toward Jared with the same intensity in her wide strides. The pair collided into each other, sending out a blast of dusty wind. I covered my face as it slapped my skin and whipped my hair in passing.

The impact rocked the building, and I braced to keep my balance. As the room slowly returned to calm, I stared at the collision spot. Neither Jared nor Lauren was in sight and it scared me to death. I looked to the floor and saw Jared's tennis shoes were still there, seeping white smoke, the rubber soles soldered to the tile.

"Jared?" My eyes watered. "This isn't funny … please answer me right now … please?"

I heard her breathing behind me, seconds before it registered in my thinking. It made goosebumps pop along my neckline, though her breath was warm and inviting against my skin.

I don't want to die.

"Pity," she responded to my thoughts.

My limbs trembled and my fingertips tingled with a feeling new to my entire body. I wanted to face my demons, but I was too terrified to turn around to her.

I peeked from the corner of my eye, but I couldn't see her. "Hey, Lauren, um … you know, there's enough Earth to go around."

"You think?"

"Of course."

"Huh."

It took all the courage I could muster, but I needed to show her I was sincere and unafraid (a lie even I didn't believe). I turned on fragile eggshells, making sure not to disturb a single one. Lauren was looking right at me, and her poppy red eyes locked dead on mine.

"We can work something out, sweetie."

"…We just did. Sweetie."

"Wait … don't kill me yet."

"Kill you? I would never," she shied.

I sighed. "Thank you, Lauren."

"Don't thank me, thank yourself."

Without warning, a sharp punch to my head made me reel—and made my hand ache. I found myself fighting a losing battle of stopping my own fists from beating me in the head and face. The vile force was supernatural and so brutal that I bled.

"Make it stop," I pleaded. "Make it stop doing that!" My nose broke and it stung, giving me a blooming headache. My cheekbone shattered and I felt wetness seeping from my ear, and my eardrum rung.

"I'll be your slave, okay? Anything. Just let me live … you'll see!" My vision started to swirl, but my fist turned scalding hot.

"Did you enjoy hurting my dad?" her sly tone turned conniving.

"I'll … I'll be your pet."

"I'm bored with you," Lauren said. "My regards to your siblings."

"Lauren! You can't do thi—"

CHAPTER 64

DETECTIVE NEESE

I'D NEVER BEEN A hostage in my own town, and yet here we were: helpless pawns, victims to an insanity and pinned down by a deviant beast that couldn't have come from this world. My reality was taking an eerie beating, with no end in sight.

The three-legged beast and its foreign rider began to choke on the atmosphere, as a faint green, protective haze fell away from its frame. The animal released a pathetic roar and dropped to the pavement with a thunderous crack, smashing the concrete into pieces and trapping its rider underneath its body. Then the damn thing and its rider dissolved: flesh, bones and organs liquefying as if doused with burning acid.

Seconds later there was nothing left of our aggressors but a slimy pond of green goo. It stank terribly. We rose to our feet from behind our cars in utter disbelief.

Were they real? They had to be.

"Is that it? Is it over?" Officer Smith asked me.

"Not sure, but we should be the ones to find out. Who still has ammo?" I asked.

Several men inspected their weapons and raised their hands.

I reloaded my pistol. "You six follow me. The rest of you secure the parking lot."

I collected my deflated bravery and led the team beyond the green pool of gory mess and inside the front entrance of what looked like an otherworldly war.

CHAPTER 65

LAUREN

DIANE'S BODY DROPPED TO its knees and tumbled to the tile, leaking out blood from her battered head. I felt empathy at the disgusting image. Or so I thought, but it was just the lowest form of pity, cleverly disguised. In a way, she was a casualty of a war neither of us had started, but that didn't change her having to still die.

Her kind always had to die. Just the way it was. The way it would always be.

But at least it was over, and all it cost me was—everything. I gazed across the floor and saw my father's body. His limbs were crooked and awkward looking, like no bones were within his skin. I knew he'd suffered dearly to help me, to give me a chance.

Look, Dad, I made it ... because of you I am here. The only thing you were ever guilty of was falling in love with a Mother Perfect.

The scar on his face was a testament to his affection for Mom and me. It had taken a long while for me to figure that out, but I'm glad I know now. I stood over my aunt's corpse and admired her perfection. Like Mom, she too sacrificed for love. I heard footsteps, and I looked along a corridor to see Zoe and Madison hurrying my way. Jacob, who was drenched in goo, and Wyatt stepped out of another corridor on the other side of the main room. They joined me and observed Aunt Geneve's body on the floor.

Tears gathered in Jacob's eyes.

Madison knelt down to her body and inspected her. "Mother Geneve is no more."

"It is indeed a sad day for Mother Perfects," Wyatt consoled. "For all Perfects who lost their life."

Zoe stood wide-eyed, looking at me. "Be that as it may. Lauren was able to kill the Fearian Seal. That is truly an amazing feat."

"This is a new era, just as Mother Geneve prophesized," Wyatt said.

Madison spread out her arms. "The Earth is ours to reign! No longer are we condemned to the shadows. No one can stop us."

Jacob glanced into a rear corridor. "More humans are coming fast, probably with guns. What's the move?"

They turned to me for answers.

I only had one.

"...I invoke Oracle Six of the Perfect Order," I said.

I could sense my words caught them off guard.

How did I know what to invoke? Who told me? And would I allow them to complete the Fearian's plan for dominance?

I faced them with nobility in my posture and a hint of arrogance in my stance. "What say you?"

They hesitated, shooting anxious glances back and forth, but I knew no one would dare contest my lineage, or my Perfect resolve.

"We will honor the order," Jacob said. "That has always been our way. It will continue to be so."

The others nodded.

"Disband until I call for you," I ordered.

They disbursed.

Oddly enough, I wasn't the least bit concerned that they might contest my decision. The battle scars now embedded in my heart were transforming my outlook—or maybe it was just the first time in my life I felt the weight of a Mother Perfect bearing down on my spirit, and I was finally willing to carry the load. For Mom, and for Aunt Geneve, and for the others who came before me, and died so I could thrive.

It was what it was ... and I was becoming more than okay with it. I cherished its gentle calling. So much that, I could never live another day without it. I motioned for Aunt Geneve's corpse to rise, and it levitated feet up without any hesitation.

Footsteps from Detective Neese and his team of armed stranglers sounded behind me, and I sifted through his fearful thoughts as he advanced forward. My heartbeat stayed steady, and Aunt Geneve and I disappeared from sight as the humans rounded the corner, with their pistols at the ready.

WOOSH!

CHAPTER 66

APPLE

I STEPPED INSIDE MY bedroom with a white cotton towel wrapped around my body and my damp hair flowing off my sexy shoulders. I stared at the flat screen hanging on my wall. The day was all but ended, and sunset brought a sense of calmness over Grand Blanc and over my gift of survival. On the screen, the newscaster stood in front of Somerset Mall, reporting on the devastation that had occurred earlier.

The property was damaged from battle and filled with local and state policemen as well as several teams of crime scene technicians. Even a couple of cadaver dogs sniffed about with their handlers in tow. A few serious looking suited men with 'FEDS' written on their blank expressions also surveyed the crime scene in the background.

"Witnesses reported seeing what they describe as two gangs battling each other for supremacy," the reporter said.

"Perfects and Fearians," I scoffed, with a snooty tone. "Report the damn news right if you're going to report it. Humans."

"Bolts of lightning that some witnesses recalled cannot be confirmed, but authorities are saying there were no survivors from the violent clash. I'm Tiffany Jones, reporting for WDIV Channel 4 News."

"Those are the words I was hoping to hear," I smiled.

I pitched the remote onto the bed.

"Idiots killed off one another, trying to be king, leaving little ol' me all by my lonesome to rule the Earth as Queen Bee." I smirked. "Life is so good—for me, anyhow."

I strutted over to my closet, just as the door opened wide and Lauren stepped inside my bedroom. My heartbeat elevated, but I played it coy, as best as possible anyway, wiping off my surprise with a shallow grin.

Disappointment shaded my cheekbones the light color of crimson.

"Lauren! Sweetie. Uh … hey."

"Hello, Apple."

If you want something done right ... right?
"You're alive. I mean ... not dead."
"It would appear so, yes."
"Great. Great ... awesome."
"You don't mind me barging in at such a late hour do you?"
"Uh. No. You're always welcome here. So. Were you a part of that ruckus at the mall earlier?" I asked. "Looks pretty bad."
"Oh. That?" She waved it off. "It was much to do about nothing, really. A lot of crazy confusion and misunderstandings, but we straightened it all out."
Lauren continued to grin. It had a sneaky undertone and I didn't like it one bit.
What are you up to, girl? It can't be good for me.
"Oh. Okay. Thank God, for a minute there..." I smiled extra big.
The moment grew awkward. Lauren stared at me, and it made my caution flare up like a forest fire in the middle of June.
"Tragic thing that happened earlier."
"What do you mean?"
"I mean Riley, silly."
"Right. Right. Poor thing." I tried sounding sympathetic. It was much harder than I imagined. "It made me want to cry when I heard about it on the local news."
"Hum." She batted her long eyelashes. "I bet. So anyway, correct me if I'm wrong, but... didn't you and I have a bit of unfinished business to attend to?"
"We did? Uh. No. No."
"Are you sure about that? Because I could have sworn ..."
I shot out a gust of air. "Full disclosure."
"I'm listening."
"That whole drama mess was Riley's gig. Jealousy, right?"
"Don't I know it?"
"But you and I are cool now. Right?"
I could no longer deny her intentions, and it was going to be either her or me. I turned away and headed for the bed, knowing I was only getting one shot, one chance to end this ordeal in my favor, even if I had to explain her death to my parents. Her casual demeanor gave me a slight edge, and I was going to make her pay for trusting me.
Now or never, girl! Kill her!
I whipped around, eyes raging pink and glove lit. Yet before I could aim, I was again startled by Lauren's close proximity. We stood face-to-

face, and I felt my destroyer glove turn impersonal. It powered down as the pendulum swung toward high distress.

"Apple?"

"Yes?"

"You weren't going to sucker punch me were you?"

"No."

"Now or never! Kill her!"

"I … I didn't think that, Lauren." I hesitated.

She stared into my eyes, her face blank. "A sewing needle in Riley's hand?"

I rolled my eyes, my words contrite. "Fine. I was overwhelmed by it all. Plus, I didn't know what else to do at the time. And now you're here scaring me, so I panicked."

"I should burn you for what you did to my Alison."

I backed off. "You … wouldn't do that to me," I said. "Your heart is too kind."

She prowled closer. "You have no idea who I am … or what's hiding in my heart."

Lauren's rage killed the television, and the bedroom lights flickered off and back on again. The silence became terrifying. It took all I had to force myself to breathe again.

"Please. I don't know what came over me. It's like there was some unseen power that wouldn't let me think on my own, like I was under someone else's control."

"Penelope the Perfect."

I frowned. "Are you saying Penelope hexed me?"

"Uh-huh. Like how you hexed Riley, before The Seal killed her. Payback's a bitch. Right?"

"Riley…? I didn't. She was just mad like me and …" Tears ran down my face. "You can't prove I did anything to Riley."

"Proof is for humans."

"Don't kill me. Being a Perfect was too much for me to handle. I'm not at fault here."

"I agree. And I'm not going to kill you, Apple."

"You're not?"

"Of course not. I genuinely care for you."

"I feel the same."

"I figured as much."

"Thank you. Thank you. I promise you I'll be a better friend from here on out. You won't regret this. Best friends again?"

"I believe I can do better than that," she said.

"What do you mean?"

"Oh, Apple."

Lauren moved quickly—no, even faster. She gripped my head with her hands, her thumbs pressed against my temples. She wasn't bigger than me, and yet I couldn't shake free. My skull throbbed from the pressure, and I levitated off the floor. I felt trapped inside my own skin, and it was a tight fit. My ears rang with an annoying echo.

"Lauren, please!"

"I think you have something of mine," she said, her eyes glowing red. "And I want it back from you."

The destroyer glove on my hand burned and glowed again. I peeked from the corner of my eye and watched it glimmer, then release from my hand. My palm felt strangely naked with it gone. It left me with a foul taste of inadequacy in my mouth.

I stared into her eyes and saw my reflection as my pink eyes turn dull brown. I almost didn't recognize them it had been so long since they described my existence.

"Lauren, what are you doing to me?"

"What do you think?"

"No."

"I banish you from my world forever."

"Anything but that!"

"What has been done by me shall never be undone, except by your death ... and I dare any one to try."

Her words were firm, and I shuddered from the absence of my Perfect gift. I felt my body run hot and cold as ripples of energy moved through it, then faded.

"There you are. Good as old."

I dropped to the carpet, landing on my knees, and braced my hands to the floor.

"Lauren?"

"One other thing. You might want to wake up extra early in the morning if you have errands to run."

"Why is that?"

"Something tells me that shiny new Mustang GT out front will have turned back into a smelly old pumpkin."

"Don't do this." I slouched, sobbing.

"Sorry, Charlie. It's done."

"Please..."

The closet door swung open without her looking to it, exposing a vacuum of wind and lustrous starry darkness. Lauren backed in and was sucked inside, and the door slammed shut and exploded with a loud boom. I ducked and covered my face while pieces of wood shot around the room. Furniture rattled and the walls shook.

I looked to my closet, but there was nothing left to see. No majestic swallow tweaking my senses, no Alexis outfits or Nuvula blouses, and no Fendi heels and Prada handbags to confirm my perfection like glass slippers.

I'm no longer Cinderella.

There was nothing left but a gaping hole in the structure of the house, and the loud ticking sound of my perfection as it slowly counted down to human, like the second hand on a grandfather clock losing steam.

Tic. Tic. Tic. Tock...

CHAPTER 67

LAUREN

THE DAYS OF TORMENT that followed my awakening slowed to a creep. No amount of deadly injuries could defeat my purpose, my perfection, but the sleepless evenings and puffy bags under my eyes added a decade to my skin, like aged wisdom.

The burden of loss makes you notice every little thing wrong with life. I'm now an anomaly, and not even the other Perfects who survived the fray can empathize with my unique disposition. Just as well, I wouldn't wish it on anyone.

No one left on Earth could understand my plight, so I felt it best to stay gone until I could handle my emotions. At times the battle was harder than dealing with Fearians.

I remained in the realm of Perfects, trying to imagine the lives of the ones that came before me, the ones I mourned: Mother, Aunt Geneve, and the other elders. I'd missed out on a whole side of Mom's existence, an important side that connected me to the parts of her that no other human could comprehend, not even Dad. I wished I would've known my Aunt Geneve under more pleasant circumstances, had her in my life to teach me things only an aunt of her lineage could teach. Aunt Jamie did her best, and her best was good, but her best wasn't perfect. It would never be perfect.

The chaos over the last few weeks was no more, and with each day and nothing new to report, the witness statements began to look more and more absurd—so absurd it had to be an elaborate hoax of some kind.

Even the authorities had difficulty putting their names on the dotted line, with no concrete evidence to back up what they swore they went through. I heard that Governor Granholm had scrutinized Detective Neese over his recount of the events in his police report. Ultimately, Detective Neese was given a short leave of absence to get his head right. If he's anything like me, it didn't help any. He knew, like I knew, what really happened, and no amount of free time was going to change the truth. The world loves to be blissful in ignorance. Still, today was a day of remembrance, a day that meant so much to me I elected to return to the realm of humans out of esteemed respect, and out of love.

WOOSH!

I opened the door and stepped inside the Holy Family Catholic Church, where my family attended services off and on over the years. The interior of the building was filled with melancholy dimness. A small crowd of familiar faces was seated at the front of the room, fifty or so in all. I walked along the center aisle, trying to ignore the whispers and growing stares that followed my journey toward the open coffin below the altar.

I looked inside the casket and saw my father. He appeared peaceful and at rest. Finally, something that only death could offer him. Dad was wearing a black suit and was clean-shaven, though the scar on his face was still evident of his gift, a gift that came with a life-threatening curse.

"Daddy ... you look good, you look safe. I'm sorry it took this for that to happen. You deserve so much more—and I'm tormented I can't give you what you've earned."

I placed my hands on the edge of the box, and the plain material transformed into an elegant stainless steel casket more befitting of a man who died with honor, a man I knew as my father. Sounds of shock filled the room, but I paid them no mind. Dad had longed to make amends for his past failures, and I needed him to know he was successful in doing so. I needed him to know he gave what only a father could give his child: everything.

I caressed his face with my hand and wiped away the scar from his jawline, returning his skin back to its perfection underneath the light stubble.

That is a much better look for you.

"Goodbye, Dad."

I turned to Aunt Jamie and Grangy, who were seated in the front row surrounded by close friends and family.

"Lauren," Aunt Jamie said. A tear ran down her cheekbone. "You came back. How did you..." her words lost power.

"You are my family."

Grangy stood to her feet. "I knew it. I knew you were special ... just like your mother was special."

"You knew about Mom?"

"Of course I did. I'm old not blind. Just didn't know you knew."

"Knew what?"

Grangy patted Aunt Jamie's hand. "I'll explain it to you later."

"So then you know I must go? It's for the best, it really is. And I'm needed elsewhere now."

"Say no more. But, if you ever get homesick ... don't you dare hesitate coming back to us. No questions asked." Grangy sobbed.

My eyes flashed fuchsia in loving gratitude, and I left them without looking back.

Their looks of admiration overshadowed the many glares of terror from the others. I walked out of the church and paused at the top of the steps, seeing police officers standing behind their patrol cars with pistols and shotguns aimed at me. Detective Neese was in the middle of the crowd, smiling slightly as he sensed his quest for human justice coming to a close.

"That'll be far enough, Lauren!" he shouted.

"Why is that?"

"Why else? You are under arrest."

"Color me curious. What legal charges are you trying to pin on me?"

"Let's start with murder, then work our way backwards," he said, gloating with a smirk.

"Hum. I have a better idea." I took a step.

The officers cocked their weapons.

"Don't make us kill you. Just ... stop."

My eyes slanted and I felt liberated when they burned bright coral, and I took a step out of spite, vanishing into thin air before anyone had the chance to test their triggers. I reappeared standing behind Detective Neese, where I wrapped my arms around his neck.

"Peek-a-boo. Guess who? I'm a Mother Perfect," I whispered to him. "Killing me is not an option for you."

"Wait!"

We disappeared in the blink of an eye, leaving his service pistol falling to the pavement.

WOOSH!

He and I arrived at our new location, and he pried open his eyes to find himself in the midst of a pride of lions, relaxing after a big kill. The wildebeest carcass had been picked bone dry and numerous flies pestered the cat's shiny coats.

His eyes danced. "An African prairie?"

"I could never harm Ali." My voice was tired. "I can barely deal with her death as it is now, I loved her that much."

"Who then?"

The lions picked up on our scent, heard our whispering voices and took notice of us, and one by one they stood on alert and prowled closer.

"You're a smart man." I popped his collar. "I'm sure you can figure it out. Someone with a drastic weight loss and bad luck touch."

I motioned with my forefinger.

"But, how do I-"

"Don't worry. Her reign of terror has ended. She's one of you again."

The strong odor of fear radiated from his pores. I smelt it. The other carnivores did too, and the largest lion growled, and moved even closer on my backside.

"Lauren?"

"Yes, Detective Neese?"

"Please don't leave me here to be eaten alive," he begged. "I don't want to die."

"… Okay. Since you asked me nicely."

The lions roared and attacked, and we disappeared into thin air with the smell of fur in my nose.

WOOSH!

CHAPTER 68

DETECTIVE NEESE

I TENSED FOR THE mauling that was on my doorstep, for the claws to rip into my flesh with excruciating agony, when the scene changed so fast I didn't have time to blink. My stomach churned acid as the other officers and our squad cars with flashing blue lights came back into view. A wave of anxiety mixed with relief washed over me, and I bent my knees and exhaled deeply, trying to gather my composure. That's when I noticed the DVD case marked 'security feed' clenched underneath my bent fingers. I was holding it so tightly I didn't even know it was there.

"Detective!" Officer Smith yelled out.

I picked up my pistol. "I'm back."

"Did she hurt you?"

"Nothing more than my pride," I said.

"How did she do that?" Officer Walton asked, his voice high pitched. "And where did she take you?"

"How? I couldn't begin to tell you. Where? Well. Let's just say I won't be going to the Detroit Zoo ever again," I said.

They looked to me, puzzled, but I didn't want to say more and risk upsetting her again.

Everyone else stood down and prepared to leave the church, but I couldn't stop myself from savoring my precious life, and pondering on Lauren's words.

So who had killed Ali?

There was only one other person left that fit the clues of the riddle.

CHAPTER 69

LAUREN

I STROLLED THE FIELD of calf-high dry weeds, letting my fingertips scrape across their tips in passing. The others walked beside me with excitement on their faces and eagerness in their steps. We made it to the picnic table at the edge of the wooded area where my dad's family first encountered Mom, and I stopped before the lucky tree that had been chosen to present a Perfect to the world.

"So, are we going home?" Jacob asked.

I didn't answer him—I didn't need to. My smile was enough.

"No longer hiding in secret among the humans?" Wyatt added. "I've been doing it for so long I'm not entirely sure I know how to stop."

I waved my hand before the tree, brushing the bark with my fingers, and painted a stroke of shining light down the center. The tree trunk split in two, exposing the portal to the other side, the home of our kind: the home of Perfects. We passed over the shimmering threshold then crossed into our own land. The force field was gone, and so were the thoughts of a selfish Fearian invasion.

"With Nolum and the others gone now, will we venture onto that side of our world?" he asked me.

"There are more important things to do first," I replied.

"I got dibs on the Counsel's palace," Jacob joked. "Who wants to arm wrestle me for the family jewels?"

"Later," I said, without looking his way.

The others followed me to the cliff, which overlooked their colony and my new home. I hadn't told them I'd been using it to be alone to gather my thoughts, or that I had already journeyed to the Fearian side of our world and had visited with the female and children survivors living without a Counsel … or a warrior to protect them. I could have destroyed them all, in a fiery instant, but chose not too. To me it felt pointless. I'm a Mother Perfect, not a monster—and humanity was something precious I still longed after.

The colony below looked deserted, and yet comforting and at peace at the same time. It had been a long time since the war for them, and the colony had begun to show signs of slow recovery. Small flowers with coral petals sprouted out over the unbeaten paths like dandelions, and the trees were fuller, some holding ripening fruits. Still, many of the buildings were damaged, dirty and in need of detailed repairs. The colony was healing, but it was still hurt.

Wyatt wiped away a tear. "Wow ... home."

"I had forgotten how much I've missed the smell of this place," Madison said. "Before the Fearians infected it with their filthy touch."

"Better than those human castles in Ireland?" Jacob asked her.

"Those castles can't compete."

He chuckled. "Thought we lost you there for a minute. Welcome back."

"Of course, we have a lot of work to do if we expect to return it to its former glory," Zoe said. "A lot of work indeed."

"No. We don't," I said.

"What do you mean?" Madison asked me.

My eyes glowed titanium and I looked to the polluted clouds above. Aunt Geneve's voice spoke strange words in my mind, and I mumbled them aloud, drawing from the wisdom of her essence. The Elders recited my charm in the background.

The clouds began to give way, and loud thunder erupted as flashes of lightning zipped across the sky. Pink sparkling raindrops fell upon the colony, dissolving the grime into streams that flowed into puddles and evaporated from sight. The dust and dirt melted away from the buildings, like a monochrome scene gaining bold color and majestic beauty.

"That's freaking hot," Zoe said, impressed.

"Am I dreaming?" Jacob admired.

Madison's mouth parted. "How... did you ... do that? No one ever said that was even an option."

"...Because not every Mother Perfect is equally matched."

"WHOA!" Wyatt screamed to the heavens. "We're going home! Come on!"

He and the others charged down the hillside toward the colony, but I stayed put. I wasn't sure if I was going to be able to let my guard down and let friendships bond, being I had no room for error, so I elected to put it on the back burner for the time being. I believed Aunt Geneve and the others would've approved of my choice.

"I know you're standing there. I can feel you," I said, without looking to the emptiness around me.

Isabelle and Harlen and Aunt Geneve appeared on my flank, wearing white linen garments. Their presence was as if phantoms, yet real enough that I could smell the honeyed myrrh simmering from their clean pores and heard the shaded grass flattening underneath their bare feet.

Although we had yet to be formally introduced it was like I had known them all of my life, and I was not at all surprised by their support.

Then mother appeared standing beside me. She didn't say a word. She just looked on at the others frolicking, as we did.

"Hope I've made you proud," I said.

I longed for a response, and finally one came. She held my hand, and the rushing heat of her touch settled into my chest, calming me—reassuring me things were on the right track.

"I love you too, Lauren," Mother said. "I love you, too."

CHAPTER 70

APPLE

THE WEEK HAD PASSED and my suspension from school was over. It had been a long time since I'd dreaded returning to these halls, and yet here I was, walking them again with reluctance. My once Perfect life was now anything but, and no one would believe me if I told them of its past existence. Sadly, the old me had returned just as Lauren had said. I knew it from the second I opened my eyes that next morning.

My Mustang GT had been repossessed once the Michigan Lottery came calling with infallible proof our lottery ticket was fraudulent. An internal investigation ensued, and now my parents were stressed they would have to sell the house at a loss just to pay back the money we spent. Luckily for me my parents were able to find useable clothing at our local Goodwill. Oddly enough, the t-shirts they found looked vaguely similar to the ones I used to wear before the big change occurred in my life.

I missed that 'big change,' like I missed the three friendships I blatantly ruined for no reason, other than blind selfishness, greed and sheer stupidity.

Things couldn't be worse at home, and now I had to face similar music playing at school. It all sounded like a broken record to the ears of a victim, though I was still the villain. I stumbled through the gauntlet of ridicule that was the main hall with my schoolbooks pressed against my healthy bosom. I thought it best to keep my head down, though it didn't matter much. The looks of disgust flew at my head like cannon balls.

"Damn, girl. What'd you eat over the weekend?" Neal asked, surrounded by a couple of fellow jocks and skinny cheerleaders. "The whole damn pig?" he jeered.

They laughed hard at my expense.

"Did you at least kill the pig first?" Max asked, snorting.

I swallowed my pride, along with the hurtful words, and was making my way by the main office when a familiar voice called out to me, getting my attention. I stopped my walk and looked to the doorway and saw Principal Ward, Vice Principal Ubly and Detective Neese standing there like cowboys at the OK Corral—and me without a revolver.

"Can we talk?" Detective Neese asked.

Two uniformed officers filtered out of the congestion and closed in behind me. I noticed the pair had their hands resting on their pistols.

"About?"

He held up a DVD case. "A recent trip you and your brother took to the Grand Blanc Library."

My breathing fell flat. "How did you find... it was self-defense."

"I don't care."

"Alison was trying to kill me."

"We'll let a jury of your peers decide that," he replied. "If you haven't killed them all."

I slouched, turning teary-eyed. "Whatevs."

Exhaling big, I dragged into the office.

"As for me, I'm going to request the city prosecutor try you as an adult."

"...Why would you do that?" I asked.

"I think you know already."

"But..."

His arrogance was infuriating and stole my words. If I were a Perfect, my retaliation would have been searing and swift. But I was no longer a Perfect, and there was no more retaliation left in me to give.

"Oh, one more thing." He leaned into my ear. "I know what you did to my good friend on those train tracks."

"What? No. I ..."

"And while I'll probably never be able to prove it to anyone who matters, you will pay for it," he snarled.

The heat off of his breath slapped my skin and I walked inside the office, trembling, terrified at the thought of what was to come.

What have I done to my life?

CHAPTER 71

KAIDEN

I LIMPED ALONG THE sidewalk and made my way up the steps and into the building. It had the feel of a hospital, yet at the same time different. I limped over to the front counter, where three ladies dressed in white nurse's uniforms were standing.

"Hello. Back for another visit?" the RN said to me.

"Is my favorite patient awake yet?"

"She has been given her morning bath and is now fresh as a daisy. Follow me."

She escorted me along a grey hall and past several closed doors. As we neared the end of the hall, she stopped at a door, stuck a key into the lock and opened it.

"You have company again," she announced, on my behalf.

I entered the padded room behind her and limped over to Bridget, who was curled in a corner, rocking back and forth. Her black pupils seemed to stare at the ceiling.

"Hey, sis," I greeted.

"When you're ready to leave, just bang on the door. I'll hear you," the RN said.

"Thanks."

She shut the door and locked me inside the padded room. I kneeled down to Bridget and brushed her nappy locks from off her forehead.

"Look at you. What has that wicked Perfect and her evil ways done to my poor human pet?"

I retrieved the jade ring Elisabeth had once stolen from us (and taken to her grave), and placed it onto Bridget's finger.

"Do you ...? I think that you do. I can see it in your pretty eyes," I teased.

The blackness shading her pupils transformed to a sparkling ocean blue, though her expression remained lifeless.

Then she spoke. "Per … Perfects."

"It's just you and me now, kid," I shared. "Normally, that might not be enough, but with nothing to lose, it's going to have to do. Lucky for you, I came prepared."

I took out the glass vial filled with Anomous' essence and popped the red lid. A mist rose from the syrupy liquid and bounced off the padded walls, the flavor decadent and full of new life.

"I would've never seen you as anything close to an equal—but, desperate times call for desperate measures … and I'm desperate."

"Des … per … ate meas … ures," Bridget stuttered.

I kissed her on the mouth, then forced the vial in between her lips. "I'm sure Anomous won't contest much."

Bridget slowly focused her gaze and regained her bearing … sort of. Her pale body shook, and white smoke shot from her nostrils and mouth. Her blue eyes flashed hazel as she levitated off the floor.

Flashes of lightning struck across the window in the door, and thunderous claps rocked the building. A funnel of wind rattled the hall, and terrified screams of nurses and doctors bounced off the corridor walls. Though the chaos outside the door continued, ramping up its intensity, calmness filled the padded room. Bridget's body ceased its tremors and landed back onto the floor.

"Where—where am I?"

"Looney bin."

"Huh?"

"Where people who've gone loco are taken. Do you not remember anything?"

"No, I don't."

"Do you remember me?"

"You're … Kaiden."

"Excellent. And I have another tale to share with you. You may not enjoy the middle of the story, but you're going to love the hell out of the new ending."

THE END